An Opening
for Murder

Maggie Kean Mysteries by Nageeba Davis

A DYING ART
AN OPENING FOR MURDER

An Opening for Murder

Nageeba Davis

BERKLEY PRIME CRIME, NEW YORK

AN OPENING FOR MURDER

A Berkley Prime Crime Book
Published by The Berkley Publishing Group,
a division of Penguin Putnam Inc.,
375 Hudson Street, New York, New York 10014.

Visit our website at
www.penguinputnam.com

Copyright © 2002 by Nageeba Davis.
Jacket art by Mary Ann Lasher.

First edition: July 2002

Library of Congress Cataloging-in-Publication Data

Davis, Nageeba.
    An opening for murder / Nageeba Davis.— 1st ed.
        p. cm
    ISBN 0-425-18493-5 alk. paper
    1. Women sculptors—Fiction. I. Title

PS3554.A93744 O64 2002
813'.6—dc21

                                                    2002019527

PRINTED IN THE UNITED STATES OF AMERICA

10   9   8   7   6   5   4   3   2   1

Dedicated to . . .

Mom and Nancy,
for all the shopping trips, phone calls, and early mornings
spent talking and laughing with our feet propped up on the
table

my husband and son,
my greatest fans

Chapter One

I was a basket case. Not your everyday "Gee, I'm a little uptight, maybe I should have a glass of wine to calm down" basket case. Nope. Not me. I'm talking real-life crazy. I'm talking nutcase—chicken with its head cut off, wacko, psycho, neurotic—in bilingual terms, *loco*.

My first show was opening in seven hours, and I was a little nervous. That's putting it mildly. Truth be told, I was a nervous wreck. My skin was blotchy, pimples were sprouting, and I was retaining water. Limp, unenthusiastic curls hung from my head, an unusual feat for someone who was normally a dead ringer for Little Orphan Annie. Minus the little and minus the red. My hair was more of a soft, sable color if you were lucky enough to catch it in a dim, candlelit room. Otherwise it was brown . . . the definition of brown. Not the rich color of bare mountain peaks in autumn, and not the color of warm buttered toast or café mocha. Just plain mousy brown. The color of swamp muck. Someone suggested highlights once, but on my head, they'd look like a family of albino earthworms squirming through my hair.

But I digress. My first venture into the sculpting world was just around the corner and I was too nervous to stand still. I was driving Mark, the manager and overseer of The Outlook, the very upscale gallery where my work was being displayed, unequivocally nuts. And that's not easy to do. This man never got ruffled. He reminded me of the soldiers who stand guard outside Buckingham Palace. The ones who never move a muscle no matter how many times you wave a hand in front of their face or whisper dirty words in their ear or describe an itch that must drive them crazy. No matter what—rain, sleet, or snow—these guys remain starch stiff, staring stoically ahead, which seems, in my opinion, to be an awful waste of healthy male bodies. I mean, let's be honest. The queen is moving up in years, and certainly no one would ever accuse her of being "a looker." So, what exactly are they guarding?

This isn't to say that Mark is cold or aloof or anything like that. In fact, he's quite the opposite. He warm and sweet and has a gentle sense about him. No matter how crazy the outside world, a strong current of peace seems to flow through him. Mark believes in quiet leadership. He can, and often does, slip into a room unannounced and calmly assess a situation without speaking a word. Then he stands completely still until the chaos and noise subsides. And surprisingly, it does. It's an amazing thing to watch. He doesn't scream or yell or, my personal favorite, offer a middle finger salute. Before you know it, though, the room is so quiet, you can hear people breathing. After several moments, he gives a few succinct directions and suddenly, once again, the earth is spinning smoothly on its axis.

But that was before *my* show. Much to Mark's distress, I'd been hovering over his back and breathing down his neck for the past five hours, questioning his every move and decision. Which was a joke, trust me. I knew next to nothing about staging an art show. But that didn't matter, and it certainly didn't stop me. They say that ignorance is bliss, and I guess, in this situation, it was. Empowered by my naivete, I suggested new colors for the walls, loudly discussed alternate traffic flow patterns, and hotly debated the placement of my different pieces.

We were now in the midst of a rather heated discussion regarding the titles for my sculptures. He was completely unperturbed and I was pulling my hair out.

"It's simply a way to focus your art, Maggie. The titles you've given your pieces are simple and direct, but they need more. People respond to patterns and organization; it's what the mind is built to do. The mind will seek order, even in the midst of chaos."

"You're saying my work is chaos?"

"Of course not. Don't try and put words in my mouth. I simply meant that it is easier for people to walk into a room filled with art and appreciate what they're seeing if there is a unifying theme."

I took a deep breath and tried to get a hold of myself. Mark was staring at me with a half-amused, half-irritated expression, and I wondered again for the thousandth time how it was possible that the two of us managed to get along. We were polar opposites, and I do mean opposites. Where Mark was quiet, organized, and neat to the umpteenth degree, I was noisy, random, and sloppy. Mark was compactly built, lean but not skinny, with a body that spoke well-modulated volumes about order and discipline. On the other hand, I managed to be bony and soft at the same time. I don't think a muscle would dare show up on my body. What would be the purpose? I'd have them slacking off in no time. I'm exaggerating, of course. Given all the molding I do, my upper body was actually rather strong, but I was still a long way from boasting a chiseled physique.

"Why can't they just walk in and observe, appreciate and buy?"

He shook his head. "Maggie, we're good friends, right?"

"I think so," I agreed cautiously.

"Then go home. It's after twelve. Eat lunch, pour yourself a glass of wine, take a hot bath, and relax. Put this out of your mind for the next few hours. I'll take good care of everything." He picked up my hand and reassuringly squeezed it. "Remember, this is my show, too. It reflects my name and my reputation, also. Believe it or not, I want everything to be as perfect as you do."

I looked into those gentle blue eyes and sighed. "I've been a bitch, haven't I?"

Mark smiled. "You're a little on edge."

I threw up my hands. "Okay, you win. Group them, tag them, and theme the whole lot of them. Just don't make it look like a Martha Stewart 'Crafts in Clay' show."

He grinned. "I'll do my best. Go home, take a nap or

whatever you do to relax, and come back this evening ready to drink champagne."

I put my arms around him and kissed his cheek. "Why are all the good men taken?"

Laughing, he tucked my arm through his and walked me toward the back. "Do me a favor and say that a little louder the next time Jamie is around. I'm not sure she feels the same way anymore."

I stopped. "You're kidding, right?"

"She tells me I'm overreacting." He shrugged. "Maybe she's right."

"Overreacting to what?"

Mark hesitated. He's extremely reticent about his personal life. I'm not sure if it's because he's embarrassed by his lousy childhood or because he *was* naturally a very private individual. Probably some of both. From the little I've been able to piece together, the man had had a crummy childhood—an overbearing mother and a father who abandoned the family when Mark was barely out of diapers. I met his mom once, and it wasn't something I'd want to do again. She defined tacky—platinum-dyed hair sprayed stiffly into place, fake stick-on nails, and a pudgy body stuffed into polyester stretch pants topped off by a loud, floral print nylon blouse. It was hard to believe she and Mark shared the same gene pool. We talked only briefly, thank God, but it didn't take a Rhodes scholar to detect the signs of a blood-sucking parasite. The way she clamped her hand around my arm grated on my nerves, and before I could disengage myself from her tentacles, she launched into the woes of being a single mother. Within minutes, she had neatly maneuvered me into feeling sorry for her as she ticked off her list of problems: she was all alone, had no money, no one cared whether she lived or died. She wrapped up the diatribe bemoaning the fact that her only son seldom managed to visit her in Golden, a small town west of Denver. By that time, "seldom" sounded too frequent. All I wanted was to get out of the room and run as fast and far away as possible. Mrs. Martyr had worn me out in record time, and I hardly knew the woman. But it did help me understand why Mark refused to open up his childhood for public viewing.

"You're not the panicky type, Mark," I added, knowing I was going to have to prod him for information. "What's happened?"

"Oh, you know, it's the small things. Difficult to explain."

"Try anyway," I insisted.

A small smile tugged at the edge of his mouth. "You are persistent, aren't you?"

I waited.

He sighed. "I'm never going to get rid of you unless I say something, right?"

I waited again.

He shook his head. "In the interest of preparing for the show, which I cannot possibly continue with you stepping on my heels, I'll talk. But you have to promise not to push for any more details than what I'm willing to give. Is it a deal?"

I nodded reluctantly. "Fine. I'll take the deal, on one condition. You have to tell enough of the story so it makes sense, minus the intimate stuff, of course. Trust me, I don't want to know what color underwear Jamie wears. But you have to tell it from start to finish. No handing out little anemic scraps of information. Okay?"

"Okay. I accept your conditions, as you do mine," he replied. "But not now, not today."

"But—"

"But nothing, Maggie. I have too much work to do to indulge in a little heart-to-heart. If the whole story is what you want, then you'll have to be patient, and wait."

I drew myself up. "How long?"

"Tomorrow. Lunch."

"Fine," I said haughtily. "But it will cost you. As an unbelievably nosy person, waiting twenty-four hours for information upsets my equilibrium. If I have to wait, then you can pay the damn bill."

"Naturally," he said, chuckling. "Given the supreme sacrifice you are making, I would expect nothing less."

"As long as you understand," I called over my shoulder as I pushed through the swinging doors into the back studio, "that I want to go to La Casa Fiesta." I didn't have to turn around to see the dismay slide over his face. Mark was much more comfortable in a fancy restaurant serving entrees drizzled with a lemon caper sauce than in a place specializing in refried beans. The phrase "chips and dip" was enough to send him shuddering.

"Come on, Maggie, have a heart," he implored.

I kept walking as though I never heard him. The poor guy was too uptight. Nothing loosened a man up more than a good sweaty bout of sex, something I couldn't help him with, or a plate of enchiladas with enough chopped jalapeños to clear up the world's sinus problems.

The sadness in Mark's voice worried me, though. He and Jamie had been dating for almost two years. I'd known them both for a little over a year, and I hated to think that Jamie felt any differently now than she did in the beginning. But I'd been married once myself, and I knew how things could change without warning.

I leaned against the counter and looked around the studio. I loved this place—the perpetual layer of white dust, the wooden shelves lined with vases and other pieces in varying stages of completion. I liked the openness and the onslaught of light. I was even partial to the cement floor. Although I did most of my work in my home studio, I came here to use the wheel and relax—my own form of yoga. I loved putting my hands in the cool water and molding the wet clay as it spun around. It called for small movements and a steady touch, and I got so lost in the spinning motion that time slipped by soundlessly.

In fact, I was here early this morning, so anxious about my show that I couldn't eat or sleep. After showering and puttering around the house for several long minutes, I threw on some clothes and drove to The Outlook. Fortunately, Mark always unlocked the back door once he arrived so people could work in the studio. I strode in, tossed my purse in the corner, and crossed the room to the cabinets where the clay was stored. Pulling out a small square, I unwrapped it and kneaded the clay until it was soft and malleable and then placed the mound in the center of the wheel. Pulling up a stool, I sat down, flipped the switch, and winced when the wheel let out a high squeaking noise as it reluctantly started to rotate. As I dipped my hands in the cool water and placed them on the clay, the motor began to hum and my nerves calmed. I felt myself sloughing off the stress and the fear of finally exposing my work to the public.

The funny thing is, I never expected to be here. When I was young, things were very different. I wanted to be a baseball player. It was a dream of mine, a really big dream, one that led the charge and made everything else pale in comparison. I was determined to be the first woman baseball player. At ten years old, I ate, slept, and dreamt baseball. Without a mother to guide me toward a more feminine pursuit, I was molded by a pushy older brother who never got over his profound disappointment that my parents' bundle of joy turned out to be a girl.

The day I was brought home from the hospital, Andy took one look through the bars of my crib, snorted his disgust, and stomped out of the room. At least that's the way I imagine the scene, because ever since I can remember, he's ignored my gender completely. My own gender, that is. Other women were a completely different matter. If you listen and believe half of what Andy says, he does very well with the opposite sex, thank you very much. To hear him talk, he's quite the stud—which is more than I needed to know.

Anyway, from the moment I was old enough to walk, Andy began wrapping my pudgy fingers around a baseball and explaining the importance of the red stitching and other intricacies of the game—all gobbledygook at the time. But to please my older brother, whom I inexplicably adored despite his merciless teasing and dogged determination to toughen me up, I became a willing student. He desperately wanted me to be one of the boys, and I just as desperately wanted to please him, so I did what he wanted. I played baseball. Before long, I could out-run, out-pitch, and out-bat any boy in the neighborhood. And as luck would have it, I grew to love America's favorite pastime.

My childhood had one purpose—to be the first woman recruited by the Yankees. I didn't want to interview the other players, I didn't want to nurse their injuries or have their babies. I wanted to *be* a Yankee. My goal in life was to hit so many home runs that people called me Babe—and not because I was looking hot. Even better, I dreamed of being the outfielder who stopped every "should-have-been-a-home run" hit, vaulting up and crashing into the fence with my arm outstretched, feeling the ball smash into my open glove.

But then mud pies walked into my life. On one hot, windless day, my brother and I started squirting each other with the hose, an activity that quickly escalated into our usual war games. Andy and I took turns with the hose, pretending it was a machine gun or a stream of arrows. It was always fun for about fifteen minutes, until Andy became a little too enthusiastic and ended up hurting me. That day, in his zest to beat up the bad guys, he pinned me to the ground, sat on my chest, and sprayed water directly into my face. I spit and sputtered and finally managed to throw him off. I was so angry, I marched off, refusing to listen to his apologies. Eventually he gave up, shrugged his shoulders, climbed onto his bike, and pedaled down the street.

After he left, I grabbed the hose and jerked it across the lawn to water the freshly planted flowers, a chore that always fell on me because I was the girl. Sulking, I flopped down, dropped the hose, and watched the water stream out, creating little gullies and valleys in the loose soil. Mesmerized, I stuck my hands in the earth, grabbed large chunks of wet dirt, and started packing them together. Ten minutes later, I had a pile of thick, semi-round, hamburger-patty mud things. Stacking them on top of each other, I leaned back to examine my work. I had created a misshapen, multitiered chocolate cake. I was hooked.

Baseball dimmed in the light of my real dream. I wanted to be a sculptor.

Fifteen years later, fifteen years of watching my brother clutch his broken heart, I was exactly that. At least I hoped to be. Tonight was the big test. After months of suggesting changes in my work, Mark had finally decided I was ready. So after a restless night of tossing and turning and sweating through my pajama top, I slipped into the studio, sat down, and created another vase I didn't need but didn't have the heart to throw away.

And now, a few hours later, I was standing in the studio again all by myself. I leaned over and touched my vase. The clay was still soft to the touch and would be for several hours, but I knew Mark would want the place spotless for tonight. Leaning over, I took a thin wire and slid it underneath the vase, separating it from the wheel. I carefully lifted the vase and carried it into the small staging room where the kiln stood and placed it on the shelf with the other pieces waiting to be fired.

I was reluctant to leave. Deep down I was scared that the show was nothing more than a figment of my imagination, and if I left—*Poof!* it would disappear. I'd always been insecure about my talent, and despite Mark's frequent pep talks, I couldn't help but wonder if I should have stuck with baseball.

But I couldn't stay. Mark had made himself perfectly clear—*get the hell out.*

My red Jeep was parked at the curb. I climbed in, grabbed the cell phone, and dialed Lisa's number. Like clockwork, she picked up on the third ring, a habit she developed in college to keep her boyfriends from thinking she was waiting by the phone for their call. She thought anything less than two rings smacked of overeagerness. I thought waiting for the third ring smacked of manipulation, but as usual, she ignored me, insisting that there was a very thin line between thoughtful maneuvering and clear deception. It didn't make sense to me then and it still doesn't. But then again, I'm hardly an expert. She's the happily married one, not me. I'm single and involved in a stormy, up and down, convoluted relationship with an Italian detective, the key word being "Italian." What else did I expect?

A groggy, muffled voice came over the line. "Hello?"

"Lisa?"

"What's wrong?" I asked. "Did I wake you? You sound funny."

"No, I'm just lying down."

"In bed? It's eleven-thirty in the morning. Are you sick?"

She sighed. "No, Maggie. Believe it or not, there are other things to do in bed than sleep."

Oh, yuck. "That's disgusting. It's like hearing about your parents having sex."

"What did you think—that Mandy just miraculously arrived on my doorstep?"

Mandy was Lisa's two-year-old daughter, cute as a button and mischievous as hell. She was also my goddaughter. "Of course not, but I don't want to hear every lurid detail, either."

"I hardly call mentioning the word bed a lurid detail, but for someone like you, it probably is."

"What's that supposed to mean?" I asked, summoning up a little indignation.

"Exactly what you think it means. You've got the best-looking, mouthwatering man this side of the Rockies following you around like a lap dog, and you tuck tail and run."

"Thanks for the interesting canine analogy," I responded dryly.

"What are best friends for?"

"Butting in where they don't belong?" I suggested.

"You'd miss me if I didn't interfere."

"So you keep saying. Listen, as much as I hate to end this little verbal sparring, I called to see if you wanted to meet me at Jamie's for a late lunch, but this probably isn't a good time," I finished lamely.

"Actually, it's the perfect time. We just finished our . . . uh . . . gardening, and Joel is off for the afternoon. He can watch Mandy."

"Then I'll meet you there in thirty minutes. That'll give

you two an extra ten minutes to finish . . . well . . . turning the soil."

"Trust me, it's been taken care of."

Gross. "Okay, make it twenty minutes. I'll be there before you, so I'll get us a table, but hang on a second while I start the car. I may need you to drop by the gallery and pick me up if this rust bucket decides to throw a tantrum," I said. I pumped the accelerator three times, waited, and pumped it again twice. The Jeep was, gently put, a seasoned piece of machinery. Actually, it was a mechanic's nightmare, not to mention mine. It was a used car when I bought it, and it had only gone from old to decrepit. Underneath this hood was a thick layer of corrosion and a temperamental engine laughing its ass off at my frustration. I had to soothe, coax, and sometimes beg to get this contraption moving.

I prayed to the great Car Dealer in the Sky, because if the engine didn't turn over real soon, this heap was heading there in a jiffy. My Jeep must have known what I was thinking, because suddenly it roared to life like a brand-new Porsche.

Lisa heard the engine and hung up while I pulled out onto Tejon, drove to Bijou, took a left, traveled down three blocks, and took another left, completing what amounted to one giant U-turn. I followed Nevada north until I hit Uintah, turned left, and caught the freeway for a few miles, exiting on Academy Boulevard. About a mile down the road, I saw the sign for Jamie's Café on the right, wedged right between Kentucky Fried Chicken and Burger King. I swerved in and parked in the back.

Climbing out, I was struck again by Jamie's choice of

location. Her small restaurant, which served sandwiches for lunch and specially blended coffees and teas, was really a front for a catering business she ran from the back of the building. She was a wonderful chef and her reputation was solid, but word of mouth was slow. Her menus were sought after by a more elite (translate that to rich) clientele than was normally found here on Fast Food Row. But evidently, her wealthy clients liked to keep her name to themselves. So she continued to depend on the walk-in business for her bread and butter.

Entering Jamie's Café was like stepping into a real French bistro, at least what I imagined one to look like—sunny yellow walls, black and white tiled floors, and wicker furniture. Starched white tablecloths and glass vases filled with fresh flowers topped the small round tables. Overflowing pots of dark green ferns hung from the ceiling. Every imaginable brand of coffee and tea lined the glossy pine shelves. A large glass case displayed delectable desserts guaranteed to satisfy any sweet tooth. Hips and thighs spontaneously ballooned just being in the same room.

I walked to the long wooden counter next to the Pastry Bin of Sin, and sat down on one of the high wooden stools, hoping to get a chance to talk to Jamie for a few minutes. Since Mark had mentioned the trouble between the two of them, I thought I might be able to get Jamie to shed some light on the problem. Although Mark had agreed to talk to me, I knew from experience what that meant. The bare minimum. But Jamie was a whole other story. If I was lucky, not only would she paint a broader and much more detailed picture, but she'd also supply me with free appetizers while we talked. Mark might not like me poking my nose in his business, but given the way he threw me out of the gallery, my curiosity (aka nosiness) was the least of his worries.

Jamie's distinctive voice floated through the swinging bar doors that separated the kitchen from the rest of the restaurant. Seconds later, Jamie came barreling through the doors, her arms loaded with plates of food. She caught sight of me and sent me one of her broad, welcoming smiles. After serving a young couple who were obviously besotted with each other, she walked back and threw her arms around me. I eased back on my chair again as she circled back behind the counter.

"Hey, girl, you sure are lookin' good," she declared, leaning on her elbows, her thick blonde hair pulled back in a ponytail.

I grinned. In baggy pants and a ratty sweatshirt, I looked anything but good. "You lie with such finesse, Jamie, but I'm willing to believe."

"I'm offended, honey. A false word has never passed these lips."

Even though I'd heard her voice a million times before, I still had to laugh. Her down-to-earth, unpretentious style totally belied the sophisticate she really was. The lady had graduated from the New York School of Culinary Arts, earning enough awards to paper the walls of her restaurant, but she insisted on sounding like she'd never cooked anything but buckwheat flapjacks. Jamie McGuire was tall, thin, and buxom, and had every guy within a fifty-yard radius salivating like Pavlov's dogs: See breasts, will drool. The first time I saw Mark and Jamie at the gallery, I knew they were perfect together. Not only were they great to look at, but more importantly, Jamie had a heart of gold. It was exactly what Mark needed to loosen him up a little and coax him out of his shell.

"I came for lunch . . . and to talk."

My tone must have raised her suspicions. "You want to swap gossip or did you have something particular in mind?"

I cleared my throat. "I just came from The Outlook, and—"

"Ah, I see. Mark sent you over to grill me, right?"

"Well, not exactly. I kind of took that mission on myself," I admitted. "He mentioned that things were strained between the two of you."

"It's nothing."

I should have backed off then, but as usual, I ignored the warning signs and plunged ahead. "He thinks you might have lost interest."

Jamie's big blue eyes went flat and her lips tightened. "How many times do I have to tell him nothing's changed? Work is stressful right now, that's all. Except for Kevin Brooks over there," she said, pointing to a thin busboy clearing plates from an empty table, "the teenage help nowadays is virtually useless. Why he stays is a mystery. I've lost two waitresses in the last week, so he's doing the work of three people right now. I'm swamped trying to run two businesses, and I haven't had a chance to interview for replacements. I don't have time to deal with Mark's insecurities, especially when they're groundless. If he can't handle a little bump in the road, then that's his problem."

"I think he can handle a bump, Jamie, if he knew what

it was or what was causing it," I said, a little surprised by her unusually cold response. "He's just worried. I don't think he's convinced that it's entirely work related, and I'm guessing that you haven't been your characteristically jovial self."

Jamie stared at me for the longest time without saying a word, then took a deep breath and let it out slowly. She dropped her head in her hands. "You're right."

Concerned, I placed my hand on her shoulder. "What's going on, Jamie? I've never seen you like this." I cleared my throat, afraid to ask the next question. "Is there someone else?"

She looked up and shook her head. "No, believe me, it's nothing like that."

"Thank God," I said, relieved. "Then what is it?"

"Nothing I can't handle," she said, forcing a smile that didn't erase the sadness in her eyes.

"But, Jamie—"

"No buts," she said, glancing over my shoulder. "Your friend Lisa just arrived and I have work to do." She stood up. "I have a lunch crowd to take care of and food for a party tonight at The Outlook—some up-and-coming artist," she said. Jamie winked and started back toward the kitchen, then stopped and turned to face me. "Don't worry, honey. Mark and I will be fine. By this point in our lives, we've both survived a whole lot worse than this."

I tried to do exactly what she said, and for the most part, I succeeded. At least during lunch. Jamie came out and chatted with Lisa, a tall beauty with thick auburn hair and hazel eyes. Between the two of them, I felt like the ugly stepsister with a wart on her nose. But lunch was kept light and frivolous. Jamie served sandwiches and regaled us with stories of her more difficult clients and their very uppity demands. She was back to her relaxed and entertaining self, even pulling up a chair, eating off my plate, and unabashedly praising her cooking between mouthfuls. By the time we left, I had convinced myself that Jamie was right, there was nothing to worry about. Things would smooth out on their own.

It wasn't the first time I'd been wrong.

Chapter Two

I drove north to Monument, a picturesque little town situated at the base of Mt. Herman, fifteen minutes north of Colorado Springs and forty minutes south of Denver. Twenty years ago, the area was a haven for retired military officers, but over the last few years, the place had exploded, bringing in all the familiar trappings of progress—fast-food restaurants, a large post office, four elementary schools, and a huge franchised grocery store. People moaned and groaned about the developments tearing down the quiet town we once knew, but the area was still small enough that we cared about one another and watched over the neighborhood kids like they were our own.

Crossing the bridge from Exit 161, I took several dirt-road shortcuts to my house. Halfway down my street, I whipped the steering wheel to the left. My back wheels fishtailed and spit out gravel as I slammed on my brakes and stopped just inches behind the black Bronco parked in my driveway.

I hopped out of the Jeep and walked toward the house.

"Nothing to do, Detective? No crimes to solve?"

Villari, my quasi-boyfriend, if there is such a thing, was sitting on my front step smoking a cigarette. He really was drop-dead gorgeous, and my stomach still did these funny little somersaults whenever I saw him, but there were problems. His cup runneth over with way too much machismo for my taste. Of course, being Italian, there was only so much he could do about that particular shortcoming. It was some kind of deeply ingrained, cultural thing. I was willing to bet that Michaelangelo strutted through the Sistine Chapel and yelled out, "Hey, yo, Pope!" whenever his bene-factor came to check his work. Sometimes I was able to overlook this personality deficit, but not always. Our rela-tionship was a frequent battle; a sort of push-pull for dom-inance between two very stubborn people who couldn't *spell* compromise, much less put it into practice. Neither one of us knew quite what to call this thing between us or where it was going, although Lisa insisted we did know but were too bullheaded to admit it. Chances are she was right.

"No crimes at the moment, unless you've found some-thing I don't know about," he replied, a direct reference to the day, over a year ago, when I had unearthed my neighbor Elizabeth's murdered body.

Villari and I met under circumstances that were hardly suited to romance; namely, he was the detective and I was his primary suspect in the investigation. Things went from bad to worse once we discovered that Elizabeth had appointed me, instead of her two surviving grandchildren, trustee of her very large estate. To this day, her grandson, Will, pestered me on a regular basis to release her money for some crazy moneymaking idea. He was king of the get rich quick scheme, and I was a major thorn in his side. I could grant the funds anytime I wanted, as long as the money was used for charity, education, or a business venture that made sense. Elizabeth's grandson had all sorts of grand ideas, but he never caught on to the "made sense" requirement. So, Will kept asking and I kept turning him down. He'd already called once this morning at the crack of dawn and I'd already hung up him. Great way to the start the day.

Actually, Elizabeth's will had surprised me as much as anyone else, but at the time, no one believed me, especially Villari. The man had the persistence of a pit bull, stalking me until the murder was solved and we tumbled into what is best described as an uneasy friendship with a large dose of sexual chemistry.

Villari ground his cigarette into the dirt with the toe of his boot.

"I really hate it when you do that." I sat down next to him.

"Yeah, I know. I'll pick it up on my way out."

"Why are you here, Villari?"

"Feel free to tromp on my ego anytime," he said, sliding his arm around my waist and pulling me toward him. "One of these days, you're going to surprise the hell out of me and actually smile when you see me." He leaned over, brushed a curl from my face, and kissed me. Then he kissed me again, deeper and deeper, until the next thing I knew, I was sitting on his lap with my arms roped around his neck. Several minutes later, he broke the kiss, leaned back a few inches, and grinned. "Well, hey."

"Hey, back," I said, smiling into those dark black eyes with the crinkly corners.

"Happy to see me?"

"Ever so slightly."

"Are you nervous yet?" he asked, lightly running his thumb over my bottom lip.

"Nervous about what Mrs. Peterson is thinking while you paw me in public, or nervous about the opening tonight?"

"Naturally I'm referring to the woman with the blue hair who is peeking through the curtains as we speak. You know she's dying for me to take advantage of you right here on the front porch. Come on, Maggie," he said, nibbling my ear, "let's show the old lady something to jump-start her pacemaker."

I laughed, wiggled out of his embrace and off his lap. "Thanks, but no thanks. She's the local gossip with a mouth the size of the Grand Canyon. I'm not interested in being the subject of her tongue-wagging."

"Fine. Ruin all her fun and mine." Villari reached over, wrapped a strand of my hair around his finger, and tugged it gently. "Then I guess we'll have to talk about your show. Nervous?"

"Only when I think about it."

"You'll do fine, Maggie. Your work is very good."

"And what do you know about sculptures?" I asked, a little too strongly.

Villari plucked my hand from my lap. "Sometimes you are just plain ornery."

I tried to pull my hand from his, but he wouldn't let go.

"I mean it, Maggie. Every time you get scared or worried or you think your pride is being wounded, you hunker down and prepare to attack before your brain has a chance to put in its two cents. Think a little. I'm not your enemy. I'm on your side, remember? I may not know squat about art, but Mark does, and I can guarantee you that he didn't plan this show so you could fall flat on your face. He thinks you're talented. I'm willing to take his word for it." He paused. "Have a little faith."

My eyes filled with tears. "I really hate this side of you. Just when we're moments away from an invigorating battle, you go and say something that turns me all mushy inside."

He smiled. "Hey, that sensitivity training must really be working."

I laughed. "The only thing that's working is your gloating mechanism. Just because you might possibly be in the vicinity of being slightly right, does not mean we're going to indulge in a group hug."

"Actually, I was thinking along the lines of something a little more intimate."

"Rein in your libido, Detective. I've got a zillion things to do before tonight."

"That's Mark's job, Maggie. All you have to do is put on a dress and show up." He hooked a finger inside the waistband of my jeans, pulled, and twisted. "Of course, the dress part might be a problem for someone who prefers to swim in her clothes rather than wear them."

"There's nothing wrong with my clothes," I said, batting his hand away.

"Everything's wrong with them."

"I suppose you'd rather see me strutting around in some tight T-shirt with a plunging neckline and shorts up to my butt."

"Damn right I would."

"It's not going to happen, Detective."

Villari let out an exaggerated sigh. "Yeah, I know. But I can dream."

I laughed. "You have a nice way of getting my mind off my worries."

"I keep telling you, sweetheart, you've done your part. Sit back and let Mark do the rest."

"That's pretty much what he told me before he threw me out of The Outlook this morning."

"You're kidding. He threw you out?"

"He implied that I was being uncooperative and demanding."

"Imagine that."

"It was not all my fault," I insisted. "Mark wasn't himself today. He and Jamie are having problems, so it's only natural that he was a little testy and impatient." I hurried on when I saw the skepticism written on Villari's face. "It's true. In fact, Mark and I are supposed to have lunch tomorrow so he can give me his tightly abbreviated side of the story."

"You went to see Jamie today, didn't you?"

"How'd you know?" I asked, surprised.

"Simple deduction, Watson. When it comes to sticking your nose into someone else's business, you're no better than Mrs. Peterson with her nose pressed against the window. You knew Mark would never spill his guts the way you want him to, so you hightailed it to Jamie's, right?"

I scowled. The man was entirely too smug. "For your information, I did not hightail anything. I drove leisurely and stopped in because I was hungry."

Villari ran his fingers through his mop of black hair. "If you say so. I'm not going to argue with you, although I don't believe a word of your story." He stood and took a step down. He leaned over, put his hands on my elbows, and pulled me up so that we were standing nose to nose. At my average height, I needed that extra six inches to look him straight in the eye.

"One of these days, Maggie, we're going to have to quit hiding behind our sniping and deal with the two of us." Before I could respond, he kissed me on the lips and took my hand. We walked to his car.

"What time do you want me to pick you up?"

"The Outlook is serving champagne at eight. Why don't you come by around seven-thirty?"

"Be ready at six, Maggie."

I sighed in defeat. "I was hoping you'd forgotten."

"Not a prayer. And I mean that literally. Mom's got a church pew named in her honor and the Pope calls collect from the Vatican to consult with her on religious matters. 'Thou shalt show up at Mom's reception' is the Eleventh

Commandment." He smiled. "You don't want to chance a flood or a drought do you?"

"Not really. I get seasick on arks," I replied, laughing at the picture he'd drawn of his mother. "Mamacita wins again. I'll be there."

Villari winced. "Someday you're going to slip and call her that in person. It won't be pretty. And I won't step in to protect you."

"Coward."

"Smart."

I threw my hands up in the classic surrender pose. "Okay. I'm all yours. Pick me up at six and we'll go visit your parents. Is the whole family going to be there?"

"Of course. Italians always travel in posses." His lips twitched as he put his forefinger under my chin and tilted my face up. "You'll enjoy yourself, I promise. Mom is really proud of you . . . the whole family is."

"And homemade lasagna is their way of patting me on the back, right?"

He shot me that full-blown grin that always knocks the wind out of me. All white teeth with a twinkle in his eye. "You're learning."

Villari got into his car and drove away.

I walked back into the house, but not before picking up Villari's cigarette butt.

TIME never moved so slowly. The afternoon just moseyed on by while I went berserk waiting for six o'clock to arrive. I spent the hours moving aimlessly from room to room, piddling around the house, which is the most I ever do, since housekeeping is never on my list of priorities. Now and then I felt twinges of guilt watching the dust pile up like snow, but I figured that, as far as faults go, it could be worse. Being messy fell somewhere between "Need to lose ten pounds" and "Send Christmas thank-you notes before July." I couldn't see St. Peter barricading the Pearly Gates because I left wet towels on the floor.

As Mark suggested, I soaked in a long, leisurely hot bath and tried to relax. That done, I pulled on a pair of flannel boxer shorts and a tank top, and lay down on the bed. I tried to nap for an hour, but my eyes insisted on staying open and my mind was whirling like mad. Once I started counting how many times I blinked in a minute, I knew that sleep was impossible. Finally, I got up and went down the hall to my converted studio.

My studio. It was all white with natural light streaming through the skylight overhead and a whole wall of windows facing south. Clay torsos in different stages of completion stood on a long wooden plank that stretched the length of the opposite wall, many of them wrapped in heavy plastic. Normally, there were more figures in the room, but with the upcoming show, I had culled out my favorite pieces and completed them. After they were sent to be bronzed, they were delivered to The Outlook for the show.

It had been a long road, getting here, getting ready for my first show. It was Elizabeth, my dear neighbor and surrogate mother, who left me the means to get the lessons I needed and the necessary first introduction to Mark. Her violent death left me angry and lonely for a long time, but at the same time, it made me more determined than ever to pursue my art. I saw this show as a tribute to Elizabeth, and I knew that when the doors opened tonight, I would feel a strong mixture of pride and sadness.

I left the room and walked down the hallway, too restless to work. I threw in a load of laundry that would mildew before I remembered to put it in the dryer, emptied the dishwasher, and reheated stale coffee. I tried to read, needlepoint, and watch television. I even tried to call Mark, but couldn't get through; he refused to take my call. Cathy, his secretary, had been instructed to tell me to go get a haircut, or better yet, buy a dress. If you ask me, everyone was overly concerned about my wardrobe.

Finally, five o'clock rolled around, and even though I was in no hurry to get to Villari's parents' house, at least I had something definite to do. I hopped in the shower, this time to bathe, not lounge around in smelly soap, and I started thinking about the evening ahead. Don't get me wrong— my opinion of Villari's family had undergone a major transformation over the past year, most of it in a very positive direction, but I was still uncomfortable being in the center of all that free-flowing emotion. My ex-husband was Italian, too, and I didn't fare any better with his family. I was still a little gun-shy when it came to accepting or expressing emotions, although Villari says I'm damned good with anger.

Stepping out of the shower, I slipped on my panties, towel-dried my hair, put some mousse in it—something I never do—and blew it dry. In deference to Mark, I brushed on some eye shadow, something else I never do, swiped on mascara, blush, and lipstick. Walking to the closet, I pulled out the dress that Lisa made me buy with one arm twisted behind my back. It was the typical little black dress, made of some soft clingy material. Given my washboard chest and flat-as-a-pancake butt, God only knows what the thing was going to cling to. It had a high front with a long scooped back, which meant I had to ditch the bra . . . no great loss . . . and the whole thing flared out at the bottom so that it swished around my calves. That was the one thing I had insisted on, that the dress be long enough for me to sit down or bend over without flashing the world a view of my butt. I completed the outfit by slipping on a pair of black strappy sandals with three inch heels—not enough of a boost to look Villari in the eye, but high enough to break an ankle.

Twirling in front of the mirror, I thought I looked good in a sluttish sort of way. For once, being skinny seemed to work in my favor. The dress went straight up and down, and so did I, like an antenna with a little head at the top. All in all, the ensemble seemed right for a night of gliding around the room, drinking champagne, schmoozing, and air-kissing people with large checkbooks.

The doorbell rang in the middle of my imaginary photo shoot for the cover of *People* magazine—move over, Julia Roberts—and I glanced at the clock, knowing it had to be exactly six o'clock. I suspected that Villari had arrived early, stood outside my door, and stared at his watch, his finger hovering right over the bell, ready to push the button at the exact moment the big hand hit the twelve. I'm surprised he didn't wear several watches all synchronized to beep at the same time. Blowing myself a kiss and sexily mouthing the words "Good luck, darling" in a bad imitation of Zsa Zsa Gabor, I picked up my shawl and walked down the hallway to meet Mr. Impatient.

I pulled open the door. I expected to see Villari pacing back and forth, but instead he was leaning against the porch rail, arms folded, his right foot crossed over his left ankle. His eyes widened in surprise and then changed to appreciation. Those same dark eyes roamed over my body, slowly, seductively, until the back of my neck warmed under his scrutiny. Maybe there really was something to this feminine thing Lisa kept harping about.

He stood and walked toward me, placing both hands on my arms and pulling me forward. "My God, Maggie, you look beautiful."

"Come on, Villari, I—"

"For once," he said, interrupting me, "forget the cute remarks, okay?" He leaned over and kissed me. "You look absolutely stunning. Enjoy it. Not only is your work going to knock them dead, but those rich old men are going to drool all over themselves trying to sidle up next to the artist."

I laughed. "A slight exaggeration," I said snootily, "but only slight."

He grinned. That gorgeous lopsided grin. I nudged him back a few inches and took my time checking him out from top to bottom, especially bottom. Obviously, I wasn't the only one who had spent time in front of the mirror tonight. Villari looked breathtakingly handsome. With wide shoulders and a strong, athletic physique, his body was perfectly proportioned. He wore a gray flannel sport coat over loose-fitting pleated black pants. His white shirt, one button opened at the collar, contrasted nicely with his tanned face. It was a far cry from his usual jeans, T-shirt, and black cowboy boots.

"You're not a bad-looking guy, for a detective."

"You're not so bad yourself, for an artist."

We started to laugh, but our eyes locked, and I was a goner. He hauled me up to his chest and my heart turned over. He placed his lips on mine, softly and gently, until I thought I'd go crazy with the sweetness. He pulled me closer, tighter, and deepened the kiss. We stayed in lip-lock heaven until I was dizzy from the lack of oxygen. Mrs. Peterson was probably tripping over the couch trying to get the binoculars.

"You do have a knack for kissing," I said against his mouth.

"Glad to hear it," he whispered, grazing my bottom lip. "Why don't you and I forget this whole shindig tonight and go bounce on the bedsprings?" For some unknown reason, Villari metamorphosed into the Marlboro Man whenever sex was involved. Like a frustrated wannabe cowboy, he lapsed into a heavy drawl and colorful expressions that, I admit, had me wanting to play the horizontal tussle.

"And miss Mamacita's little reception?" I teased.

He groaned. "Ever since I was five years old and she caught me checking out Sally Hall's fanny behind our garage, that woman has found a way to interrupt my sex life." Villari drew back, ran his hands down my arms, and smiled. "You look lovely, Maggie."

I was ready to chuck the dress right then, but I couldn't. "Let's go, my Texan Don Juan, before things get out of hand. I can already feel your mother's aura—the air is starting to smell like oregano."

A harvest moon hung like a pale peach against the ash-colored sky. The autumn breeze was crisp and cold, fluttering through the trees and softly tickling the pine needles. I shivered, pulled the shawl around my shoulders, and held Villari's hand as we walked down the driveway to his car.

I don't remember much about the ride to his mother's except that I was surprisingly calm and relaxed. Maybe it was the warmth and security emanating from Villari's hand, and I hoped, other parts of his body. Or maybe because this was *it*. My show. The real thing. Everything that happened from here on in was out of my control. I could rant or rave, complain or whine, it didn't matter. The world was going to march forward whether I liked it or not.

I just wish Destiny had been a little kinder.

MAMACITA set out a spread that blew me away. Petite and fragile-looking, the woman was strong enough to put a lumberjack to shame. Somehow she cooks, cleans house, pampers her husband, and manages to keep four grown kids in line by the omnipotent power of "the look." I'd been the recipient of that look once, and trust me, once was more than enough.

The first time Villari dragged me to his parents' house, I was not a happy camper. I was really nervous, and more than a little angry, but she and I got along surprisingly well. There was a downside, though. Villari's mother decided rather quickly that I was a strong candidate to fill the exalted position of potential wife for her eldest son. She'd been in heavy matchmaking mode ever since.

It seemed the whole clan was jammed in the front doorway when we arrived. After all these months, I still found myself bracing against the onslaught of well-meaning emotions that seemed to gush forth from Villari's family, but with his hand placed firmly and reassuringly at the small of my back, he urged me forward. After a flurry of exclamations and kisses from sisters, brothers, aunts, uncles, cousins—first/second/three times removed—grandparents, and godparents, Mrs. Villari extended her hand, took mine in hers, and pulled me toward her. Like the eye of a hurricane, she was a calm port in the storm. She put her arms around me and hugged me gently, her eyes sparkling with excitement and, I believed, pride.

"Maggie, what a night! Your first show, a grand opening and," she said, her eyes snapping with merriment, "your first dress." She patted my cheek and laughed. "You must be starving. Come. I will get you a plate. It would not do for you to arrive at The Outlook only to faint away in hunger."

My stomach felt a little jumpy, a little shaky, everything but hungry, but I'd given up trying to convince these people that spaghetti was not a cure-all. If pasta on a nervous stomach made me throw up, that was too bad; she would not take no for an answer, and I didn't have the heart to disappoint her. Fortunately, I had remembered to bring a roll of antacids.

Following Mamacita to the buffet table, I was suddenly swung around and swooped up in a huge bear hug, and I didn't have to look to know it was Villari's father. He was a giant of a man, by any standard, as big as his wife was small. His voice boomed, his eyes twinkled, and he laughed heartily. It was impossible to feel anything but happiness around Franco Villari, the man I nicknamed Papa Frank, an Americanized version he graciously accepted.

He took my hand and held it up high over my head, twirling me in circles like a ballerina. Normally, a move like that would embarrass the hell out of me, but Villari's father embraced the world with such enthusiasm that I didn't have any choice but to enjoy it right along with him.

"You look lovely, Miss Maggie. Still too skinny, but lovely just the same." He leaned toward his son, who had miraculously dislodged himself from the band of relatives and appeared at his side. "You'd better keep a close watch on her tonight, son. There will be lots of eligible, rich young men who will be very interested in taking this young lady off your hands."

"Yeah," I said, taunting him, "maybe someone a lot less bossy and disagreeable."

"Honey, you could take the most mild-mannered sweetheart of a guy and turn him into a raving maniac in less than an hour."

"Stop them now, Franco, or we'll have a battle on our hands," Mamacita interjected, handing me a plate heaped with food. "These two fight like Mafioso. They make Gotti and Gravano look like best friends."

"Just like you and me, no?" he asked, winking.

Mamacita rolled her eyes and leaned toward me, whispering, "The man is a respected doctor, but when he gets amorous, he insists on sounding like a man fresh off the boat."

I thought of Villari's tendency to speak in country-bumpkin cliches and nodded my head in understanding. Taking the fork from her hand, I dug in and made an attempt to look hungry.

An hour later, the room began to empty as people finished eating and headed to The Outlook in separate cars. Villari and I stayed at the house drinking coffee until everyone left. He wanted me to make a grand entrance—an idea I balked at. But Villari insisted on it and he wouldn't budge, even after I pointed out that other works by different artists were also being displayed. It didn't matter. I was the featured artist and that's all he cared about. We almost came to blows over it, but the detective held firm, saying it was my night to be in the limelight and he wasn't going to let me slink off into a corner.

We arrived about twenty minutes after his parents. Andy was the first one I saw when Villari opened the thick glass door for me. He was standing next to one of my favorite pieces, a sculpture of a woman gardening. As I walked in, he glanced up, caught my eye, and smiled. He held my gaze and I knew he recognized the figure as our mother, taken from the same picture my father commissioned into a portrait after she died.

The Outlook took my breath away. The place had been completely transformed from the craziness I had witnessed this morning. Awashed in light, the floors gleamed. Huge landscape canvases hung on stark-white backgrounds. Cone-shaped spotlights illuminated my figures, casting long shadows against the walls. The sculptures were strategically placed between pictures, tucked into corners, and grouped in the middle of the room. Nameplates were neatly typed in black letters—each title, each figure falling perfectly under the heading of *A Journey*, the title of my show. The whole scene was beyond my wildest expectations and the first thing that popped into my head was the thought that Mark should have kicked me out a lot sooner.

"Here you go, sis," Andy said, handing me a flute of champagne, slipping his arm through mine. We left Villari and walked around the room together, stopping here and there to appreciate the different art. We didn't speak much, and except for the bright smiles and murmurs of congratulations, people left us alone.

"Listen, Maggie," my brother said, his voice soft and hesitant, "I need to apologize."

I stopped and turned in surprise. "For what?"

He looked down at the ground and then back at me, his expression regretful. "I just didn't know."

"You're talking Swahili here. What didn't you know?"

"That you were so damn talented."

I smiled. "Gee, Andy, I appreciate the compliment, I really do, but why the apology?"

"Because I should have known. I'm your brother and I didn't know. I guess I thought this was more or less a hobby of yours. When you took a leave of absence from your teaching job to pursue this full-time, I was more than a little worried. I never realized how good—I mean, really good— you were."

"Well, thanks, I guess. I'm not sure whether to be glad

that you think I'm good or irritated that you didn't think I would be."

"Let's go with the *glad* feeling," he suggested, grinning. "I'd sure hate to have to pin you to the ground on your big night."

"In your dreams, big brother. You have bad knees, remember? One swift kick in the right direction and you'd fall to the ground like a drunken sailor."

We were interrupted before he could respond.

"You can't have her to yourself all night, Andy," Lisa said, coming up behind us. She was sipping champagne with her husband, Joel. "The artist needs to mingle tonight with the beautiful people, which does not include her older brother." Lisa hugged me tightly with one arm and we pressed cheeks together to avoid smudging our lipstick. Joel stood there staring at me openmouthed.

"What's wrong with you?" I demanded. "Your brain have a charley horse?"

Joel grinned. "You sure do clean up nicely."

"Ain't it the truth," Andy piped in.

"I swear, put on a dress and you guys go brain dead."

"I've known you for a lot of years, Maggie, and this is the first time I can actually *see* that you're a woman. A very attractive woman, as a matter of fact," Joel added.

"You noticed, huh?" Villari said, suddenly standing beside me, slipping his arm around my waist.

"You'd have to be blind not to notice her in that outfit."

I turned to Lisa. "What's the matter with Joel? He's never been this nice to me. Usually he chucks me on the chin and heads out to watch television with a beer in his hand."

Lisa shrugged, the edges of her lips twitching. "I told you the dress worked. If you'd let me, I could do some amazing things for your wardrobe."

"No, thanks. I've already got a headache with all this unleashed testosterone."

"Then let's go introduce ourselves around the room and leave the men to their sports and favorite power tools."

Suddenly panicked, I hung back. "Uh, Lisa, I think I'll stay and swap baseball stats."

"Oh, no you don't," she said, wrapping her manicured hand around my arm and pulling me away from Villari. "Mark has already instructed me to dislodge you from your brother and your boyfriend. He wants us to circle the place and meet people. I'm not about to ignore his orders."

"You do it," I pleaded. "You're great at this sort of thing and I'm horrible. Just flounce around the room and charm everyone into opening their checkbooks."

"First of all," Lisa said pointedly, "I don't flounce. Second, I don't know a thing about art—"

"What's to know? Just throw in a few words about capturing the essence or fluid lines—"

"And third, everyone knows who you are. They started whispering the moment you arrived."

"They have? How would they know me?"

"Because, you idiot, your father has tripped all over himself bragging about his little girl."

I blinked in confusion. "You're kidding, right?"

Lisa glanced back at the guys, who had already forgotten us. "Come on." She led me to a large painting, which we pretended to examine. "You do know he's here, right?"

"Of course. I invited him."

"Have you spoken to him yet?"

"No. I haven't had the chance."

"Then you need to." Lisa regarded me soberly. "This show has affected him, Maggie. I can't explain it. It's touched something deep inside."

"He's the same, Lisa, trust me on this," I said dryly.

"I'm serious. He's always been a handsome man, but so withdrawn and wounded-looking, even with Sherri around. But tonight, his eyes are alive. He looks . . . I don't know . . . happy."

"My dad doesn't know how to be happy. He swings from a little distant to inaccessible. Sherri's the only one who gets through to him." I shook my head. "You've got the wrong guy, Lisa."

"It's him, Maggie. I know your dad. Go talk to him."

"Where is he, anyway?"

"By the bar. I think he's waiting for you."

Lisa was right. I peeked over her shoulder and saw my father sharing a small table with Sherri, my stepmother. He was a very regal-looking man, and even sitting, it was obvious that he was tall and quite lean. His thick white hair, hair that always reminded me of Bob Barker from *The Price is Right,* was neatly combed. Sherri leaned over and whispered something in his ear, probably commenting on some act of phoniness or snobbery, and they both started laughing. Sherri was awfully good for him. My stepmother was a middle-aged lady with flaming red hair and sharp blue eyes. She had a strong, acerbic sense of humor and no tolerance for insincerity, two traits that should have conflicted with her job as the owner of an exclusive boutique. But her clients fell in love with her immediately, or soon afterward, once they realized she spoke her mind because she really did care about them. Who else could say "That dress makes your hips look as wide as a barn" and get away with it? But Sherri insisted that deep down, women already knew the real truth about their bodies, and they didn't need some twig of a salesgirl insisting that a Lycra skirt looked divine stretched across a size sixteen butt.

As if on cue, my father lifted his head and glanced across the room, catching my eye. His eyes met mine, and the laughter fell away. His unwavering look paralyzed me, rooted me to the spot. I was more accustomed to disinterest or ambivalence from him. But tonight, at this moment, his piercing, flint-gray eyes were focused on me and I didn't know how to take the next step.

Apparently, Lisa did. She placed the palm of her hand on my back and pushed me from behind. I stumbled on the death stilts strapped to my feet, but miraculously stayed upright. With wobbly ankles and a pounding heart, I started across the room. *Enough of this,* I admonished myself, *it's just your dad, the same guy who woke up every morning of your childhood and drank coffee at the kitchen table, his skinny white calves sticking out beneath his ratty old robe.* I pulled my shoulders back and strode confidently to his table.

My father stood quietly and reached for me. Taking both my hands in his, he said, "Your mother would have been proud."

"She would?" I asked, surprised. My father seldom spoke of my mother, and never with emotion.

"Oh, most definitely. As I am." He squeezed my hands. "She was an artist, you know."

I shook my head. This was the first I'd heard about it. Dad was stingy with information.

"A frustrated artist, she would say. She majored in art and planned to paint, but we met and fell in love." He lifted his shoulders. "Then Andy came along, and you were not too far behind. Suddenly, her life was very much into diapers and baby food and that sort of thing." He shook his head at the question he read on my face. "No, she never regretted it, Maggie. She loved being a mother. Painting was put on hold until the two of you started school . . . but she got sick . . . and then she was gone." His eyes softened. "But tonight, she is here. We are proud of our daughter."

Tears filled my eyes.

"Your smart mouth, though," he said, lightening the moment, "I'm not sure where you got that."

"Self-preservation. How else was I going to survive Andy?"

My father hugged me gently, then released me. "You'd better go, Maggie. I don't want to monopolize your time, especially not with Mark bearing down on me."

"I don't blame you," I said sympathetically. "Maybe I could sic Sherri on him. She's the only one I know who can stand up to a guard dog and have him licking out of her hand."

"She does have a knack for wearing down stubborn men," he agreed, turning to look at Sherri. She was still sitting at the table, contentedly sipping her drink and watching the two of us.

"You two go ahead and talk like I'm not here," she said, waving her hand dismissively. "When you need a bulldog like me, you'll remember this conversation."

"I need one now, Sherri. Mark is going to corral me into Conversation Hell with some guy sporting a big gut and a bad toupee."

"My, don't you have a cheery outlook on life," she replied drolly.

"I do, really," I insisted, hurrying on when she raised her eyebrow in disbelief. "I do see the glass as half full, I'm just extremely annoyed that someone drank the top half."

She shook her head. "I'm not sure that makes a lick of sense, darling, but you are your father's daughter, and I'm sure that in some convoluted way, that philosophy ties everything together in your world. Fortunately, I don't have to understand it to appreciate it." She stood and held out her hand to my father. "Come, Robert. Let's go admire the art. Whether she likes it or not, Maggie really does need to make herself available to interested patrons." Leaning toward me, she gave me a quick hug and smiled. "You look beautiful tonight, which is not easy for me to admit, since that dress did not come from my store."

"I was gun-shy," I said, smiling. "Calling someone the Toothpick Twin doesn't exactly invite repeat business."

"You'd be surprised, honey. Besides, you *are* a toothpick," she declared. "But in shimmering black, skinny becomes svelte . . . very chic. Tonight you are a waif with an attitude."

"Thanks, I think."

"Don't mention it. Now go on before Mark has a coronary." Seconds later, she and my father were swallowed by the crowd and I was standing in the shadows by the bar. It was a short reprieve, though, as I suspected it would be. Lisa crossed the room, grabbed my hand, and led me toward the middle of the room, where Mark was standing beside a short, squat man examining my sculpture *The Kite*—one of my larger pieces. It was of a young girl running, playing in a field of tall grass, the wind lifting her long hair as her kite rises in the sky. It's a sculpture of movement and spirit, of the fearlessness of youth and the belief that life can be, should be, everything you want.

Mark looked up. "Ah, Maggie, here you are." He touched my arm, and although his lips were smiling, there was no missing the lecture in his eyes that scolded: "And where the hell have you been?"

I smiled right back at him. "Yes, here I am," I replied, with eyes that said: "Back off, buddy."

Once the pissing contest was over, he tugged me closer and introduced me. "This is Henry Duran. He's an old friend of mine."

Henry Duran was the oddest-looking man I'd ever met. He was completely bald except for thin strips of hair on the sides—strips dyed so black, I expected to see shoe polish drizzling over his ears. His face was round and pudgy, which was not so unusual, but the green-and-white checked pants topped with the pink polo shirt clashed badly, especially against the backdrop of black jackets and evening dresses. If he spun around fast enough, he would have been mistaken for a strobe light. There was no doubt in my mind that he was divorced. No sane woman could look at that outfit without bolting to a lawyer. To top it off, the man was chomping and chewing on an unlit cigar, switching it from one side of his mouth to the other, like a cow chewing its cud. I didn't know where Mark had picked up this specimen of humanity, but if this represented the best and brightest patron of the arts, I was in a heap of trouble.

Still, I didn't want to be rude. I held out my hand. "It's nice to meet you, Mr. Duran."

He grabbed my hand in his big meaty paw and shook it until he jarred my shoulder loose. "Damn good work, Ms. Kean," he said, pulling his unlit cigar out and jabbing the air to make his point. "Like I was telling Mark here, you've got a lot of talent. I like what I see." He stuck his cigar back in his mouth, pushed it to the side, and growled around it. "The problem is, it's a little too soft for my taste. I'm partial to work with a little more edge."

Not knowing how to respond, I just nodded my head.

"Don't get me wrong, that's not a statement on what you've done here tonight, it just happens to be my personal likes at this particular time. I've been collecting art for a lot of years, and believe you me, I've gone through some wild-ass stages . . . reminds me of teenagers—one minute they're randy as hell, the next minute they're carrying a gun to defend our country. Ain't no rhyme or reason in life. You got two choices, take it as it comes or fight every second of it. There's an old saying, 'It's easier to ride the horse in the direction it's going.' Otherwise, in the end, you'll lose every time. Same with art."

Who was this man? I was afraid to even look at Mark for fear of laughing out loud or shaking my head in disbelief.

46

He was still going on about his art collection, still punctuating the air with his cigar for emphasis.

"You've got to go with what you've got inside. I mean, good artists take a chance, even if it isn't what everybody wants to see or what they're used to. You've got to grab your privates and dive in and to hell with what everyone says. If it weren't for van Gogh and Picasso and a whole list of brave people, we'd still be looking at dark oil paintings of sissy boys in blue knickers and fat women rolling on the grass." He stopped, hitched up his pants, and then pointed at my kite sculpture. "Now, this is a good example. At one time, I would have snatched this up before you could blink an eye. That was when I was married and in love for the first time and I thought the world looked pretty damn good. But a lot of time has passed and the world's looking a little rough around the edges, a little tarnished—like me, I guess, and I'm looking for something that I can think on."

Henry Duran was probably the most interesting man I'd ever met and, without being aware of it, he was luring me into his world with its mix of good ole boy meanderings and philosophical thoughts. A germ of an idea was forming in my brain. I was pretty sure Mark wouldn't like it—in fact, I could already imagine his face tightening, but I threw caution to the wind. I didn't have any privates to grab on to, but I could dive in as well as the next man.

"I appreciate your opinion, Mr. Duran, and—"

"Uh-oh. I've offended you, haven't I? Anytime a woman starts a line with 'I appreciate,' there's gonna be problems down the line."

I shook my head. "Actually, no. I really *do* appreciate your opinion. And although I might not be able to state it quite as colorfully as you did, I understand what you're saying. When we were planning this show, not only were we trying to display my best work, but we wanted to tie it together under a unifying theme." I glanced at Mark, who had slipped into Zen-land and now appeared ultra-calm and collected, except for the nasty tic fluttering beneath his left eye. Taking a deep breath for courage, I plunged on. "Anyway, for one reason or another, one piece was left out, and I think it might be more to your liking." The words tumbled out of my mouth like I'd been born selling my work. I sounded like an insurance salesman. "It's raw," I said, "with a coarse, unrefined finish. The form is undefined and blunt, for lack of a better word. But it has strength and power to it. At least that's what I was going for. I don't even have a title for it."

"Well, do I get to see the thing or are we just flapping party tongues?"

"It's here. In the back."

"Some kind of storeroom?"

"Not exactly," Mark explained. "The Outlook actually has a full-size studio attached to it, where artists work on their pottery or sculptures. Some artists bring in their paintings and sketches for group critiques. There's a storage area, too, that is available for unfinished works, or in this case, for pieces that weren't selected for exhibition. We keep them here for people like yourself, who would want to see more of a particular artist's work." He looked at me and smiled, as well as he could smile with his teeth clenched.

My jaw dropped during this little explanation. The studio

part was true—artists did work back there, but Mark did not store my sculpture for convenience; he left it back there because he *hated* the thing.

"Let's go then," Duran said, waving his cigar around. "Can you leave this little get-together for a bit?"

"Happily," I replied.

Duran's bushy eyebrows shot up and he threw his head back and roared. "I know what you mean, Ms. Kean," he said. "All that time and effort to get dolled up, and for what? To rub elbows with other dolled-up people who couldn't find their backside with two hands in broad daylight."

The man had a real interesting way with words. I loved it.

He stuck his cigar in his mouth, and crooked his elbow for me. "Lead the way, Ms. Kean."

I slipped my hand around his arm and led him through the crowds. No doubt we made a funny picture, he and I, Mr. Sturdy in the Wind and the Toothpick Twin.

I caught Jamie's eye right before I pushed open the door leading to the studio. She was busily serving food from the long tables that had been set up next to the bar, but stopped for a second to send me a thumbs-up sign. I smiled and guided Duran into the back. As we stepped through the door, I blinked a few times to adjust to the bright fluorescent lights. I saw right away that Mark had rearranged everything in the room and it took me a few moments to find my sculpture in the far corner by the back door. Moving toward it, I noticed a strange smell. I glanced at Duran and, given the way his nose was wrinkling, knew he'd noticed the same thing. The smell grew stronger as we drew closer to the firing room. Thinking something was burning, I opened the door and was nearly knocked backward by the stench. Convinced that something was on fire, I plugged my nose, ducked into the room, and hurried toward the kiln. I reached out, unlatched the small peep window on the door, and jerked it open.

I froze.

Numb. I was numb, unable to move. My legs, my arms, were paralyzed with something—I couldn't name it, couldn't describe the feeling that washed over me. A dead man was curled in the kiln, *burned*. Charred clothes stuck to his flesh, peeling at the edges. Next to the walls of the kiln, the body was burned so dark, almost purple, the skin a hard, dull surface. The rest was a blur of scalded flesh and dried blood. I was riveted to the scene, so appalled, so horrified, I simply didn't, *couldn't,* think about looking away. My mind was frozen solid, nothing worked anymore. My brain had detached itself from the rest of my body in order to survive.

Disjointed questions coursed through my mind. How long had the body been there? Was he alive when he was shoved in the kiln? What was the temperature? Did he yell for help? And if he did, why didn't anyone come? Did he pound the walls? Who was he? Who was he?

Then in a flash, I heard a loud noise, a piercing frightened scream. It came from far away, then grew louder and louder until my ears filled with the noise. Moments passed before I realized the sound came from my mouth. My lips were opened wide and my throat burned with the effort. Once I started, I couldn't stop, my voice shattering the block of ice my mind had become. I screamed and screamed, until I heard footsteps and people . . . and finally, I turned away.

Villari arrived at my side, took one look, and cursed. Grabbing me around the waist, he dragged me from the site. I fought him; I don't know why. My arms flailed, my feet kicked, until I was thrown over his shoulder in a fireman's carry and carted away. He strode across the room, pushed through the double doors leading into, and out of, the studio, and carried me into the museum and put me down. He propped me up against the far wall and pushed his face within inches of mine.

"Maggie, listen to me," he demanded.

When I didn't answer, he took my chin in his hand and held it firmly, forcing me to look at him, to focus on him. "I have to leave. I have to take care of the body."

I shook my head. "You can't take care of a corpse, Detective. He's gone already," I said, snapping my fingers. "Just like that."

"Maggie, you've got to hold yourself together, just for a little while. I know this is a shock, but I've got a crime scene that's being tromped on and I can't stay here with you. Can you stay here by yourself, at least until I get some back up?"

"I've got her, Sam." Andy's head came up over Villari's shoulder. "Go do what you have to do. Maggie and I will be fine . . . as fine as you can be after witnessing that—whatever that was."

Villari drew me close for an instant. He hugged me hard and then released me into Andy's ready arms. I felt like a rag doll being passed from person to person, but every ounce of energy I ever possessed had drained from my body.

"I'll send the EMTs to check her over as soon as they arrive," Villari said worriedly.

"I'm okay," I said weakly, my face pressed into Andy's chest.

Villari reached out and stroked my hair. "I know you are, Maggie." I could feel them exchanging looks over the top of my head. "I'll be back as soon as I can," he said. He turned and left the room. The hinges squeaked as he strode through the swinging doors back into the studio.

Andy and I stood silently for several long minutes. I didn't know what to say or what to think. A strange sensation, a sense of blankness, of nothingness, permeated my mind. I didn't know what to call it or how to describe it, because I couldn't feel *anything*. A dead body was not new to me. I'd been through it before when I discovered Elizabeth, but that was so different. Elizabeth was my neighbor, someone I cared about. The instant I saw her body, the anger I felt toward her murderer slipped in and absorbed the shock. Right away, I was mad—furious, actually. I didn't have to think, or feel, because the rage took over and propelled me through the days. Sometimes it was the only thing that kept me going.

But this time, I felt numb. Empty and hollow. This time, the body had no name. The anonymous victim. I knew he belonged to someone and lived somewhere, maybe one of those three-story houses up on the ridge that overlooked the eastern plains. He probably had kids, a boy and a girl, and a big friendly mutt that licked and slobbered on strangers and barked at the neighbors. This man had a life beyond the walls of the searing oven that claimed his life. I knew it, but I still couldn't feel anything.

I raised my face and placed my palms on Andy's chest. "Who would do such a thing?"

He sighed. "Evil, Maggie. Someone very evil."

"The smell, Andy, I didn't notice it at first. I was showing Mr. Duran around, showing him my sculpture, and then this smell hit my nose, this horrible odor that was so out of place. I just followed it to the room, where the kiln was, and I opened the door and stood in the staging area and almost gagged. It didn't make any sense, firing clay never smelled like that. I knew something was wrong. Something was burning, so I ran to the kiln and popped the latch and . . ."

My legs buckled and I started to collapse. My brother quickly slipped one arm around my back and one underneath my legs and lifted me into the air before I hit the ground. He carried me to the table by the bar, the same one Sherri and my father had sat at earlier in the evening. With his right foot, Andy hooked a chair leg, jerked it out, and put me down. He pulled up another seat and sat down opposite me.

"You all right?" he asked, concern etched across his face.

"Yeah, I'm okay. Sorry about that. I didn't mean to pass out on you."

"Don't worry about it—you didn't really faint, you sort of folded," he said, a ghost of a smile touching his lips. "Gave me a chance to feel manly, having to carry you."

"Hope I wasn't too heavy," I replied, playing along.

"No problem. I lifted with my knees."

I shook my head. "I can't believe we're making jokes at a time like this."

Andy reached over and took my hand. "Right now that's all we can do."

"I know, but it seems wrong somehow."

"There's no right and wrong in this situation, Maggie. There's no rule book on how to act or react when someone is murdered in the back room while people are drinking champagne in the front."

"You're probably right. It's just that I don't feel anything."

"That's your body's way of protecting you. Once you're convinced that you're safe, the shock will wear off and you'll be inundated with feelings. They might not make sense, but eventually, you'll feel everything."

"And how did you get to be such an expert?"

"I'm a sports columnist, remember? The same thing happens when a player gets hurt. Initially, if the injury is bad enough, he'll immediately go into shock and he won't feel anything. If things are really desperate, he'll pass out. The body just shuts everything down. Sometimes the shock is more dangerous than the actual injury."

"If I'm suffering from anything, it's an 'I can't believe this really happened' shock. Who would do such a thing? Why would they do it? The sheer evilness is mind-boggling."

"That's an unanswerable question, Maggie. Even if Villari uncovers the who, I don't think you'll ever understand the why." He paused as he stared past my shoulder and off into the distance. "How are you feeling?"

"Better. Better than I was. Not as good as I could be. Why?"

"Because life as you know it is about to change. You've got a whole gaggle of people who want to talk to you, and they're headed this way."

"Oh, my God, Andy, I'm not ready to talk to anybody."

"I don't think you've got a choice, sis. The guy heading up this group looks pretty damn grim and determined. I recognize some of the reporters—"

"Reporters?" I groaned.

"I can probably stave them off for a while, but Head Honcho there is another story."

I covered my face. "I can't look. How did they find out so quickly?"

"Police scanners. Once a call goes out to the EMTs, the reporters are all over it." He gave my hand one last squeeze and stood. "Come on, guys, let's leave these two alone," Andy said, casually stepping in front of one reporter and effectively herding the group to the other side of the room.

"Ms. Kean?"

I looked up to see a tall lean man with black hair, thick eyebrows, and a square jaw. He was dressed in a dark gray suit, stiff white shirt, and a blue, perfectly knotted tie. A heavy overcoat was draped over his arm. Probing blue eyes stared down at me.

"That's me."

He indicated the chair next to mine. "May I?"

I shrugged.

The Robert Stack look-alike unbuttoned his suit coat,

laid his jacket over the back of the chair, and sat down. "I understand you found the body."

"Yes."

He studied me closely. "Want to tell me about it?"

"Not particularly."

"Not a big fan of the police, are you?"

"Not particularly."

"Any reason why?"

I thought briefly about repeating my "not particularly" refrain again, but I didn't think humor was this guy's strong suit. Besides, I knew I was being unfair. My uncooperative response was just a knee-jerk reaction. I'd had quite a chip on my shoulder when Elizabeth was murdered and I was immediately cast as the prime suspect. But my feelings toward cops had softened this past year since Villari and I had become involved, no matter how loosely I defined that term.

"Look, Officer—"

"Lieutenant. Lieutenant Baxter."

"I've been down this road before, Lieutenant, and it's not pleasant."

"Murder is never entertainment, Ms. Kean," he said dryly. "It's violent, messy, and in this case, particularly gruesome."

"Unfortunately, I've discovered that . . . a couple of times."

He frowned.

"This is the second victim I've found, Lieutenant Baxter. I found my first body over a year ago in my front yard, so I'm not new to the process. And as much as I want to help you find the murderer, I know what to expect over the next few hours, and I'm not looking forward to it. You guys will question me until dawn, questions that will sound suspiciously like you're accusing me of the crime, and when one lieutenant finishes interrogating me, you'll substitute another lieutenant to start over and take me down the same damn road." I leaned forward. "I'll make you a deal. Gather together all your men and anyone else who wants to hear the story. I'll tell it from start to finish, all details included, one time. I'll even serve the coffee."

"I know this is difficult," he said, "but this is nonnegotiable. We don't make deals with the witnesses."

"According to John Grisham you do," I replied. "What about those 'You tell us what we need to know and we'll reduce the charges from murder two to manslaughter' incidents?"

"That's called plea-bargaining with suspects or defendants. Real life is a little more complex than what you see on prime-time television, and I don't have the time to explain the process to you," he said, folding his hands together. "Ms. Kean, the process is there for a reason. It may seem long and drawn out, even arduous, but the procedure has a purpose."

"I know," I said, relenting. "I realize you're gathering information, not trying to arrest me for murder."

"Not unless you killed the man," he said, with just the hint of a question in his voice.

"No, I didn't," I said. "I'm not in the habit of hoisting people into kilns."

"Then it's highly unlikely that we'll be locking you up in the near future—unless you refuse to cooperate with us, at which point the charges would be obstruction, withholding information, and any other charge I can trump up for waylaying our investigation."

I guess Lieutenant Baxter was sending me a free warning. Cooperate or else.

"I see you've met Maggie."

I jumped at the voice behind me. I turned around and hurled myself at Villari, wrapping my arms around his waist.

"You okay, honey?" he murmured as he stroked my back.

"I guess so," I mumbled, my face mashed against his chest.

"She giving you trouble, Lieutenant?"

I heard the scrape of the chair as the lieutenant stood and extended his hand. "Well, Sam, I had no idea that this was the woman who's been occupying your time lately. No, she's been very helpful, although," he said, raising both eyebrows, "I can see how she could be quite a handful."

"Wouldn't have it any other way," Villari replied, awkwardly shaking the lieutenant's hand while I hung on, "except when I'm working a murder investigation. As you can see, she's not the easiest person to deal with under stress."

I untangled myself from Villari's embrace and stepped back. "I'm right here, you know," I said, glaring at the two of them. "A murder's been committed. Shouldn't you be out gathering a clue or two instead of dissecting my personality?"

"How kind of you to remind me, Ms. Kean," Baxter said wryly. "But if you remember, gathering a clue is why I'm talking to you in the first place. Perhaps we should get started."

Villari's eyes narrowed as he looked from me to Lieutenant Baxter, then back to me. "Are you telling me that you haven't told John what you saw? There's a dead body a hundred feet from here and you've been busy showing off your stubborn streak? I didn't expect you to be chummy, you never are when you're upset, but I sure as hell didn't expect you to sit here wasting the man's time."

I tried, but I couldn't hold his gaze.

"Back off a little, Sam. We haven't had time to do anything but introduce ourselves. Ms. Kean and I were just getting started when you walked up."

I gaped at Baxter, surprised that he would cover for me, even a little. It's not that I'd been unhelpful, but I hadn't been exactly accommodating, either. Given the gravity of the situation, it didn't really matter whether the lieutenant and I were best buddies or mortal enemies. A man had died and maybe, just maybe, I knew something that would help find the killer.

Villari turned to Lieutenant Baxter. "John, I've got to get back. The captain should arrive any minute now—in fact, I'm surprised he's not here now. When he gets here, we can divide up the questioning and decide how to proceed." He paused and then glanced purposefully in my direction. "I'll let you finish your interview with Maggie. Let me know if she's anything less than cooperative. I'm very adept at wringing her neck."

Villari and I never did get along well at crime scenes.

"Well, Ms. Kean, shall we get started?" Lieutenant Baxter

said, offering me the chair I had vaulted from just a few moments ago.

I sat down.

Without preamble, Baxter began. "Why don't we start from the beginning, and work our way from there. The more you can tell me, the more specific you can be, the better off we are." He pulled out a small notepad, flipped it open, and laid it on the table. He took a pen from his pocket and made a small notation.

"This is your work," he said, glancing around the room. "Am I correct?"

I nodded.

"Can you explain why you were in the back room?"

"Mr. Duran wanted to see one of my sculptures that was left out of the show."

"I see. And who is Mr. Duran?"

We continued on with Baxter asking questions and me answering them. It wasn't always easy, but I did manage to answer his questions with a minimum amount of flak. Now and then he would jot something down. He paid rapt attention to insignificant details. Sometimes I wondered whether Baxter was taking notes or just brushing up on his doodling skills.

People kept coming by. I could see them in my peripheral vision, but nobody came any closer than five feet of me. They hung around a little while, paced the area, and shot worried looks in my direction. After a few minutes, they left to talk to someone or wander aimlessly around the room. As far as I could tell, there was still a bunch of people left in the gallery. Apparently, the cops had locked the door and told the guests they couldn't leave until further notice. I was sure everybody had been questioned closely, but no one else had the dubious honor of having found the body.

"Why did you go into the room with the kiln? Your sculpture was in the adjacent area."

I hesitated. The question itself was enough to make my stomach churn. Bile rose in the back of my throat and I swallowed convulsively to keep myself from throwing up on Baxter's calfskin loafers.

He waited.

"The smell." Beads of perspiration popped out on my forehead and I swiped the moisture with the back of my hand. I'm sure I looked as guilty as if I'd killed the man myself, but of all the details I had hoped to blot out of my memory, the smell was the main one. It buried itself in my clothes, my hair, and my scalp. I knew I could wash and scrub and scrape until my skin was raw, but the smell would never leave. It was part of me now. Part of who I was.

"I . . . we . . . went in the back room. I was going to show him the sculpture—"

"Duran?"

"Yes. We were walking when . . . when this smell curled up into my nose . . . like one of those old Disney cartoons where the fragrance from a hot apple pie grabs a character by the nose and pulls. That's just how I felt. Except the odor was unlike anything I'd ever experienced. I couldn't place the source. For a brief second, I thought maybe it was from the restaurant next door, but then this burning smell kept pulling at me. Finally, I turned toward the firing room. By that time, I was sure something was burning." I stopped, unable to continue.

"Take it slow and easy, Ms. Kean. We're almost done."

I tried to compose myself, to calm my breathing. I took in great gulps of air and let them out slowly. My body was shaking like a leaf, but I knew I had to finish this . . . at least once. I stared directly at Lieutenant Baxter and went on. "I wasn't thinking logically. I mean, burned clay has a distinctive odor . . . I know it . . . sometimes the kiln . . . the temperature is too high for the size of the piece, or it's kept on too long . . . this wasn't like that . . . but I couldn't imagine what it was. When I reached the firing room, I pulled the door open and this acrid odor almost knocked me off my feet . . . but I still had no idea. I just knew that something was burning. I sort of lunged toward the kiln, unlatched the peephole—"

"Peephole?"

I nodded. "That's what I call it, anyway. There's a frame or lid that covers a small window on the outside of the kiln. It allows you to see inside without opening the door." I paused a moment. "I flipped up the lid and looked through. That's when I saw the body."

Baxter was quietly scribbling on his notepad.

"And as I'm looking at this body, I remember thinking, *Oh, it was the hair,* because I've singed my hair before and I recognized the smell." I was babbling now, on my own accord, because my nerves were shot and the only other option was to grab Baxter's damn pencil and tattoo his forehead. "All the time I'm thinking these crazy thoughts and questions, I'm screaming my head off, although I didn't know that right away. The rest is pretty much history."

The lieutenant stopped writing and glanced at me. "Could you identify the victim?"

I shook my head. "No, I didn't recognize the man."

Baxter flipped the cover on his notepad and slipped it into his pocket. He stood, rebuttoned his suit, and gathered his coat. Then he spoke in a very calm, businesslike voice. "Ms. Kean, thank you for your cooperation. I realize this was difficult for you, and if I could have spared you, I would have done so. This murder was exceptionally grisly, and I apologize for having to make you relive it once again."

I was beginning to like this guy with the starched shirt and stiff neck. A little conservative for my taste, but at least he seemed to understand what I was going through.

"This is Officer Blake, Ms. Kean," he continued, gesturing toward a cop who had suddenly appeared by his side. "He'll take over the questioning now."

"I was afraid of that," I said. "Look, all I did was find the body. I didn't kill the guy," I insisted, "which you must believe, or I'd be down at the station answering questions into a tape recorder. I don't even *know* the guy."

"I am keeping you here to answer further questions about what happened this evening. It pays to be thorough. You are quite right in your assessment, though. I don't believe you were involved in this man's death, but if I should change my mind at any point, you'll be the first to know."

"No wonder you and Villari are friends," I muttered under my breath as he started to leave.

He stopped and turned toward me. "Friendship has nothing to do with it. I respect him. He respects me. We catch killers. And you," he added, "are not Sam's usual type, but I daresay, you are exactly what he needs."

"And what is that supposed to mean?"

"Simple. You must drive him straight up the wall."

"Great. Another matchmaker," I mumbled to myself as he walked away. I looked over at my new companion. "Well, Officer Blake, what would you like to know?"

He pulled out a notepad and pencil. "Let's start from the beginning, shall we?"

Yes, we shall. And we did. Over and over again.

SOMEONE shook my shoulder. "Maggie? Maggie, wake up."

Reluctantly, I swam to the surface. I opened my eyes, my lids heavy and lethargic, still struggling against a dreamless sleep. Images were blurry and distorted, and I squinted until the world slowly clicked into focus. I lifted my head off my crossed arms where I had fallen asleep.

"Maggie?"

I yawned and looked across the table. "Villari? What time is it?"

"Around four in the morning," he replied, checking his watch. "Are you okay?"

"Yeah, I'm fine," I said, rubbing the knot in my neck.

Villari stood and held out his hand. His face was drained of color and dark smudges of exhaustion underlined his eyes. I put my hand in his and he tugged me from my chair. Pulling me toward him, he gazed at me through weary eyes. I could only guess at how many deaths a man could see before the horror took its irreparable toll. I raised up on my toes and gently kissed his lips.

He smiled tiredly. "Let me take you home, Maggie."

"Are you through here?"

"No, but there's no reason for you to stay any longer. I can drop you off at home and grab something to eat before I come back."

"Do they know what happened?"

He shook his head.

"Do they know who the person was?"

"A man named Jeff Riley. Mark identified him."

"How could he . . ." I stopped. The words caught in my throat.

"We were lucky, if you can call it that. The kiln was turned on later than usual or possibly at the time of death, so the temperature wasn't where it could have been. Much hotter and the body would have been unrecognizable. Fortunately, there were some discernible features and jewelry so that Mark was able to put a name to the body fairly quickly." Villari ran a hand over his stubbled jaw. "Apparently he is, or was, on the board of directors here at the museum. You didn't know him?"

"The name sounds familiar, but I didn't know him. I've probably seen his name somewhere around here, or maybe Mark has mentioned him, but we never met." Until tonight.

Villari took one look at my face and gathered me in his arms. "Put it out of your mind, Maggie, just for a few hours. I know that sounds impossible, but try." He pressed his lips against the top of my head. "Come on, you need to get some sleep. And I need to eat something before I pass out."

"Where is everybody?" I asked as we crossed the empty showroom. "It's so quiet."

Villari pushed open the front door. "You wouldn't say that if you walked into the studio. The place is still crazy, but they're using the back door to get in and out."

"Why?"

"Easier access. The alley's wide enough for a car and the parking lot is convenient. Besides, it minimizes the panic quota. The fewer cops and medics people see, the less nervous they get and the easier it is to get information."

We stopped at Villari's black Bronco. I leaned my head against his shoulder and waited while he dug in his pocket for his keys. "When did this happen, Villari? I mean, was Riley at the party tonight with the rest of us? Why did he go into the studio? Did someone suggest he step into the kiln and try it out for size while they flipped on the switch?" I sighed. "I don't get any of this."

Wordlessly, Villari helped me into the car and shut the passenger door. He walked around to the driver's side and slid in. He turned in his seat, his tar-black eyes even darker than usual in the dim light, and reached for my hand. "Maggie, I don't want you involved in this—"

"I'm already involved. I found the body, remember?"

"Yes, I remember. I'm the one who carried you out of the room. Do you remember *that*?"

"Yes, but—"

"No, buts. You've given your statement. There's nothing else for you to do. This was not a random death, Maggie. Someone very methodically and deliberately killed a man tonight. At this point, we don't know why the murder was committed, but we have to proceed on the assumption that the person might be planning to kill again. And with your knack for barreling right into the middle of things, there's a good chance you could get hurt in the cross fire."

"Villari, Jeff Riley is a stranger to me. I can't be in any danger. This has nothing to do with me."

"Maggie, I've seen people killed over some pretty stupid things, like driving too slow in the fast lane. You found the body. The person who did this might decide to do the same thing to you."

I shivered involuntarily. "You're scaring me, Villari."

"I don't want to scare you, Maggie, but I do want you to be cautious."

"But what possible reason would the murderer have to come after me?"

"Maybe you came into the room right after Riley was put in the kiln. Maybe the murderer was still hiding in the studio somewhere and is afraid you heard him leave. Maybe he thinks you saw something he left behind, something you as an artist would know was out of place, but a bunch of cops would never recognize. Maybe there's something that *ought* to be there, but isn't." With one hand on the steering wheel, Villari nervously ran his fingers through his hair with the other hand, a habit he exhibited whenever he was frustrated or upset. "It's probably nothing, Maggie, but killers don't like to leave loose ends."

"And I'm a loose end?" I wondered aloud.

"Possibly."

We drove the rest of the way home in silence.

Chapter Three

I didn't sleep well, not that I expected to. After Villari's ominous warning about the killer coming after me, it was hard to feel comfortable, even in familiar surroundings. Two hours later, I gave up and got out of bed. Pulling on sweatpants and my father's old flannel shirt, I plodded down the hallway to the kitchen and turned on the coffee. As I waited for it to percolate, I gazed out the window. The sun had dyed the sky in broad swatches of orange and yellow, a perfect backdrop for the tall pine trees and blue spruce that provided the last remaining splotches of green on the horizon. Nature seemed oblivious to last night's tragedy, and morning arrived bathed in its palette of fall colors.

I poured myself a cup of coffee and moved into the living room. Dropping down on my plump, oversized couch, I rested my head against the back of the sofa and held the mug in my lap. I wondered if Villari had finished by now, if the body had been removed, if all the notes and photographs had been taken. He often talked about the importance of the first twenty-four hours in gathering enough evidence to track down a killer, but in this case, what kind of clues would be left on a guy who was burned to death?

The phone rang shrilly, startling me from my macabre thoughts.

"Hello?"

"Maggie? It's your father. I'm calling to see how you're holding up."

"I'm fine, Dad, really."

"They wouldn't let me get anywhere near you last night."

And so began a barrage of calls that seemed to last forever. At one point, I seriously considered taking the phone off the hook, but I didn't have the heart to follow through, not when people were calling to express their concern. So I kept picking up the phone, reassuring everyone that yes, I was fine, yes, it was horrible, and no, I didn't need them to come and keep me company.

I did, however, need to get the hell out of the house. Maybe I was too guilt-ridden to turn off the phone, but if I wasn't here to answer—well, then it was out of my hands. Before the phone could ring again, I put down my very cold coffee and ran down the hallway to my bedroom. In record time, I stripped down to my skivvies, slipped on a pair of jeans and a man's undershirt, and tugged on my favorite gray USAF Academy sweatshirt. Looking down at myself, I could almost hear Villari groan—in dismay, not passion. I shrugged and headed out to the Jeep.

My first instinct was to go to the gallery, but I knew Villari would have a conniption if he saw me anywhere near the place. I thought about going to Andy's or Lisa's or even my father's house, but I wasn't looking for sympathy. I was trying to sort this out in my brain, but I had so many questions and so little information that it settled in the bottom of my stomach like a truckload of bricks—a thought that made me realize how hungry I was. My stomach was growling like crazy. So I pointed the car to the only place I could think of at a time like this.

The café was quiet when I walked in, a few men in business suits drinking coffee and reading the paper. There was a small line at the register, people ordering pastries and a hot drink to go. Kevin, his blonde hair falling in his eyes, was behind the register, surprising me a little. When I was his age, I didn't think the world existed before noon. I scanned the room, looking for a quiet little table, when my eyes fell on Mark sitting at a booth in the back corner reading the newspaper. I moved toward him and tapped him on the shoulder.

He glanced up and did a double take. "Maggie!" he exclaimed. Mark stood and hugged me tightly before insisting that I join him. "I tried calling you several times this morning, but the line was busy," he said as we sat down. "I finally gave up and decided to try again later. I assumed you would be inundated with calls for the next couple of hours."

"That's why I'm here," I admitted. "The phone was driving me crazy. I know everybody means well, but I ended up repeating myself over and over, parroting what I'd just said to the person before. After a while, everyone started blending together and I kept forgetting who I was talking to."

"Same thing happened at the museum, except it was the media calling. I'm surprised you didn't hear from them."

"I might have if I'd stuck around long enough, although I don't know what I could tell them. I didn't even know the man."

"Yes, but you found him. That's a pretty grisly angle they'd love to pursue."

"How nice."

"Yeah, cream of the crop, those guys." He took a sip of coffee. "Besides, just because you say you didn't know the guy, doesn't mean they'll believe you. Jeff Riley was a member of the board of directors. They're going to wonder why you didn't know one of the people who had to approve your show."

Bewildered, I shook my head. "But so did the rest of the board members, and I don't know them, either. As a matter of fact, I don't know the name of the custodian who works at The Outlook . . . or the guy who sets up the lighting. Does that make me guilty of something?"

"Not to me, but this is a big story, and the media has to print something. Your boyfriend has been pretty close-mouthed about the murder, and that makes life very difficult for people who live and die by deadlines." He folded his newspaper. "Until Sam releases some information or they have enough time to uncover the real facts, they're going to connect dots that may or may not have a damned thing to do with reality."

I looked up to see Kevin at our table, pad in hand. "Can I get you anything?"

"Just coffee," I said. My appetite had suddenly disappeared. "I'm not really hungry."

"Bring her a cinnamon roll, heated," Mark interjected. "You've got to eat something, Maggie. You need more than nerves to keep you going."

"Okay," I said, nodding at Kevin. When he left, I turned to Mark. "What happens next?"

"Newspaper and TV reporters will continue to descend on The Outlook like vultures until this thing dies down, no pun intended. The studio is off-limits to everyone but the cops who secured it as a crime scene. Basically, all future shows will be pushed back until the studio is reopened. I'll be assuming more responsibility for now until the board approves another member. The gallery will open in a few days, which works to our advantage."

"Why's that?"

"Because even though no one wants to capitalize on a tragedy, the fact remains," he said, "that your work is getting a tremendous amount of media coverage."

"A guy gets murdered and they're talking about my sculptures?"

"Connect all the dots, Maggie. Every broadcast starts with a reporter standing outside The Outlook talking about the gallery, your opening, and the murder that took place. In their mind, it all fits together somehow. Whether it's true or not, it doesn't really matter. But your name was mentioned several times and the picture of *The Garden* that was on the flyer was blown up for the TV audience. All in all, you've gotten good press and I expect a lot of people will come to the gallery, even if it's for slightly sinister reasons."

While Mark was talking, Kevin placed the cinnamon roll and coffee in front of me. "I don't want to sound callous, but did anyone outside of the mainstream press review the opening?"

He arched his eyebrows. "You mean a real-life art critic?"

"Fine, Mark. Make me feel lower than a worm for asking," I said, tearing the roll, "but yes, I do want to know if there was anything written about my show besides Jeff Riley's murder. I know how that sounds, but I can't help asking."

"Although I hate to admit it, I wondered the same thing." Mark leaned forward. "To answer your question, your work wasn't officially reviewed. The reporter who was assigned to view your sculptures arrived fashionably late, and unfortunately, by the time he showed up, the police had already locked the doors and posted a man out front."

I paused. "When did you see Riley?"

"Not right away. The moment you started screaming, Sam was there in a flash. I never saw a guy react so quickly . . . the rest of us just stood there like idiots until it sunk in that someone was in trouble." He reached over and took a bite of my roll. "And from that point on, the room was off-limits to everyone until I was brought in to try and identify the body."

"How did you know what happened?"

"Sam came out and pulled me aside. He told me everything he knew, which wasn't much at the time. But by then,

I knew most of it because Duran had already given me the story."

"Duran? My God, I forgot all about him. He was there, too."

"The police separated you. I'm sure they wanted to hear the story from two different perspectives. More information that way."

"When did Duran leave?" I asked. "Almost everyone was gone when Villari took me home."

"Quite a bit earlier. He gave his statement a couple of times and they released him."

"They were a lot easier on him than me."

"Big money speaks volumes. Not to mention, he was probably a lot less annoying."

I made a face at Mark. "After a rocky start, I was a perfect witness. Baxter and I got along fairly well, considering what had happened." I took a sip of coffee. "Why was Jeff Riley murdered, Mark?"

"I have no idea, Maggie. He was a genuinely nice man. Handsome, too. Over six feet tall, pretty athletic—at least that's what the girls in the office always said." Mark shook his head. "It's too bad, too, because Jeff really cared about The Outlook. Most people on the board put in their hours and go home; they're more interested in having their name on the roster than they are in really helping the gallery. But Jeff was a lot like Elizabeth. He rolled up his sleeves and dove right in. In fact, I believe she was the one who brought his name to the board."

"Is this a private conversation, or can I join in?"

Mark's face tensed just a fraction before he forced a smile

as Jamie approached our table with a pot of coffee. "Certainly. We're not saying anything you haven't heard already."

"Give me a second," she said after refilling our cups. "Let me tell Kevin I'm going on break for a few minutes." She left and went into the back, where the waiter had disappeared only moments before.

"What was that?" I asked, leaning forward.

"What was what?"

"That pinched look you gave Jamie."

"You're exaggerating, Maggie. She asked if she could join us and I agreed."

"You were about as inviting as a rattlesnake."

"Maybe," he said mildly.

"No maybe about it. You're sitting in her café. Did you think she was going to pretend that she didn't see you?"

"I don't know what I thought. I want to think I'm imagining this . . . rift between us. But it's there. I can feel it, Maggie," he said, his voice strained. "I came here this morning to get away from the phones, that was part of it. But I also came because I've always dropped by in the morning. I keep hoping that if I act like everything is the same, then they really will be the same." The sadness in his eyes was unmistakable. "But they're not. She's avoiding me."

I shook my head. "But Jamie walked over here on her own. That hardly fits the 'avoiding you' profile."

"Maybe. But I can't shake the feeling that she's hiding something."

"She's just overworked, Mark. She told me so herself."

He lifted his brows. "And when did she tell you this?"

"Yesterday. And drop the look. I admit I was being nosy, but I was worried about you. So sue me."

"We'll tackle this tendency of yours to butt in some other time. Jamie's coming."

In between sips of coffee and finishing off the cinnamon roll, I watched Mark struggle to talk naturally to Jamie. The two of them were so uncomfortable, it was almost comical. They looked everywhere except at each other, and studiously avoided touching without seeming too obvious. Everyone did his or her best to keep up the appearance of normalcy, throwing in our quota of inane chatter, but it was useless. Conversation dried up in no time. Until now, I had thought Mark and Jamie were simply facing the typical problems that all couples experience, but watching them interact, or rather, *not* interact, convinced me that this was much more serious. But I didn't see how I could help the two of them while they sparred in some silent war.

"Was Sam able to tell you anything?" Jamie asked.

"No," I said, shaking my head. "Then again, he never does. If I want to know anything, I have to find out myself."

"I'm sure he loves having you underfoot while he's trying to solve a murder," Mark said dryly.

"He didn't have a lot of information when he drove me home last night," I said to Jamie, pointedly ignoring Mark's sarcasm.

"How well did you know Jeff Riley?"

"I didn't know him at all, but Mark did. Apparently, he was very involved with The Outlook."

Mark nodded. "I knew Jeff as well as most people know their coworkers. We didn't socialize together, except at

77

openings, but I saw him almost daily, since he worked on the gallery's finances."

"Are you going to take over that job, too?" I asked, knowing that Mark already had his hand in almost every aspect of running the place. I didn't see how he could take on more responsibility.

"I can't. I'm swamped as it is. As I said, I'll take his place on the board for a while, but I don't have the time or the background to oversee the finances like Jeff did." Mark ran his finger around the rim of his cup. "Fortunately, Mr. Prestwood called with someone in mind."

"Who is Mr. Prestwood?" Jamie asked.

"Another member of the board." Mark's gaze met mine. "He was also a very good friend of Elizabeth Boyer's, the friend of Maggie's who was murdered over a year ago."

"I remember," Jamie said, reaching out to squeeze my hand. "That was a hard time for you."

I nodded. "It still hurts, but I'm learning to handle it little by little." I turned to Mark. "What did Prestwood have to say?"

"Actually, I talked to him last night after you found Jeff. He wanted to come down to the gallery right then, but I told him to stay home—the police had barricaded the doors and wouldn't let anyone in or out, including the art critic you were asking about earlier. Once I knew it was Jeff who had died—"

"Was killed," I interrupted.

"You're right. Jeff Riley was murdered. It's nothing to be polite about."

"Why did you call this Mr. Prestwood?" Jamie asked.

"Because he's on the board and because he's an attorney."

"Why would you need an attorney?"

"Because it occurred at The Outlook. It only made sense that the board's attorney should be made aware of any criminal activity that takes place on the premises. Especially the murder of another board member. Anyway," Mark continued, "he called this morning and suggested that he send an associate of his over to ease the transition until we find someone else to take Jeff's place."

"That sounds so callous, doesn't it?" I said, shaking my head. "Out with the old . . . in with the new."

"I hate it. Even Prestwood, for all his British stoicism, had a hard time saying Jeff's name without choking up. But bills and salaries have to be paid, and the truth is, I was thankful for his help. In fact," Mark said, glancing at his watch, "I'm supposed to meet Dylan Michaels at the gallery in half an hour."

"I'll go with you," I said immediately.

Mark tilted his head. "Now, why would you want to come?"

"I don't know. I just want to go. It was my show and I want to check everything over, make sure my pieces weren't touched. Besides, I'd like to walk through the place and give myself something different to remember about last night. Right now, my opening is synonymous with death. I'd like to change that."

"And exactly how do you propose to do that?" he asked, his eyes narrowing.

I squirmed beneath his unwavering stare. "I promise not to touch anything. I just need to be there."

"This makes absolutely no sense, Maggie, but I don't have the time or the inclination to fight with you. I'll leave that to Sam. You know he'll have a fit if he sees you anywhere close to the studio, especially if he thinks you're snooping around where you shouldn't be."

"He won't see me. I'm very good at ducking out of sight. And you won't even know I'm around."

Mark shook his head. "Fine, then. Let's go." He turned toward Jamie and gently touched her arm. "May I see you later?" It was the first sign of familiarity, of tenderness, I'd seen him display.

"Of course," she said, scooting out of the booth with Mark following right behind. As they stood, Jamie gazed at Mark, her eyes sad and wistful. For a fleeting moment, his face softened. I expected him to gather her in his arms and kiss her, but a stiff expression quickly slipped over his face and he retreated back into his shell.

"Are you coming, Maggie?" he asked tensely.

I nodded and slid off the bench, afraid to say anything. I pulled a few dollars from my purse and placed them on the table. Jamie protested, but I insisted that Kevin deserved to be paid and tipped.

"Breakfast was great, Jamie." I said, giving her shoulder a light squeeze. "I'll be back sooner than later, I'm sure." I walked past Mark, who still hadn't moved, and headed toward the exit. "I'll see you at the gallery."

Mark nodded. He brushed a chaste kiss on Jamie's cheek. "I'm coming."

Once outside, I headed toward my Jeep with Mark by my side. "I don't get it."

"Get what?"

"Your reaction. Wasn't it just yesterday that you told me Jamie had lost interest in you?" I asked, barging on without waiting for an answer. "Then today, instead of being sweet or charming, or something semi-approachable, you act like you can't bear to be in the same room with her. An ice cube is warmer than you were." I rummaged in my purse for my keys. "And Jamie does the same about-face. Yesterday she acts like she's pissed as hell at you, and today she's all gushy-eyed." I climbed into the Jeep, crossed my fingers, and turned the key. The engine sputtered a little, but eventually caught hold and started running, if not exactly purring. I rolled down the window.

Mark gripped the top of the door and leaned his head into my car. "If it's any consolation, I don't understand it, either," he said loudly, trying to talk over the racket my motor was making. "When I'm not with her, I'm upset about the way things have deteriorated over the past month, but when I'm with her, I freeze and push her away. She probably has a similar reaction, only the other way around."

"Have you guys talked about this?"

He shrugged. "Yes and not really."

"That certainly covers all the bases."

"But it's the truth. We have talked about it. She says it's work and I don't believe her. I haven't pushed her about it, though, so we keep shadow-boxing."

"Then somebody needs to ring the bell and get this fight over with, otherwise the relationship is on a fast track to nowhere."

"Final words from Dear Abby herself?" he asked, amusement turning up his lips.

"Cute," I said, "but you know I'm right." I gunned the motor for emphasis, but it sounded more like pots and pans clattering to the ground than the thundering sound I was hoping for.

Mark laughed, smacked the door with his palms, and waved me off.

MINUTES later, I pulled into a spot across the street from The Outlook, just in front of Acacia Park. Mark wasn't too far behind. He'd been on my tail the entire time, refusing to go around and pass me. I didn't know if he was trying to irritate me or if he was seriously concerned about whether the Jeep had enough working parts to get me to the gallery safely. I turned off the ignition and hopped out. Mark parked next to me in his extra-fancy Lexus, of which I was very envious but would never admit it, and waited for me to lock my car door.

"You have to promise to stay away from the studio, Maggie. The police have cordoned off the area out back, but I'm not convinced the yellow tape would stop you from going anywhere."

"I promise," I said, my mouth going dry. I was taking a big chance coming here. The way my luck was going, Villari would step outside for a cigarette, take one look, and kill me on the spot.

"There are probably some reporters hanging around back, so let's get in before one decides to circle the building and catches us—or you, rather. Unlike you, I'm allowed to be here."

"You worry too much," I said, taking his arm.

Traffic was fairly light and we hurried across the street. As we stepped onto the sidewalk, I saw a man sitting on the three-foot stone wall that fenced in the flower beds surrounding The Outlook. He wore long nylon gym pants, a bright orange T-shirt, and a pair of Birkenstocks with socks. Narrow sunglasses wrapped around his face, and his blonde hair was pulled back in a ponytail. His legs were stretched out in front of him, one ankle crossed over the other. He was a nice-looking guy—okay, a *great*-looking guy, in that sun worshipping, broad shouldered, California Dreamin' sort of way. If you like that type.

He glanced up as we approached, but he remained silent and returned to his people-watching. The gallery was located in the center of the downtown square, one of the many reasons it was so successful. It was the perfect place to check out the female population as they strolled down the streets and ducked into the small boutiques and café's that lined the area.

When Mark inserted a key into the front door, however, the guy angled his head toward us, thought for a second, and then stood.

"Excuse me, but are you Mark Gossett?"

Mark stared intently at the man. "Yes, but the gallery is closed right now," he said curtly. Mark acted as though the guy was going to jump him, steal his keys, and burglarize the place right there in broad daylight, with half the precinct working in the back.

"I'm Dylan Michaels," he said, sticking out his hand. "Robert Prestwood set up this meeting."

Mark shook the man's hand "I apologize for my reaction. I was expecting you, but with everything that has gone on, I'm a little suspicious of everyone. And, quite honestly, I didn't expect you to look . . ." Mark faltered.

"Like an overgrown surfer?" He grinned and broke out the dimples.

Mark held up his hands in surrender. "I guess I'm guilty of stereotyping here. But I did expect someone a little more . . . professional-looking."

"A stodgy little number cruncher with a pocket protector and a mustard-stained tie? Don't worry, you're not the first person to mistake me for the pool boy," he said, chuckling at Mark's dubious expression.

The fact is, Golden Boy had a great-looking smile and a toasty-brown tan, but on closer inspection, he also sported a small beer belly, a chin that was starting to loosen, and a high forehead. He had nice strong shoulders, but his torso was thick and his thighs were like tree trunks. He could be described as husky, a word that falls in the same category as stout, stocky, and even chunky, words that circle but never quite hit the fat mark. He was an all-around big guy—built like someone who played linebacker on his high school football team but forgot to push the plate away when his exercise program was reduced to sharpening pencils and finagling numbers.

"The thing is," he continued, "accountants have notoriously bad taste in clothes and I'm on a one-man mission to change that image."

Mark lifted one brow as his eyes settled on the neon orange T-shirt with the message *Bean Counters Are a Gas!* scrawled across the front.

"If you say so."

Dylan Michaels laughed. "That's the same reaction I get from Bob." He turned in my direction, pushed his glasses on top of his head, and looked me up and down with the prettiest pair of sea-green eyes I'd ever seen. "You must be Maggie Kean."

"And why must I?"

He tilted his head toward the window. "The flyer. You look just like your picture, only more attractive."

"I don't know what office you're running for, but you've got my vote."

"Just your vote?" he asked, his eyes gleaming with humor.

"For now," I teased. I looked over to catch Mark's reflection in the plate-glass door staring back at me with the oddest look on his face. Okay, I'd been a lousy flirt when I was young, and given that little display of verbal virtuosity, I was no better fifteen years later, but what was the harm in trying? Given half a chance, I would have continued swapping wordplay with the Sunshine Boy, but Mark was looking at me like I'd just asked Dylan Michaels to strip down to his underwear so I could rub oil on his back.

Finally, Mark turned the key, pushed open the door, and led the way through the darkened museum and down the hallway to an office on the left side. He flipped a switch and the room flooded with light.

"I'll leave you guys alone so you can work," I said, moving

from the doorway so Michaels, no petite little thing, could get into the room.

"Don't do anything that's going to alert Sam. I don't want him in here breathing down my neck," Mark warned as I started back out the door.

"Villari's never going to know I was here."

"He'd better not," he said, looking up from the files on the desk. "Don't come running to me if you get into trouble. From here on out, I don't know you, don't know how you got in here, don't know what you're looking for, got it?"

"What is this, *Mission: Impossible?*" That got an amused grin from Blondie, but a scowl from Mark. Between the murder last night and his relationship with Jamie, the horizon probably looked a little bleak. "Don't worry, if Villari catches me, I'll take the heat. I'm used to it." I turned to Mr. Sunshine and smiled my widest toothpaste-commercial smile. "Nice to meet you. Hope to see you around."

"You can count on it, Ms. Kean," he said, pinning me with his emerald eyes.

"Call me Maggie," I insisted.

"With pleasure."

His gaze was friendly and open, but I had a sneaky feeling that this guy with the ingratiating smile could charm the pants off anyone. Well, almost anyone. I was immune to his charisma for several reasons, the main one being that Villari would try to beat the crap out of him if he thought the guy was hitting on me. Then again, I wasn't sure whether Michaels thought that a girl wearing saggy jeans would be worth the trouble.

．　　．　　．

THE gallery was large and dark, sort of dusky gray with the lights off, but shafts of natural light streamed through the front door and the skylights. The sculptures hadn't moved, the pictures were still on the wall, everything looked exactly the way it had last night. But nothing was the same. Everything felt different. All the glitter, all the shining glory was gone. In the dim light, the walls cast the sallow complexion of a sick person. The air carried the stench of disinfectant and ammonia. What had seemed bright and luminous the evening before had lost its luster. Death has a way of doing that.

I walked around the room several times, touching my pieces one by one, drawing strength from the fact that they were still there, that they still existed. The figures were cool and smooth, and I could feel the strength of each piece beneath my fingertips. I needed that strength, especially after last night and . . . especially now, when I could hear the studio door swing open and footsteps heading down the hallway. There was only one man who had a gait like that, whose walk was as distinctive as a set of fingerprints. Even with the vibrating echoes distorting the sound, I knew it was Villari striding toward Mark's office. And I knew that I needed to get the hell out of that room.

Fortunately, the detective hadn't seen me, and I held my breath until I heard his deep voice as he spoke to Mark and Michaels. I slipped out the front door, looked both ways, and sprinted across the road. I didn't see Villari's car, which gave rise to a small sliver of hope. Maybe he hadn't seen the

Jeep. Maybe I could get in and out undetected. My guess was that he had arrived earlier that morning, or had returned after dropping me off and never left. But my hunches have a higher ratio of inaccuracies than the Weather Channel. I wouldn't bet my last dollar on either one.

Reaching the Jeep, I yanked open the door, and jumped in. I turned the key and . . . nothing.

The Jeep refused to budge. Right there in broad daylight, the moment I needed a clean getaway, the thing dies on me. Bonnie and Clyde would have dumped this clunker in a heartbeat.

Disgusted, I climbed out of the car and lifted the hood—step one on the first page of the owner's manual and the only step I understood. I didn't know the first thing about engines, nor did I care, but Andy had insisted that all independent women needed to know the fundamentals of auto mechanics. I tried, I really did, but it just didn't register. All I saw were a bunch of wires snaking in and out of chunks of metal. The carburetor looked like the radiator and the pistons looked like spark plugs. It made no sense to me. But I couldn't whine about that now. I was caught in a severe time crunch here without a spare minute to call big brother or even a tow truck for a lift. So I followed the age-old tradition of mechanically-challenged car owners—I jiggled things around. There was enough corrosion in there to keep anything from sparking or chugging or whatever the parts were supposed to do. After a few minutes, I slammed down the hood, got back into the Jeep, and turned the key.

And, miracle of all miracles, the motor turned over. It

was an anemic rumble, but I would take what I could get. Throwing my hands up in victory, I shifted the car into reverse and pulled out onto Tejon. I glanced into the rear-view mirror then and recognized a familiar figure with a shaggy black mane coming through the doorway. Without thinking, I revved the car, jammed it into first, and lurched forward. I made enough noise to wake the dead, no pun intended, and if Villari hadn't noticed me before, no doubt he did then. Sooner or later, I'd have to face him and explain what I was doing at the gallery, but at least I had postponed the inevitable lecture.

Normally, Villari would have jumped into his car and followed me home, but with the investigation under way, I was banking on the hope that he didn't have the free time he needed to tear me limb from limb. That guy had a real problem with my presence around a crime scene. Maybe I should suggest therapy.

I took the Bijou entrance onto the freeway. I drove north for several miles and exited on North Academy, thinking I might as well pick up a few groceries and art supplies while I was in the Springs. This side trip accomplished a lot of things: I could actually stock the refrigerator with something besides coffee, and more importantly, if Villari somehow managed to get away and drive to my house, I wouldn't be there to meet him.

The traffic on the north end of town never failed to surprise me. The Springs had grown in leaps and bounds over the last ten years, and the expansion was really obvious on this main thoroughfare. Usually, I avoided the area, but today I was thankful for the vans and SUVs on both sides.

They provided added camouflage, just in case Villari had decided to track me down.

I pulled up at a stoplight not too far from Jamie's Café and replayed this morning's visit in my head. The tension between Mark and Jamie was thick enough to cut with a knife, but it was also obvious that a strong current of attraction still ran underneath. As I mused on the situation, I cut my eyes toward the bistro and caught a glimpse of Jamie striding quickly—and judging from her body language, angrily—toward a dark green luxury car. A man sat in the driver's seat wearing sunglasses and a cap pulled low over his head. Jamie yanked the door open, jumped in, and slammed it shut. I watched the man check over his shoulder as he started to pull out of the parking space, but I wasn't close enough to get a good look at him. I couldn't see the man, but I just knew he was some creepy, fishy character.

The light turned green and I made an immediate, no-brainer decision. I was going to indulge my curiosity and follow them. Maybe this guy had something to do with the problems between Mark and Jamie. If he did, I wasn't sure what I'd do with the information, but I would deal with that issue later. I took a quick right into the driveway of a convenience store two doors up from the café so I would be behind Jamie and the stranger. I cranked a hard, screeching U-turn in the lot, narrowly missing three parked cars, and pulled forward until I could see past the small lube shop that stood between me and the café. Inching ahead wasn't a problem, but doing it quietly in the Racket Machine was nearly impossible. Hopefully, the traffic noise would drown out the Jeep's clattering as it idled.

The stranger waited for an opening in traffic and merged slowly. I let a burgundy Honda Accord pass and then pulled out onto Academy. I knew very little about tailing someone, but I knew enough to keep one or two cars between Mr. Fishy and me. Admittedly, I didn't know anything about this guy ferrying Jamie around, but an uneasy feeling in my gut made me awfully glad I wasn't on his Christmas list.

It wasn't hard to keep a safe distance between us, but my hands were clammy and my fingers grew stiff from holding the wheel so tightly. Mr. F. drove like an old woman—kept to one lane and stayed under the speed limit, making my life easier. As a tailing novice, I wasn't ready for squealing tires and a pedal-to-the-metal chase heading in the wrong direction down one-way streets. The bad guy kept heading south, and except for the occasional stoplights, the trip was uneventful. After a while, I started to relax my grip to let the blood flow into my fingertips. Maybe I was overreacting. For all I knew, this guy was Jamie's favorite cousin and he was taking her for a visit to Grandmother's house. *Whom the big, bad wolf had just swallowed.*

After twenty minutes of monotonous driving, Mr. Fishy put on his blinker and turned right into a residential area. By the time I reached the corner, I had no choice but to make the turn myself or give up the whole idea. I was sorely tempted to do just that, but some inexplicable feeling urged me on. Hastily, I turned right. The stranger was a couple of blocks ahead, but without a car in front of me, I slowed even further to increase the distance between us. We continued this way for several miles, following the road past clusters of low-income housing projects, apartment buildings, and, further up, multiple neighborhoods of single-family dwellings. As the road climbed, the ponderosas, Douglas firs, and other trees grew denser and the yards became more lush and manicured. The road narrowed, threading its way up the mountain, making it harder and harder to follow the sedan incognito. I couldn't see beyond the increasing switchbacks, but I couldn't afford to get any closer. My car was wheezing around every bend and I was starting to feel rather silly about this little excursion. What if Jamie and her companion were checking out the views or visiting mutual friends in one of the mini-mansions cuddling the mountain? How was I going to explain my sudden appearance? *Me? Oh, I was just in the neighborhood and thought I'd pursue you and your friend up the mountain.*

Finally, I realized I couldn't go any further without being spotted or breaking down. As the sedan disappeared around the next curve, I glanced into the rearview mirror and noticed a black pickup truck quickly approaching my Jeep. I cranked down the window, stuck out my arm, and waved to the guy, motioning for him to go around me. But instead of passing me, he slowed down and backed off, putting several car lengths between us. I took another bend and glanced back. There he was again . . . speeding up, moving stealthily to the butt of my Jeep like a male dog sniffing a female in heat. Then he backed off again. Curve after curve, it was the same thing. Tailgate . . . back off. Tailgate . . . back off. After several minutes of playing cat and mouse, the truck drew closer and closer until it loomed menacingly in my rearview mirror. Irritated, I turned around to scowl at the guy, but I couldn't see anything except the grill of his truck filling my back window. I didn't want to play games with a man driving a machine strong and powerful enough to squash my Jeep like a bug. Suddenly nervous, I quickly scanned the side of the road looking for a shoulder space wide enough to pull out of the way of the demon truck. Seeing nothing, I gripped the steering wheel tightly and flicked a glance out the side mirror, growing more frightened as the truck backed off, gained speed, and moved rapidly forward. My heart leaped in my throat as I read the familiar words: *Objects in mirror are closer than they appear.* The meaning had just dented my brain when I felt a strong jolt against my bumper. The Jeep lurched on impact and I slammed back hard against my seat. My head smacked the headrest, but I managed to control the car and keep it on the road facing straight ahead. Panicked, I jammed down on the accelerator, but the Junkmobile, already pressed to the limit, was barely lugging up the mountain. I checked the mirror. The truck had backed off again, but I couldn't see anything beyond a pale-skinned driver wearing sunglasses and a dark knit cap covering his hair. Seconds later, his truck bore down on my tail and I braced myself for another hit. It was harder this time, but before I could react, the black pickup swerved out from behind, drew up even with the Jeep, and then cut sharply in front of me, so sharply, I stood on my brakes and yanked the steering wheel to the right, right into the mountain.

For several long moments, I sat in the car, my hands shaking on the wheel, forcing myself to draw in deep breaths, breaths that felt like I was sucking a thick milkshake through a straw. By the time I was calm enough to focus, the black truck was long gone, too late for me to get a license number or any real description of the vehicle beyond big and black. Neither one would be much help for identification purposes.

Besides, who would I tell? What would I tell? Would anybody believe me if I said someone in a black truck tried to run me off the road? That someone hit my fender, not once but twice, and then cut in front of me so quickly that I ran into the side of the mountain? Did this have anything to do with last night's murder, or was it some overeager teenager showing off his new driving skills in his parents' truck? If I went to the cops, I would have to endure several hours of repeated questioning, and I wasn't sure I had the energy to sustain another interrogation. And what would they do—make me look through a book of black truck mug shots? I knew nothing, could identify no one—did I really need to say that I had no information over and over again to some uniformed cop? Did I want to put myself in the position of explaining why the hell I was traveling way out in the country boondocks when I lived twenty miles in the opposite direction?

Running on sheer nerves, I forced myself to unlatch my seatbelt and climb out of the Jeep to inspect the damage. I held on to the door until the wobbling in my legs had settled into a minor tremble and walked around to the front. The front grill had stopped just short of a pile of basketball-sized rocks, like a nose smashed up against a windowpane, but there was little damage other than scratches made by scrub oak limbs and other bushes. I moved carefully over the rock-strewn dirt toward the back of the car to inspect the damage where I had been hit. Surprisingly, I only found a dent the size of a large coaster, which fit in quite well with all the other dents and dings on the bumper. Quickly checking under the car, I breathed a sigh of relief when there were no signs of oil or other leaking liquids.

Making my way back around to the driver's seat, I clambered in and prayed that the car still worked. After several aborted starts, the Jeep reluctantly rumbled to life. Carefully checking over my shoulder, I backed out slowly onto the narrow road where it was too tight to navigate a U-turn. I drove ahead for a brief stretch, scared shitless that a black truck was just around the corner waiting to mow me down. When I finally spotted a wide area on the right side, I pulled in, turned around, and headed back down the mountain toward home.

It took almost thirty minutes to reach Monument, a long half-hour of checking my mirror for threatening cars. It wasn't until I had pulled into my driveway, thrown the gearshift into first, pulled up the emergency break, and shut off the car that I saw the smoke seeping from the sides in front. I jumped out, ran around, and stupidly reached for the hood, which was hotter than hell. Jerking my hand back, I wrapped the sleeve of my sweatshirt around my fingers and managed to move the lever and push up the hood. I lifted it a few inches and stumbled backward when a gray cloud came billowing out. After several minutes of coughing and fanning the air, I was finally able to prop up the cover. I didn't bother checking out the engine, since jiggling wouldn't accomplish anything but a trip to the hospital with third-degree burns. I simply stood there and sighed.

There was no denying it now. The Jeep was due for an extensive, i.e., very expensive, overhaul, something Andy had been badgering me about for several months now.

I left the hood up to give the motor a chance to cool down, and walked into the house. The rooms were chilly, and I shivered as I turned up the thermostat. The Indian summer was beginning to cool; the nights were cold enough now to require the heater. Fall swept quickly through Colorado, the sun sliding lower on the horizon, its rays slanting across the fields. The aspen fluttered gold for just a few weeks before the limbs dropped their leaves and stood bare for winter.

I grabbed a blanket, wrapped it around my shoulders, and picked up the phone to dial a number I knew by heart.

"Sports, Andy speaking."

"Sculptures, sister speaking."

"Hey, Maggie, what's up? Everything all right?" he asked, his voice laced with concern.

"Everything's fine, considering what's happened in the last twenty-four hours," I replied, not wanting to talk about the semi-crash on the mountain. "Actually, I'm calling to ask for the name of a good mechanic. The Jeep's on its last leg."

"Honey, that thing ran over its last leg a year ago. If you take it in to get it fixed, they're going to charge you a small fortune, and deservedly so. You're going to have to break down and buy yourself a new car."

"Maybe, but I don't want to rush into anything. The right mechanic might be able to resurrect the thing for another few months or so. A year if I'm lucky."

"I think the Second Coming is more likely."

"It's worth a try. There's some sentimental value there, if nothing else."

"That piece of crap isn't worth the price of a phone call, but I'll give you the number because I can tell by the tone of your voice that you're determined to be stubborn about this."

"Why is it that I'm being reasonable when I agree with you and stubborn when I don't?"

"Forget I said anything. You're not pulling me into some feminist argument just because you're too damned cheap to open your wallet."

"I'm not cheap," I retorted, "just frugal. It's not like I've got money to burn."

"With the percentage you get as trustee for Elizabeth's estate, you have more than enough to spring for a down payment. I'm talking reliable transportation here, Maggie, not a Ferrari."

He was right about that, actually. Being trustee gave me a fairly decent income for watching over Elizabeth's estate and protecting her money from her grandson's wild ideas, but I hated the thought of touching the money. Right now, that money was all I had to support myself during this year-long sabbatical from teaching and I wanted to use it carefully.

"You're probably right, but—"

"I usually am," he said.

"That's what you say—on a regular basis, I might add—but I still want to give it one last shot, Andy. Maybe it's something simple like a loose hose problem."

He sighed in exasperation. "You're a mechanical moron, you know that, right?"

I didn't bother responding.

"Fine. Grab a pencil. There's a good man right up in Monument. His name is Roy. Here's the number."

I jotted the digits on a pad. "Thanks, Andy. Always a pleasure doing business with you."

"Yeah, yeah."

"Before we hang up, what's the topic today?"

"Golf."

"Well, that ought to take up two lines. How are you going to fill up the rest of your column?"

He chuckled. "Just because you hate the game doesn't mean the rest of the world feels the same way."

"I don't hate golf. It's no different than any other sport, really. Men are enamored with the idea of a stick in some form, a ball, and some place to put or send the ball. I don't get it, but I've learned to accept it. You know I love baseball. But golf . . . now that just seems like a colossal waste of time. Look at pool," I said, warming up. "Same concept, right? Put the ball in the hole. But rather than destroying good land and traipsing over miles of an artificially created oasis to hit the little white ball into the hole, pool does the same thing on an eight by four foot rectangle of green felt. You get the same game in less time, with less money and prettier balls."

"Are you through?"

I could practically see Andy rolling his eyes.

"If you want me to be. I could go on, you know."

"Yes, I do know. That's why I'm ending this conversation now."

Before good-bye was halfway out, I heard the click in my ear. Andy and I frequently hung up on each other, our own special code of caring. Smiling, the first time I'd smiled all day, I called the garage and was able to make an appointment to take the Jeep in that afternoon. The only problem was whether the car would move once it cooled down. I was still debating about calling for a tow truck when someone rapped sharply on the door. My stomach lurched and my heart thudded against my chest. I quickly scanned the room trying to measure my chances of escaping. Not only did I recognize Villari's signature knock, but judging from the precise staccato sound, I could gauge his mood. The man was royally pissed.

Reluctantly, I opened the door. Villari walked silently past me, but I didn't need words to know how he was feeling. One look at his clenched jaw and rigid spine and I knew I was in deep trouble. I closed the door and followed him into the kitchen, where he immediately started pacing.

He stopped and glared at me. "Do you want to tell me why you were at The Outlook this morning? I don't need to ask why you tore out of the parking lot like a bat out of hell."

I held up my hand like a traffic cop. "Before you launch into a major tirade, give me a chance to explain."

"This *is* your chance. You've got exactly sixty seconds to justify your presence at a murder scene. Personally, I can't wait to hear how you rationalize coming down to the gallery less than"—he glanced at his watch—"sixteen hours after you stumbled onto a dead body."

"First of all, I wasn't anywhere close to the kiln. I didn't trample on any yellow tape; I didn't even peek into the studio. Contrary to popular belief, I do not get my jollies hanging out at murder scenes. I do not stalk dead victims. I hate cadavers. I'm partial to live, breathing, healthy people."

"Then why revisit the scene?"

"I just told you—I didn't even come close to the kiln. I went to check my sculptures."

"I don't understand," he said, shaking his head like a wet dog.

"This is a little hard to explain . . . and it doesn't really make sense, but last night was the biggest night of my life, and it all went down the tubes fairly quickly, not," I hastened to add, "that I blame Jeff Riley, obviously, but everything started out so wonderfully. It was magical. Then I took one step in the wrong direction, and reality came crashing down."

"Keep going," he said.

"I went, Detective, because all I've been able to picture in my mind for the last sixteen hours is Jeff Riley's body. And as sorry as I am for what happened to him, I don't want his death looming up in my brain every time I close my eyes," I retorted. "I went to The Outlook to touch my sculptures, to see that they were real, to remind myself that there was some beauty to last night, that I hadn't made it all up."

Villari took a step forward. I stood my ground. He took another step, his face hard and uncompromising. One more step and he covered the distance between the two of us. He looked down at me, pinning me with his eyes. Standing my ground was appearing less and less attractive. At this point, running like the wind in the opposite direction held a whole lot more promise.

He reached out and grasped both my upper arms. I thought I detected a bit of softening in his face, a smoother brow, but it was probably the result of severe wishful thinking.

"Personally, that whole story doesn't wash, but then, it wasn't my show and I didn't discover the victim. Practically speaking, I don't know why you wouldn't do everything in your power to stay away from something as unspeakably brutal as what you saw last night," he said. "But what makes sense to me and what makes sense to you is often diametrically opposed."

No truer words had ever been spoken. The guy's brain worked like a meter. Check everything twice, record the results, account for each second, and give nothing away for free. I believed in free-flowing matter, in random molecular bonding and a universe that cruised on the laid-back law of c'est la vie.

"However, in this instance, we only need to agree on one thing."

I eyed him warily. "What's that?"

"The fact that you are not to step foot on the premises or anywhere near the vicinity of the murder—not until I give you the go ahead and Mark reopens the place for the public."

"What possible difference does it make if I go into the gallery?"

"For a normal person, it wouldn't make a damn bit of difference. But as touching as your little explanation was, it wasn't the whole story."

"And what exactly is that supposed to mean?"

"It means that you're nosy. Don't forget, this is Episode Two in *Maggie Finds a Body.*"

"Look, Detective, it's not like I go around searching for deceased people."

"Murder victims, Maggie. And I'm not accusing you of looking for them, but I am saying you don't know when to back off once they're found. We've been here before, Maggie, when Elizabeth was killed. I didn't like it then, either, but knowing how close you were to her, I understood your need to find the murderer." He took a deep breath and loosened his grip long enough to run one hand through his hair. "I don't want you running off half-cocked, poking and prodding where you don't belong just to fulfill your innate need to snoop."

"I'm not going to . . ." I trailed off. His superior, bossy attitude bothered me, but there was enough truth to what he was saying that I couldn't really fight him.

"Listen to me carefully, Maggie. Jeff Riley worked for the IRS in a high-level capacity. I can't give you all the details, but he was in a position to make a lot of people angry. Shady characters with enough money to exact revenge. Do you understand what I'm saying?"

I nodded reluctantly.

"I don't want you anywhere near the murder scene until we've cleared the case. It's bad enough that you found the body."

Alarm crawled up my spine. "Am I in danger?" I asked, thinking about the little run-in on the mountain.

"Not if you stay away from this point forward. As long as the murderer believes that your involvement was purely innocent, you'll be fine. If you happened to stumble across a clue that threatens his or her exposure, however, that's a different story. That's why I want you to stay the hell out of this investigation."

"You think the killer is still around?" I asked incredulously.

"Maybe. Until we know more for sure, we have to assume that he or she is close enough to observe the aftermath of the murder."

"Okay, you've convinced me. I don't like it, but I'll do it."

Villari released my arms and cradled my face in his hands. "Then you admit you were curious about what was going on at the museum?"

"I admit nothing," I said stubbornly.

"That's my girl," he said, a faint smile playing at his lips. "Closemouthed to the end."

"You wouldn't respect me any other way."

Villari bent down and kissed me. He was surprisingly gentle, given the intensity of his anger a few moments ago. I slid my arms around his neck and sighed as he slipped one hand down to the curve of my back and pulled me closer. I could feel the strength of his body and the heat that radiated from him. Slow, sweet kisses grew harder, more demanding, and I parted my lips to taste him. He caressed and stroked and searched and explored until the world began to spin.

His passion seared a direct path to my lower anatomy, which was now begging for equal time. Villari raised his head and gazed at me with dark molasses eyes.

"Promise me you'll keep out of the investigation, Maggie," he whispered, lightly brushing a kiss across my forehead. "I'm getting used to having you around."

"My, you do know how to charm the ladies."

He shrugged. "It's a genetic knack, passed down through the Villari men. My father, to hear him tell it, was quite the ladies' man before he was married. Of course, once he met my mother, it was all over for him. He says she stole his heart the moment he set eyes on her."

"My guess is she cracked his ribs, grabbed his heart, and yanked it right out of his chest," I said, "with no anesthesia."

He laughed. "One of these days, my mother's going to do the same thing to you. You're going to fall in love with her." Villari ran his fingers through my hair and pushed a curl behind my ear. Following the path of his fingers, his lips nibbled my earlobe and nuzzled my neck. Tingling shivers skipped down my back. "Maggie?"

"Hmmmm?"

"Why don't we step into my office and finish our business in more comfortable accommodations?" he said suggestively. Before I had a chance to answer, Villari had one hand around my waist and the other underneath my legs and was heading down the hall toward the bedroom.

"Isn't it a little early for intimate relations?"

"Mrs. Peterson might think so, but since I'm taking *you* and not a seventy-five-year-old woman, I think it's the perfect time." He placed me on the sheets and sat down next to me, his expression suddenly serious. "Honey, there's something here between us."

"Of course, there is. And in a few minutes, I'll get to see and enjoy it."

"Drop the smart remarks, Maggie," he said simply. "I know you're uncomfortable with the idea of our relationship, although I haven't completely figured out why. But whether you're afraid or not doesn't change the fact that there is an us."

I propped myself up on both elbows. "I don't mind that there's an us, as you call it. I just don't know exactly what that means."

"It means whatever we want it to mean."

"Explain that."

"For me, a level of trust, of passion—of commitment."

I thought about his words and the feeling behind them before I spoke. "I've been alone a long time, Villari. My mom died when I was young and my dad abandoned me in his grief. Andy did his best to take care of me, but he was only a couple of years older than I was when it all happened." I hesitated, trying to put my thoughts into words. "I don't want to be melodramatic, and I try not to let my past rule my life, but the fact is, I grew up very independent. I had to."

"It's part of what I admire about you, Maggie," he said, sitting on the edge of the bed.

"But independence has its downside; I don't trust easily. It's hard for me to let people into my life. If Elizabeth were here today, she'd vouch for that. She just bulldozed her way through my defenses."

"So what are you trying to say?"

"I guess I'm saying I like the way things are now. We have fun together, in between our many fights, we make up well, and I don't see why we need to mess with that."

"I'll tell you why," he replied, his gaze as soft as a caress. "Underneath that fiercely self-reliant exterior with the smart mouth is a vulnerable woman."

"Oh, please, that's such a cliche. Hard and crusty on the outside, soft and sensitive on the inside."

"True, but I have proof."

"Which is?"

"Your underwear."

"My underwear?"

"Yep. You wear serviceable underwear, briefs not bikinis, and a white bra without lace."

"Is this line of reasoning going anywhere?"

"Your underwear is so bland, it doesn't even qualify as lingerie. It's tough, sensible, and the ultimate attempt to repel the opposite sex. It's your last line of defense. But when I take it off, you're all woman underneath. No barbs, no thorns, no nothing. Just pure sweetness and passion."

"That is the biggest bunch of psychological crap I've ever heard."

Villari grinned. "Probably, but you obviously need more time to digest the fact that a relationship is not the equivalent of daily fiber. More importantly, Mr. Ed is getting restless."

"Mr. Ed?"

"Yeah. An old friend of mine." Villari pulled my arms down and rolled on top of me. "I think it's time I introduced you."

Mr. Ed and I got along just fine.

Chapter Four

The phone rang while we were lying on the bed, arms intertwined and big smiles all around. I wanted to ignore it, but I couldn't. Without turning, I stretched one arm behind me and groped around on the nightstand. Keeping my eyes locked on Villari, I lifted the receiver and placed it next to my ear.

"This better be important," I muttered.

"Don't know much about buttering up a client, do you?"

I knew that voice. I'd never forget that deep growly voice, not after last night. I sat up in bed. "Sorry about that, Mr. Duran. I was . . . uh . . . distracted."

He chuckled. "Got a visitor, do you?"

"Pardon me?"

"Ah, hell, honey. I'm seventy-four years old. Grant you, it's been a while, but I'm not too old to remember that tone of voice . . . smooth as ten-year-old scotch . . . and a little flustered to be caught butt naked."

I would have choked on my coffee if I'd been drinking any.

"I'd bet my jewels you've been tangling in the sheets with that cop I met last night."

"How . . . how . . . ?" I sputtered.

"I saw him last night. Men don't haul women over their shoulders, even good-looking ones like yourself, unless there's some pretty strong feelings flowing underneath. Too easy to get a hernia, and believe me, those things are hell when a man's trying to dance the horizontal, if you catch my drift."

Boy, did I. Blood suffused my face. I glanced over at Villari, who was lying on his back now, one arm draped over his eyes. I had one man falling asleep on me and one man embarrassing me to death. I didn't know what to do with either one.

Mustering up whatever remnants of dignity I had left, I spoke into the phone. "How can I help you, Mr. Duran?"

"Aw, hell, I went too far, didn't I? My first wife, the true love of my life, was always trying to rein in this mouth of mine. It just runs off like a hound dog chasing a jackrabbit—no idea where it's going, just got to take off on a tear now and then. Didn't mean no harm."

Deep down, I knew that, but I was still too shell-shocked to say anything.

"Looks like I dug myself a deep hole this time, but if you give me half a chance, I'll do my damndest to make things right." He paused. "Mark gave me your number—now, don't get all riled up, he wouldn't do that for anyone except me. Known him a long time, since he was a little thing. He was my neighbor years ago. Watched him grow up into a fine man in spite of that mother of his. Have you met her? All helpless on the outside and cold as a well-digger's ass on the inside. But that's another story. Reason I'm calling is because we didn't get a chance to finish our business last night. Lousy thing for you to see."

Lousy for Jeff Riley, too.

"Course, it's going to happen to all of us sooner or later. That one was a little uglier than most, but the result was the same. I saw some mighty bad things in the war, but in the end, no matter how bloody or blown up, a body was just a body once the spirit up and left. It seemed to make sense to me . . . the body being God's way of protecting the spirit."

It seemed as good a philosophy as anything else I'd ever heard. I wasn't very religious myself, although I grew up Catholic and attended all the classes and Masses that were required at the time. The Church would label me a lapsed or inactive Catholic, but in reality, I wasn't anything. At least, nothing that fell under the heading of an organized religion. Maybe it was because I'd lost my mother at such a young age, and in every way but physically, I lost my father at the same time. Going to church didn't bring either of them back. No matter how hard I prayed or tried to bargain for my parents, the Man Upstairs just wasn't willing to deal. Over the years, Mass grew to be more of a habit than anything else. Finally I stopped looking for comfort or answers, and my Catholic upbringing became a thing of the past. After Elizabeth was killed last year, the senselessness of the crime convinced me that there were no real explanations, nothing black and white, nothing you could hold in the palm of your hand. There was no correct response on a multiple-choice test. Even *Jeopardy!* couldn't form a question for the answer "Innocent deaths and murder."

Maybe Duran was right. Maybe the body was there to protect the soul or the spirit or whatever it is that separates the living from the dead. If that's true, though, the whole concept definitely needed a little fine-tuning. Considering all the deaths I'd witnessed in my own lifetime, I wasn't particularly impressed with the body's job performance.

"You still there?" Duran groused in my ear.

"Yeah, sorry. I was thinking about what you said."

"Well, now, that's refreshing to hear. Not many people listen to a word I say, especially you young folks. Think you know everything about everything. Of course, I'm not necessarily lumping you in that group. Just speaking generally."

"Thanks, I guess," I replied.

"You're probably eager to get back to that young man of yours and wondering when I was going to get around to explaining the purpose of my call."

"I am curious," I admitted. And eager to get back to Villari, which I did not admit.

"Like I told Mark, I like your stuff. I especially liked that piece you started to show me there in the back before all hell broke loose."

"But you never saw it."

"Well, yeah, I did. In all that pandemonium, I managed to get over and take a look."

My heart started racing. In the middle of everything that happened, I'd forgotten about Duran and his possible interest in the sculpture that Mark had banned to outer Siberia.

"Thing is, it was damned good. Complicated and simple at the same time."

If Duran were in charge, my next show would be hailed as "Good Stuff!"

"But . . ." he said.

The inevitable precursor to disappointment.

"It's still not exactly what I'm looking for. I was wondering how you felt about developing a piece just for me— custom-made."

"You want to commission a sculpture?"

"If you'd be willing."

"From me?"

"Well, hell, girl, I'm not in the habit of wasting my time jawing on the phone for no reason."

"No, I guess you wouldn't . . . uh . . . jaw just to pass the time." How in the world did someone conjugate the verb *to jaw*? "I'd be very interested in working with you," I said.

"Good. I was hoping you'd meet me here at the house. I'd like to show you what I've collected over the years. Might be easier for you to understand my thinking on this."

"That would be fine, Mr. Duran," I said in a voice that sounded much calmer than the pounding going on in my chest.

"Call me Hank. God knows I've got hemorrhoids older

than you, but I sure as hell don't like being reminded of it. Between the poor circulation, indigestion, and cataracts, my body's doing a fine job of that already."

I cleared my throat. "If you insist, then, Hank it is."

"Good. Now, when can you get over here?"

Villari turned on his side, threw one arm across the top of my thighs, and crunched the pillow underneath his head. His broad shoulders tapered down to his waist to where the sheet was loosely draped across his hips. My mouth went dry at the sight.

I turned back to the phone. "Would this evening work for you? Or sometime tomorrow?"

"Why don't you come over tomorrow around supper time."

"I don't want to interrupt—"

"Don't you worry about anything. I'll have Mary throw on another steak or make a bigger pot of chili. It's plain food, but good. Guaranteed to stick to your bones. I've got to warn you about Mary, though. She's not happy unless your plate is cleaned off, so come good and hungry." He paused, and then spoke as if the thought just occurred to him. "Of course, considering the way you spend your afternoons, that shouldn't be a problem."

I didn't know whether to smack the man or laugh.

Hanging up the phone, I scooted down under the covers and rolled toward the naked man in my bed. I laid one hand on top of his hip and leaned in to kiss him. He opened his chocolate eyes and slanted me his special smile, that endearing irregular smile that sort of loped across his face.

"Who was that?" he mumbled.

"Henry, I mean Hank," I amended. "Duran."

"The guy who was with you when you found Riley's body?"

I nodded. "Uh-huh. He's the reason I was there in the first place. I was showing him a sculpture that was relegated to the studio because Mark was being difficult."

"Hated it, huh?"

"Yep. But apparently Duran liked it. At least the idea of it."

"What's he calling you about? Shouldn't he be negotiating with Mark?"

"Are all cops just innately suspicious?"

Villari bent his elbow and propped his head on the palm of his hand. "If they aren't, they will be after spending a month on the job. And if they want to stay alive, they develop it even faster."

"What a crummy way to make a living," I said, rolling onto my back and staring at the ceiling.

"Um, I don't know," he said, sensuously trailing his index finger from my nose over my lips to the valley between my breasts. "It has its perks."

"I see." My voice hitched as he drew small lazy circles that brushed closer and closer to two particularly sensitive bumps on my chest. "But in this case, the perks are pretty small."

"Let me be the judge of that."

I tried to focus on his voice instead of his fingertips, but it wasn't easy. "I'm supposed to meet with him."

His fingers stopped moving. "Where?"

"At his house. For dinner."

"I'm going with you."

"Like hell."

"You've got a problem with that?"

I turned to face him. "As a matter of fact, I do. He's not the murderer. He's not dangerous."

"Exactly how do you know this?"

"First of all, Duran was with me when I found the body. I saw the look on his face and he was as shocked as I was. There's no way he could have faked that. Second, it was my idea to take him back to the studio, not his, and he went along without protest. Now, why would a murderer kill somebody, throw him in the oven, and then show up at a party only a few hundred yards away? And then go back and view his handiwork? Third, and most important, you're not my bodyguard. You tried this once before and it got us off on the wrong foot, and I'm not going to replay the same fight again."

Villari's face tightened and anger flickered in his eyes. "If I may respond? Last night you were too busy screaming to notice the expression on Duran's face, and it's not unheard of for a killer to murder someone and then stuff the body someplace nearby. It gives them a sense of having out-smarted the cops. They *like* the risk. It's akin to having illicit sex . . . it's the adventure of the act that makes it exciting. And lastly, as your lover and potentially something much more, I have every intention of keeping you as safe as possible, and if I need to shadow you day and night, then that's what I'll do."

I let out an exasperated sigh. "But Duran? I don't know, it's hard to believe that someone who looks like they buy their pants from Checks "R" Us, could possibly be a murderer."

"I'm not saying he is, Maggie. But it doesn't hurt to be cautious."

There wasn't much I could say to that. It was the smart, sensible approach. Apparently, Jeff Riley hadn't been careful enough, and I had no desire to meet the same fate. Just as I was about to capitulate, the phone rang. I shot a frustrated glance at Villari, muttered something about these interruptions becoming a major pain in the butt, and turned over to grab the receiver.

"Hello?"

"Maggie? It's Mark."

"Funny you should call. I just got off the phone with Duran."

"I figured as much. The guy doesn't waste any time. Once he got your number . . . by the way, are you okay about me giving it to him? I have a policy against that, but I've known Hank a long time."

"Don't worry . . . he explained it to me. Besides, you can hand out my number to anyone if there's work and money involved."

"Then good. When do you meet with him?"

"Tomorrow around supper time," I said, repeating Duran's terminology, "which, by the way, is what time?"

Mark chuckled. "Around five-thirty or six. He eats pretty early."

"That's probably to give his body enough time to fully digest the plate of dead cow he's serving."

"Actually, Mary makes a good steak. Just don't leave anything on your plate."

"I've already been warned. Don't worry. When I finish eating, I'll tear off a chunk of bread with my teeth and sop up the blood, butter, gravy, and any other liquid sloshing around on the plate. The lady will love me."

"I don't think you need to go that far," Mark said dryly. "Just take an appetite with you and you'll do fine."

"Is there anything I should know ahead of time?"

"Not really. Hank is pretty straightforward. He'll let you know what he wants."

"In very descriptive terms, I'm sure," I murmured.

"You noticed, huh?"

"It's hard to miss a two-by-four smashing into the side of my head."

"That's Hank, all right." He laughed. "But he's a good man. He's helped me through a lot of bad times."

Coming from Mark, this was a huge emotional admission. "Someday you're going to have to explain that to me."

"Mmm. Someday. But not today," he said. "Besides, the real reason I called is to let you know that Jeff Riley's memorial service is tomorrow at eleven o'clock at St. Mary's downtown, followed by a reception at his house."

It sounded like a very civilized afternoon tea party. "I don't know, Mark . . ."

"I wasn't sure how you'd feel about it, Maggie. I'm not suggesting anything one way or the other. I'm just letting you know the time and place. The board members will be attending. Some of the artists and most of the office staff are going, too, but you need to make up your own mind."

"I'll think about it, Mark."

"Don't worry. I'll see you if you're there."

"Mark," I said, catching him before he hung up. "Sorry about missing lunch with you today."

"It's not a problem, Maggie. When Sam came walking into the office, I figured you'd be skipping out the front door. We'll get together another time."

I glanced sideways at the detective lying next to me. "Thanks for understanding." I put the receiver back and rolled over again to gaze into Villari's face. He looked at me, concern etched in the lines fanning out from his eyes.

"What's going on?"

I repeated Mark's conversation, realizing afterward that Villari already knew about the service. "I assume you're going?" I asked, remembering his presence at Elizabeth's service.

"No, Baxter is officially the lead on this case. He'll be there," he said. "I've got some other things I'm following on my own." He leaned over and kissed the tip of my nose. "You know, there's no real reason for you to attend."

"I knew you'd say that. You're very predictable, Detective."

He shrugged. "Maybe. But that goes two ways. I've got a strong hunch you'll be heading off to the service tomorrow whether I like the idea or not."

I turned somber. "True, but I wouldn't go just to be difficult."

"Then why?"

"Respect." The word popped out before I had a chance to stop and examine it. "It's true—I didn't know Jeff Riley, but in an inexplicable way, I feel tied to him . . . like a war veteran. It's like we've been in a battle together, like we're bound by something bigger than the two of us. Other than birth or sex, what's more intimate than death?"

"Maggie, I—"

"I know," I said hurriedly, "it doesn't make any sense. I wasn't there when he died, but I was the first person to see him afterward. He was sort of curled up, most of his skin was black, and . . ." I covered my face, trying to block out the gruesome pictures flashing through my brain.

"Shhh," Villari began, gently pulling my hands from my eyes. "If you need to go, Maggie—if it will help you—then go."

"He deserves to have his dignity restored, Villari," I said brokenly. "I'd like to be there."

"Then it's decided. Go," he said, caressing my cheek with his thumb, "but be aware of the people around you. Be safe."

I smiled wanly. "Always a cop."

His lips fell into his crooked grin. "Always a pain."

"Well, now that that's settled, what do we do next?"

"We go back to what we were doing before Mark called."

"Which was?" I asked coyly, thinking he was revving up for Round Two.

"Arguing about the fact that I'm coming with you to Duran's house tomorrow."

"Okay. Let's say I consent to having you tag along," I said, shocking Villari by acquiescing so quickly—but what choice did I have with his hand surreptitiously slipping underneath the sheet? "How am I going to explain your presence?"

"Tell him you couldn't bear to be away from me," he replied, grinning lasciviously.

"That's hitting below the belt, Villari," I murmured. "Literally."

"Complaining?"

"If I did, you might stop."

"Not a chance, honey. Not a chance."

Once Villari left, I lolled around in bed awhile, feeling wonderfully lazy and decadent. He was a great lover, not that I had many notches in my belt for comparison, but he was easy on the eyes and I was always left satisfied, both physically and emotionally. What more could a girl want? I couldn't deny that I was deeply in like with him, but I couldn't see beyond that. Or admit beyond that. Fortunately, the detective seemed willing to step back and give me some space—a phrase that sounded like a bunch of psychological hooey, but it was what I needed. I didn't respond well to being pushed; all I did was push back, whether I really wanted to or not. And with Villari, I'd found that a little pushing quickly escalated into some heavy shoving, and the next thing you knew, well, it wasn't a pretty sight.

The faint scent of sex still hugged the sheets as I buried my face in the pillow and stretched out beneath the covers. I closed my eyes against the light spilling through the window and tried to nap for a couple of hours, but my mind was not as relaxed as my body. Last night's murder lingered on the outskirts of my thoughts, while my brain tried to make sense of Duran's offer and my father's sudden interest in his daughter. Then there was Jamie's excursion into the mountains and my own close call on the winding roads. Was it innocent or, as Mark believed, was she hiding something? Was someone trying to scare me off, or was it some dangerous high school prank?

I was too restless to lie in bed for long. Piddling away the hours doing nothing, accomplishing nothing, was usually my idea of a perfect afternoon, but not today. The heavy hand of Catholic guilt was making me squirm—the saints and archangels have big problems with couch potatoes. No doubt St. Peter was there this very minute, thumbing through his book, placing yet another black tally mark beside my name, right alongside the other demerits that were lessening my chances of reaching the Holy Gates. The premarital sex probably didn't help, either.

Throwing off the covers, I stood and walked toward the bathroom, naked as the day I was born. Growing up in an all-male household, with my father ignoring me and Andy treating me like his eunuch brother, it was hard to understand why I've always been modest about my girlie physique. Under Villari's tutelage and gentle persuasion, however, I'd relaxed a little. Not that I was singing from the mountain tops à la Julie Andrews about my sexy body, but I could at least look at myself now without cringing.

Shrugging into my bathrobe, I stared at my reflection in the full-length mirror hanging from the bathroom door. I held my microphone, aka the hairbrush, to my mouth and began swinging my hips in the ever-popular one-two metronome style while singing, " 'This girl is a woman now, she's learning how to love. This girl is a woman now, she's found out what it's all about. And she's learning, learning to live!' "

By the time I reached the end, I was belting out the last line at the top of my lungs. I didn't have an ounce of rhythm or talent, but I sang with a whole lot of off-tune gusto. If Gary Puckett heard me singing, he'd probably dive into the nearest kiln and beg his band members, the Union Gap, to lock the door behind him.

Chapter Five

I had Lisa follow me down to the garage and wait while I spoke to the mechanic. Roy took one look under the hood and started clucking like a mother hen whose chicks had been caught in the evil clutches of sly Mr. Fox. He shook his head, wrung his oily red rag before shoving it into his back pocket, and reluctantly admitted that he could have the Jeep ready by tomorrow morning. Given the pained expression on his face, he was one spark plug away from turning my name in to the Department of Abused Vehicles, where my car would be permanently removed from my driveway and I would be handed a lifetime bus ticket.

Lisa dropped me off at home, where I spent the evening covering the basic domestic chores. I threw in a load of laundry, vacuumed a couple of rooms, and rinsed a few dishes. As far as I was concerned, cleaning the house was like pulling weeds. It was a never-ending process of fighting an enemy that refused to die and kept reappearing at an alarming rate. If Roy thought I was a lousy car owner, I could only imagine what Martha Stewart would think of me as a housekeeper.

That night I fell asleep thinking about Jeff Riley and his burned body, contorted images that kept flickering across the front of my brain. The way Villari talked, Riley had probably racked up a long line of enemies. Working for the IRS would dampen anyone's chances of being crowned Mr. Popularity, but would it be enough of a motive to kill someone? Villari would raise his left eyebrow at my naivete. After all, wearing the wrong color in the wrong part of town could earn you a shot in the head. Uncontrollable rage was in vogue now. Get fired, send a letter bomb. Catch your wife in bed with another guy, shoot the two of them and then turn the gun on yourself. Feel depressed, grab a semiautomatic weapon and mow down a group of kids. And always blame everyone else.

Thoughts and picture fragments kept whirring through my head like helicopter blades. I tried to slow my thoughts down, but to no avail. As bad as I felt about Jeff Riley's death, I had a million unanswered questions, especially about his murder. How could he have been killed less than a hundred yards away without anyone hearing? Granted, there was a party going on in the next room, but surely the noise wasn't loud enough to cover the sounds of someone being wrestled into a big oven. I didn't know Riley, but common sense says he would have screamed or fought back . . . unless he was dead first. Someone could have carried him into the studio and dumped him like a sack of garbage . . . no muss, no fuss. Of course, there were plenty of problems with this theory. Dead people are heavy—thus the term "dead weight." I didn't know how big Riley was—there was no way to tell from what I had witnessed—but Mark had said he was tall. Given that the average male weighed over 170 pounds, how could anyone haul that much weight through the parking lot and into the workroom without looking conspicuous? Surely someone would have said *something*:

"What's that heavy thing you're carrying on your shoulder?" innocent bystander asks.
"Just a pedestal for the art show," murderer responds.
"Those blood spots certainly add a nice touch."
"I thought so," murderer growls.

Or:

"My, that's a real big garbage bag you're dragging across the floor."
"Yes, it is, isn't it?" bad guy says.
"There's a finger poking out of that small tear," Good Samaritan points out helpfully. "You might want to try double-bagging."

I could feel a migraine coming on. All this analyzing was getting me nowhere. I punched the pillow, tossed and turned several times, and finally fell asleep singing "99 Bottles of Beer." I used to count sheep when I had insomnia, but the woolly animals kept bashing their shins on the fence and breaking their legs, and I had to cart them off to Lamb Hospital before they were slit open and hung up for mutton.

Somewhere between the forty-second bottle and Riley's blackened hand, I fell into an uneasy sleep. It was after nine when I awoke the next morning, and a dull headache had gathered itself behind my right eye. As my stomach toyed with nausea, I dragged myself out of bed, washed three aspirin down with a glass of water, and stumbled into the bathroom. I was either fighting the beginnings of the flu, or my body was succumbing to the stress of everything that had happened over the last two days. I stood under the shower and let the hot water beat down over my back until my neck muscles began to relax and the water grew lukewarm. Drying off, I pulled on a long-sleeved T-shirt and threw on a pair of rumpled fatigues I'd found at the Salvation Army.

Lisa picked me up at ten o'clock and dropped me off at Roy's Garage, where I had to endure a ten-minute dissertation on the hazards of neglecting my automobile before he handed the keys over. Maybe it was my lousy mood, but I could have sworn Roy was sending me a veiled threat. *Change the oil, or else* . . . I rolled my eyes and stuck my tongue out when he turned his back toward the cash register. Not a particularly mature response, but it made me feel better.

By the time I got home, I had less than thirty minutes before the memorial service. I stuffed my legs into black hose that fit like sausage casings, threw on my one black skirt, and topped it off with a tailored white shirt. I didn't look great, but this was a memorial service, not a fashion show. I wanted to show my respect, not pick up a guy.

With five minutes to spare, I arrived at the church and slipped into a pew in the back, too far away to see the immediate family. Riley's body had not been released to the family yet, and even though there was no coffin and no body to view, I still took comfort in being close to the exit. I had barely sat down when someone poked my arm. I looked up to see Dylan Michaels quietly nudging me. Grabbing my purse, I scooted over a few inches. As he settled in, Michaels turned and sent me a conspiratorial wink. I had no idea what we were conspiring against, but the incessant queasiness in my stomach settled a little and I smiled back.

The service was mostly a blur. In choked voices, people gave loving tributes to a man I'd never met. The pastor had the unenviable job of trying to impart comfort and spiritual meaning to an insane situation. How do you explain a heinous murder to a wife? As hard as I tried, I couldn't maintain my focus for very long. My attention meandered as speakers stood and singers sang and the pastor led the congregation in prayer. I was here to show my respect, but I couldn't deny that I also wanted to get out as soon as possible. I knew, better than anybody in this church, where Jeff Riley really was at this moment— on a cold steel table down at the coroner's. I knew exactly what the remains of his body looked like, and all the heartfelt eulogies in the world couldn't stave off the creepy feeling that threatened to suffocate me.

Just when I thought I was going to go crazy, Dylan Michaels laid his hand over mine, as if he could hear my unspoken thoughts. He pinned me with those seawater eyes until the rest of the world, the colors and the noise, began to recede in the background, and I knew that he understood how difficult this was for me. He laced his fingers through mine and a strange sensation fluttered in the pit of my stomach. After what seemed a very long time, but was probably no more than several seconds, I tore my eyes away from his. I could sense him turing toward the front of the church, but I didn't move. I couldn't begin to articulate the thoughts swirling around in my head, and I was much too cowardly to examine them any closer. But the funny feeling stayed and our hands remained intertwined.

At the end of the service, I removed my hand and gestured toward the outside aisle. He nodded and followed me to the exit as friends and family moved in single file toward the front of the church to offer their condolences. Although I couldn't see Mark, I assumed that he was somewhere in line, but I didn't wait around to see. Once Michaels and I were outside, I took a deep breath and let it out slowly.

"Thanks for your help in there," I said. "For a moment, I thought I was going to lose it."

"My pleasure. You did look a little frayed around the edges."

"I didn't expect to react that way," I admitted. "I thought I'd already been through the worst."

"Grief is a funny thing. It comes and goes according to its own plan, and you just have to take hold of the wave and ride it until it wears itself out."

"An interesting comparison."

He chuckled. "Surfing covers it all. You can ride the wave, lose the wave, or be annihilated by the wave—all analogies for life. With a little imagination, some hand signals, and a vocabulary of less than twenty words, you can talk about anything and everything."

"A real gift, I guess, although it might be a little out of place here in landlocked country."

"Not a problem. We simply switch metaphors. Snowboarding is just as effective. You can surf the mountain, catch an edge and eat it, or make a mistake and be obliterated."

I laughed. It felt good to laugh again, especially when he joined me.

"Are you going to the reception, Maggie?" he asked.

"No. There doesn't seem to be any reason for me to go there. Are you?"

"Yeah. I didn't know Jeff Riley all that well, but we met a few times at different social functions. We knew many of the same people, so I thought I'd go. Besides, I need to pull a few files from his office at home. If Joanne, his wife, doesn't mind, I thought I'd take them with me."

"That could be a little awkward."

He shrugged. "Maybe. Maybe not. I'm banking that there are enough family members supporting her today that she won't mind giving me access to his office. The longer I wait, the longer she'll be alone and the harder it will be for her to allow someone into his office to rummage around in his desk."

"Well, good luck then." I thrust out my hand.

He took my hand and sandwiched it between the two of his. "It was nice seeing you, Maggie. I hope the next time we meet will be in better circumstances."

"I'm sure it will be," I replied lamely. He released my hand and I turned to go. I looked over my shoulder to wave at Michaels and walked right smack into the one guy I had hoped to avoid. I didn't have anything against Baxter, not really. I just don't particularly like being around cops during a homicide investigation. They keep popping up, crowding me, staring me down. Makes me feel claustrophobic. Okay, okay, chalk it up to paranoia.

"Sam told me you'd be here."

"He said the same about you."

Baxter gave me a thin smile, easy enough to do with two thin lips, as he straightened his tie. This was definitely a guy who didn't like to get mussed up. He was wearing yet another dark suit, crisp white shirt, and a striped red tie. He couldn't look more like a politician or rich CEO if he tried. I didn't know where he got the money for a wardrobe that was obviously custom-tailored, fitting his body with hardly a wrinkle. I just didn't see Baxter walking into a regular store with disco tunes piped over the speakers and buying something off the rack. Too lowbrow.

"I assume you're going to the reception?"

"I don't know why you'd assume one way or the other," I replied. I felt Michaels come up behind me and rest his hand lightly on my shoulder, a gesture I interpreted to mean *Easy does it.* Must be part of that surfer mentality. He shot Baxter a look I couldn't interpret before striding away and leaving me alone with the man.

Baxter shrugged and picked a nonexistent piece of lint off his jacket.

"Just making casual conversation, Ms. Kean. It's a social skill you could brush up on."

Easy does it. Without a word, I swung around and took off for the parking lot. I didn't think he'd follow me, but just in case he tried, I strode as fast as I could without breaking into a run. I didn't want to give him the chance to call me back and ask a few more questions. Somewhere in the back of my mind, I knew I was overreacting to this guy, to all cops, for that matter. Baxter was simply trying to find a murderer and he was asking for my cooperation. But my initial response was to resist him. Even knowing Villari as I did, I couldn't shake the feeling that I was being examined under a microscope, that somehow I could end up in jail if I didn't fight back. I was trying to squelch those feelings as much as possible, but that didn't mean I wanted to hang out with the guy.

As I approached the Jeep, my heart shot to my throat and clogged up the air passages. With no oxygen flowing to my brain, I stood paralyzed, surrounded by cars, as my eyes zeroed in on the large black pickup discreetly parked in the corner of the lot. For a second, I couldn't breathe, couldn't think. I didn't know if it was the same truck or not, but I couldn't completely dismiss its appearance as pure coincidence. Finally, I shook myself out of my stupor, took a deep breath to calm my pounding heart, and gathered my thoughts. With one fluid motion, I grabbed my glasses out of my purse, slipped them on, and peered across the hood at the license plate. Memorizing the numbers and letters, I wrenched the door to the Jeep open and climbed in. Grabbing a notepad from the dashboard, I tore off a page and quickly jotted *PQD4685* at the top. I carefully folded the sheet and shoved it into my wallet, glancing up now and then to see if a man with a bloodless pallor and knit cap came sauntering out to the car.

I debated hanging around until the owner of the truck came out or getting the hell out of there. It only made sense to stick close and see who the driver was, but there were a couple of problems with this, namely time, feeling stupid, recognizing the guy, and the ultimate question— *If it's him, then what?* I had no idea how long it would take the line of sympathizers to make their way outside, and I felt ridiculous spying on someone in broad daylight in the back of a church just because he drove a black truck—hey, welcome to Colorado, where everyone drives a truck. The chances that the driver was the same guy who followed me up the mountain were slim to nothing, and even if it were him, would I recognize him? All I remember is a crocheted hat and skin the color of bird poop. And of course, if it's him, what would I do? Yell for Baxter and tell him this is the man who followed me up the mountain yesterday and forced me off the road—a little incident I forgot to tell him about?

I decided on the drive as fast and far away as possible option. If I saw the truck again, which I could now identify by the license plate, I'd talk to Villari about it and deal with the anger/yelling/lecture/threats that would follow.

I was anxious to gun the motor and shoot out of the parking lot, but when I turned the key—there was nothing. Not a sound. Not a clank, a squeal, a halfhearted sputter . . . nothing. A lead rock dropped to the bottom of my stomach and I started pounding my forehead on the steering wheel. I was beyond caring whether I hurt the Jeep's feelings or not. I was through coaxing and stroking this pile of scrap metal into some semblance of transportation. Tomorrow I was getting the damned thing towed to Roy's "Treat It with Compassion" Garage and demanding my money back. Then I was unloading this rust heap in the town's garbage dump and saying good riddance.

"Something wrong?"

I broke off the string of creative invectives spewing from my mouth and turned to stare into the amused face of Dylan Michaels. "Not really. I just love hanging around a parking lot after a memorial service. Nothing like a group of grief-stricken people to lift your spirits."

"That bad, huh?"

"Worse. This pile of crap doesn't deserve to be called a car. This little sweetheart is taking one last ride on the asphalt highway straight to the Junkpile Morgue."

"Tell you what. Why don't you let me drive you home?"

"That's okay," I said sulkily. "I can get a friend to pick me up."

"It would be my pleasure," he said. "Of course, I still need to stop and talk to Jeff Riley's widow and pick up a couple of files, but that shouldn't take too long."

I thought for a few moments and decided to go along with him. I hated to bother Lisa again, and who knew how long it would take Villari to get away? "If you don't mind, I'll take you up on your offer."

"Good," Michaels said.

I grabbed my purse and scrambled from the car, kicking the door shut. If Roy had seen me, I would have been arrested for vehicular brutality and then for Murder One right after I lassoed him with my shoulder purse and twisted the long handle around his skinny neck until his self-righteous little eyes bugged out. Not that I was hostile.

Michaels led me to his car, a new Chrysler 300M, and opened the passenger door. He walked around and slid in on the driver's side and turned the key. The motor turned over immediately and the engine sounded like a contented man snoring after sex. I swallowed my envy, but it wasn't easy. It kept backing up my throat, especially when Michaels merged into traffic, smooth as silk.

We didn't say much on the way over. I started thinking about standing face-to-face with Riley's widow, and an uneasy feeling crept up my spine. We had never met, but I had found her husband's body. I didn't know what to expect or how she would feel once she realized who I was. Maybe it wouldn't make any difference—I mean, dead was dead. Or maybe it would be enough to send her screaming from the house. There wasn't anything I could do about it now, though, and I tried to push the thought out of my head. Of course, once I did that, my car problems jumped back to the forefront and I got angry all over again. I wasn't sure which was worse.

A long line of parked cars snaked their way down the curved driveway and out into the street. Jeff Riley lived— used to live—in a newer neighborhood populated with sprawling houses encircled by sweeping decks offering panoramic views of the mountains. Michaels squeezed into a small space between a champagne-colored Mercedes and another expensive car brandishing some sort of hood ornament. We left the car and walked up the driveway towards Riley's Mediterranean-style house, where the simple lines, curved arches, and rounded corners quietly suggested money and lots of it. We entered a courtyard filled with enough plants to qualify as a nursery, and stopped at the wooden front door. It was open a few inches, and rather than knock, we stepped inside.

If I were the gasping type, I would have gasped here. The interior of the house was a continuation of the outside—more simple lines and round arches. Salmon-colored Mexican pavers, glossed to a high sheen, covered the floors. The walls were painted a soft white, like baby's breath in floral arrangements. A mixture of stone, wood, marble, and other natural textures lent the house a very comfortable, homey feel. There was no ostentation or haughty grandeur. Colorful rugs decorated the floors and the walls, and I would have bet my last dime that they were authentic Native American weavings—not something the Rileys picked up at Wal-Mart.

Michaels put his hand on the small of my back and lightly steered me toward the corner of the room, where a slender lady, about my height with salt and pepper hair, stood talking to another couple. I assumed this was Riley's widow and I stiffened. But Michaels kept walking, so I couldn't do much except go along until we stood a respectful distance behind a husband and wife team who were speaking in low, sympathetic tones. After one last hand squeeze, the two people left and Michaels moved forward. He took her hand, leaned over, and pecked her lightly on the cheek.

"You okay?" he asked her.

His question took me by surprise, not so much the words, but how he asked them. Like he really wanted to know. He looked directly into her eyes and patiently waited for her answer. There was no polite murmuring, no looking over her shoulder or at the ground in order to avoid her gaze. Michaels really wanted to know how she was, and he was in no hurry. She must have felt his sincerity, because tears began to well in her eyes.

"Just barely," she said, her voice a little shaky.

Michaels nodded. "What can I do?"

There it was again. Simple and direct.

Joanne Riley managed a small, sad smile. "Bring back my Jeff."

She barely got the words out, when Michaels wrapped his arms around her in one giant bear hug. "Ah, Joanne, if only I could."

She didn't weep or sob, but simply laid her head on his shoulder and closed her eyes. A few tears trickled down her cheeks. She never said a word, but the sadness was so palpable, I had to turn away.

We stood there, the three of us, for a long time. Michaels stood with Joanne Riley in his arms and me sort of hanging out on the perimeter like an errant electron. After what seemed to me an interminable length of time, the two of them pulled apart and Jeff Riley's widow turned to face me.

"My name is Joanne Riley," she said, her voice a little stronger.

That's all it took. My legs turned to Jell-O, my stomach hit the floor and my intestines were sending signs of: "Big trouble, boss." I didn't have Michaels's soothing manner or comforting gaze. I wanted to tuck tail and run like hell. In my defense, I didn't know this woman or her dead husband, although I was forever intricately linked with his body. What was I going to say? *Hi. My name is Maggie Kean and I happened upon your husband's roasted body.* But there was nowhere to turn, and she was staring at me with the saddest blue eyes I'd ever seen in my life.

"My name is Maggie Kean."

She looked at me quizzically.

"I work at The Outlook."

"You're an artist?"

I nodded. "Yes."

"Jeff loved art," she said, looking down at her hands.

I didn't say anything. I didn't have the words or the composure to work the magic that came so easily to Michaels, and I certainly didn't want to launch into a long conversation with Riley's widow. I have a lousy tendency to babble like crazy when I'm uncomfortable, and I was seconds away from spewing a torrent of unnecessary words. I reached out and touched Joanne Riley's shoulder and looked over at Michaels with what I hoped was my most beseeching "get me out of here" look. Thank God the man was not as dense as the average card-carrying member of Testosterone Unlimited. In one smooth motion, he stepped in and saved the day. At least mine. There wasn't much we could do for hers.

"Joanne, I need to ask you a favor."

She didn't even hesitate. "Anything, Dylan."

At this rate, Michaels could ask for anything and get it. He had an unbelievably mesmerizing effect on her . . . well, to tell the truth, I wasn't totally immune to his charm, either. Not that this subtle, underneath the surface flirtation would lead anywhere . . . but he did have a hypnotic style that seemed to draw women in without their knowledge. It was a funny thing, though. The guy didn't look like your typical Lothario. We're not talking about rock-hard abs and massive, well-developed pecs. This was not a man who caused women to swoon from his sheer maleness or the thought of unbridled passionate sex. Michaels was no hard-body. He wasn't fat, exactly, but he was pushing the envelope—an awfully hefty envelope.

Still . . . the guy was mesmerizing. He had a wonderful, almost goofy smile, and eyes that bored into you with an intensity that held you rooted to the spot. When he talked to a woman, he talked to her as though she was a real person, not a life-support system for breasts.

"I've stepped in to help at The Outlook, but I need a few of the files your husband kept at home."

She nodded. "Of course. The gallery meant the world to Jeff. He was a bit of a frustrated artist, you know. He tried his hand at painting and produced some horrific stuff. He could add fifteen numbers in his head, but as hard as he tried, he couldn't draw anything beyond a stick figure. Most of his pictures are almost unrecognizable." She turned to face me. "He used to laugh and call it abstract art, but the truth is, it was just terrible."

"I won't stay long, Joanne." He paused. "I promise not to disturb anything."

She shook her head and gestured toward the hallway. "Don't be ridiculous. Jeff loved that place. He would have hated for things to fall apart. Go and take what you need and don't be afraid to move things around if you have to. Turning his office into a shrine isn't going to bring him back."

Walking down the hallway, I couldn't help but marvel at how resilient people could be. I didn't doubt that Joanne Riley would live through some terribly lonely times, but I did believe she would survive them. She seemed to have an iron core that I found admirable—and enviable. It was a strength I wasn't sure I possessed.

Michaels pushed open the door to Riley's office. It looked like a typical work space—a little more upscale than the average office, but very familiar all the same. There were bookshelves along the walls, a small sofa, and two leather chairs. A computer, fax machine, and telephone sat on top of a large desk. Papers were stacked in small, neat piles, a metal container held a fistful of sharpened pencils, and a wooden file cabinet stood guard behind the desk. A legal pad filled with long columns of numbers sat sideways in the middle of a desk that was already beginning to gather dust. Life doesn't stop for the dead.

I hung back as Michaels strode into the office, seemingly without reservation, to Riley's file cabinet and pulled out the top drawer. I, on the other hand, took several moments to gather my meager courage and walk into the room, fully expecting a ghostly hand to reach out and stop me from moving any further. Once I reached his desk, however, and realized that I was still breathing on my own and all my organs were still intact, I started to relax a little. It was eerie standing in a dead man's office, but I pushed the thoughts out of my head and tried to concentrate on something, anything.

As if he could read my mind, Michaels spoke up. "Why don't you look through his desk. Pull out anything that has to do with The Outlook."

Great. Just when I was hoping to do nothing more than lean against the desk for support, the guy hands me a chore. "This was my first opening, you know," I said, resisting his efforts to get me into the swing of things. "I don't know many people at the gallery very well except for Mark. I'm probably not the best person for this job."

Michaels stopped riffling through the files and looked over his shoulder at me. Humor flashed in his eyes and the edges of his mouth quirked upward. "A little freaked out, huh?"

I drew myself up, stiffened my spine, and clenched my fists, ready to battle it out with him. But he kept looking at me with that amused but empathetic expression, and all the fight drained out of me. I just didn't have the energy.

"Totally," I admitted, slouching against the wall.

He walked over, grabbed me firmly by the arms, straightened me up, and placed me squarely on my feet. "Then don't think about it. Just do what you have to do."

"That's easy to say," I said morosely.

"You're right. It is easy to say and it's hard to do, but not impossible. You had nothing to do with his death, and the sooner you accept that fact, and I mean truly accept it, the faster you'll be able to erase the image that keeps bouncing back in your brain."

I shuddered. "I'm not sure I'll ever forget what he looked like."

"You won't. You won't ever forget what he looked like the night you found him. The image is branded on your brain until the day you die. But *you* are not dead," he insisted. "You're alive and well, and you've got to move on. One day at a time, one step at a time. Just like Joanne out there."

I looked up into his eyes. "You used to be a coach, right?"

His face relaxed a little. "Why do you ask?"

"Nobody but a coach can whip out a rah-rah speech on the fly," I said. "Baseball?"

He eyes crinkled and his mouth twitched. "Nope."

"Football? Soccer?"

He shook his head. "Give it up. I've never been a coach."

"A sales manager, then. Or a male cheerleader!"

He grimaced. "None of those."

"You were something, I know it," I persisted. "You're good with people, Michaels. You had Riley's widow eating out of your hand, and I don't mean that in a derogatory way. From what you told me, the two of you are good acquaintances, but you had her responding to you like you were lifelong friends. And me . . ." I stopped.

"What about you?" he prompted.

"I don't know you at all, and yet you talk like you're inside my head," I admitted, heat flushing my cheeks. This conversation kept swerving into areas that threw me off guard, leaving me flustered and uncomfortable. I was never quite sure whether Michaels's response to me was just his normal par-for-the-course reaction to any woman he ran across, or whether there was an underlying male-female interest involved. He was such an ingratiating creature that it was hard to tell if that was romance glinting in his eye or just an allergic reaction to the ragweed in the air. In direct contrast to Michaels's easygoing *I care about you* style, Villari was about as subtle as a scud missile. Villari never beat around the bush, never tried to get in my head—in fact, I think he was a little afraid to spend too much time nosing around my brain. He wanted me big time, though, in bed, out of bed, and anywhere in between. His intentions were laid out on a platter, right out there for everyone to see, and he went after what he wanted with a vengeance. I liked that in a man. Of course, Michaels's softer, but just as lethal, approach wasn't too bad, either.

"It's not that hard to know what you're thinking, Maggie. It's written all over your face."

Oh, shit.

Michaels took one look at my face and burst out laughing.

"What are you laughing at?" I demanded.

"Your expression. You look like I just caught you with your pants down."

"You didn't catch anything," I said coolly.

"I wish I had," he said suggestively, eyebrows waggling.

It was the worst Groucho Marx imitation I'd ever seen, and I had to laugh, quickly dissipating any tension in the room, or whatever it was that was standing between us. Michaels was so laid back and casual, I wasn't sure the word "undercurrent" was even in his vocabulary.

"I think I'll check Riley's desk," I said.

"Good idea," Michaels replied with a quick wink before turning back to the filing cabinet.

I still didn't like the whole business of touching a dead man's things, especially one I didn't know. But I took Michaels's advice and forced the thought out of my mind and quickly pulled out the bottom right-hand drawer, the only one deep and wide enough to hold files. Sure enough, there were at least fifty folders, all neatly labeled and alphabetized. I flipped through the files, but as I expected, nothing jumped out at me. I shut the drawer and pulled out the smaller one on top. There was nothing there but pencils, pens, erasers, notepads, and the like, all meticulously organized and lined in ABC order so that the highlighters were placed before the notepads and after the erasers.

Shutting the drawer firmly, I decided to ferret through the stacks of papers on top of his desk, a daunting task for someone who flunked algebra and couldn't add numbers without a calculator. I sat down in his well-worn leather chair and pulled a batch of papers toward me. I thumbed through the pages as fast as I could, swallowing the bile that threatened to come up as I felt Riley's burned, disfigured ghost standing behind me watching. I went through four stacks the same way, plowing through the mounds of paper like a mad woman and pushing them away as soon as I could. I stared at the fifth stack. *Forget it,* I thought.

Nothing made sense, and poking through a dead man's papers seemed almost sacrilegious. I looked over at Michaels, who was still making slow, methodical progress through the file cabinet. Every once in a while, he would stop, pull out a folder, and place it on top of a growing stack of files. I leaned back and watched him work.

"Getting bored?" he asked, stopping long enough to glance over his shoulder.

"A little," I admitted. "And more than a little creeped out."

"How so?"

"I'm sitting in a chair that *used* to belong to a guy that *used* to be alive."

"A little unsettling?"

"Oh, just a little," I said dryly, putting my foot on the ground to stop the chair from swiveling back and forth.

"I'm almost done."

"You're still on the first drawer," I complained.

"I know. But the guy was fastidious."

"So?"

"He cross-referenced everything. He has files for The Outlook, files for the individual artists, files for companies that extended grants, files for potential business investors, and so forth." He sighed and draped his arms over the drawer. "I thought I'd be able to come in, fetch one Outlook file, and be on my merry way."

"Can I help?"

He nodded. "Go get something to eat or drink."

"What?"

"It makes me nervous having you sit there with nothing to do. You tend to fidget, you know."

"I do not," I countered. "I just get a little restless when I'm digging through dead people's personal effects."

"Listen," he said, his voice taking on tired edge, "it's no picnic for me, either. But I'll be damned if I'm going to come back and do this all over again because I was in too big of a hurry and missed something important."

I stood. "Fine. I'll go get a Coke or something. Do you want anything?"

He shook his head. "Just want to get through these files and run," he muttered to himself.

I left the room then, shutting the door quietly behind me. I wanted to jump and kick my heels together—I felt that vibrant and alive once I left Riley's office. But my mood darkened again when I looked ahead and saw Riley's wife surrounded by yet another group of well-meaning, sympathetic friends. I did the only thing I could think of at the time. I veered off at the first right and headed down a hallway that led to what I soon discovered was the kitchen.

Unlike the living room, where the guests were gathered and the atmosphere was subdued and quiet, the kitchen was one big, well-lit center of bustling activity. Waiters hurried from one place to another, food in one hand, grabbing things with another, before heading out the door to serve. White-aproned people stood behind the stove flipping, stirring, and spicing food in gleaming silver pans, and it hit me once more that Jeff Riley was not your run-of-the-mill dead person. He was, or had been, a very important, certainly successful, member of the community. This was a rich man's wake. No small-town noodle casseroles and drinks served in paper cups in this place. People came to pay their respects, and received a gourmet meal in return. Judging by the amount of food and alcohol that was heading out the door, grieving took a whole lot of sustenance.

At first, the kitchen's hustle and bustle felt like balm

to my battered and weirded-out heart. But the longer I watched, the more bothered I was by the sheer impersonalness of the whole proceedings. Joanne Riley may have really loved her husband, but jeez. If you loved someone with all your heart, how did you muster up the strength and sensibility to order a caterer and organize a quasi-banquet for a large crowd of melancholy, soon to be very drunk, souls?

"We need more wine," a large, big-boned redhead called out as she burst through the door holding up a little round tray littered with dirty glasses and crumpled cocktail napkins.

"Check the garage. The boxes are stacked up against the west wall," someone yelled back.

"Like I don't have enough to do already," the redhead muttered, smoothing her hair and trying to tuck long strands into a frazzled ponytail.

"I'll go," I said, pushing myself from the wall.

"Who are you?" she asked suspiciously.

I didn't think my patented *None of your damned business* would be appropriate, considering I didn't really belong here and I was using the kitchen as a hideout. I felt like a cornered animal, with a creepy dead man's office on one side and a lot of commiserating, sympathetic noises on the other. The only place to go was thataway, and in this instance, thataway was the garage.

"A friend of the family," I answered.

She wasn't buying it. "Why aren't you out with the others?"

Nosy little thing. "I *was* out there. It got to be a little overwhelming."

"Well, I don't think the guests should be helping the help, if you know what I mean."

"Look," I said impatiently. "By the time you finish interrogating me, I could have picked the grapes off the vines myself. All I did was offer to help. You can sit here and question me all you want, or I can run out, grab a box, and bring it back in while you're unloading your tray. It's your call."

She shrugged and sank down into a chair. "Okay, suit yourself." Wearily, she slipped off a shoe and began rubbing the arch of her foot through a hole in her stocking. "But you ought to do something about that nasty disposition of yours. It really puts people off," she added crankily.

Great. Everyone's a critic. "I'll try and keep that in mind," I murmured as I moved past her. "By the way, which way is the garage?"

Big Red looked up at me. "You're a friend and you don't know where the garage is?"

"I don't know where my spleen is, either," I snapped back. "Just point."

She raised her hand and stuck out her thumb like she was hitchhiking. "Over there. Past the stove, down the hallway to your left."

I stepped past her, dodging several people zigzagging back and forth like a flock of decapitated chickens. I found the door leading into the garage, turned the knob, and walked into a room that was bigger than my entire house put together . . . not to mention a whole lot cleaner. The walls were painted, the floor was glossy, some kind of stained cement, and the car—oh, Lord, the car . . . all I could do was drool. The only thing this great hulking machine had in common with my low-down, miserable, worthless Jeep was the fact that it rode on four tires. Which wasn't true, actually. My Jeep only *sat* on four tires.

Holding my breath just like I did moments before losing my virginity, I held out my fingers and trailed them over the sleek black hood of the Mercedes S600. Before I knew it, I was standing on the driver's side, right by the door. Without thinking, without caring about just how wrong this was, I glanced over my shoulder and lifted the door handle at the same time. Quickly, before my sanity returned, I ducked into the car and quietly closed the door. I leaned back, sinking into the luxurious leather seat, and shut my eyes. It was sheer heaven. After years of fighting cracked seats, rusted hinges, and corroded parts that didn't move, I was sitting in a car that deserved the name "car."

After several glorious moments of inhaling the heady scent of what big money can buy, I opened my eyes and checked out the interior. I pumped the brake, ran my fingers over the thick steering wheel, the teak panels, the new CD player. A cell phone, a pair of sunglasses, and a small notepad were thrown carelessly on the passenger seat. As I contemplated the idea of slipping on the very expensive sunglasses, the number scrawled across the top of the page caught my eye. I shook my head. *It can't be.*

But sure enough, as I leaned over and peered closely through the gray light, the seven digits jumped out at me again. Punch those numbers on the phone and somebody at Jamie's Café would answer. I didn't know why the restaurant's number would be on the front seat, and Joanne Riley wasn't here to answer my questions. There was another phone number scribbled underneath. Without stopping to analyze my actions, I tore off the top sheet, folded it in half, and quickly stuffed it into my pocket. I hurried out of the car and shut the door. Spotting the wine stacked against the wall, the kind that comes in individual bottles instead of cardboard containers, I picked up a box and returned to the kitchen.

"Don't do me any favors next time, okay?" Carrottop said, tapping her foot and checking her watch. "Maybe I should check your pockets in case you found something out there you couldn't live without."

With no warning, I dumped the box into her arms and smiled in satisfaction as she grunted and fumbled to hold on to it. "Touch me and you'll enjoy nine fingers for the rest of your life." I turned and walked out of the kitchen and down the hall.

I retraced my steps to Riley's office in time to see Michaels shutting the bottom drawer. He looked up at the sound of my footsteps. He stood, brushed his hands off, and grabbed the stack of files off the top of the file cabinet. "Ready to go?"

"I was ready before we got here."

A slow grin slid across his face. "Yes, I know."

I frowned at him. "That obvious, huh?"

"Maggie, a herd of laughing hyenas are more subtle than the expression on your face."

"I thought I was being stoic."

He laughed and ruffled my hair with his free hand. "You thought wrong." He walked past me and I followed him, but I was less than happy. In fact, I was really annoyed. Any romantic thoughts I might have been harboring about Michaels just dissipated into thin air. I may not have big breasts or legs that ran the length of the Amazon, but I sure didn't deserve to have my hair ruffled like a young boy whose gonads hadn't dropped. I practically stomped down the hallway and past the sympathy room, where I happened to see Baxter glance up from leaning against the fireplace to watch me storm out the door.

Michaels was nice enough to drop me off at my house, which was really out of his way and beyond the call of duty, but conversation was short and stilted. Every once in a while I caught him looking over at me, a strange, quizzical look on his face, but I didn't care whether he understood my sudden silence or not. In the back of my mind, I knew I was semi-sulking for no reason—I mean, beyond offering a friendly chauffeuring service, Michaels and I had no relationship. And I didn't want one. Not really. Villari and I could barely figure out what to do with each other; what would I do with Bachelor Number Two thrown into the equation? The whole non-situation was giving me a headache and I was glad when we finally reached my house.

I was pulling on the door handle when Michael put

his hand on my forearm. "Obviously, I've insulted you somehow. I apologize for that."

I held up my hand to stop him. "First of all, there's nothing to apologize for. You were very supportive during the service, which was difficult for me, and you were kind enough to bring me home today. I appreciate both. But the bottom line is, although we have a common interest in The Outlook, we are nothing more than strangers caught in the middle of some very unusual circumstances."

"I'm not sure what you're trying to say," he said, male confusion written all over his face.

I sighed. "That we have nothing in common. We're simply acquaintances who have been extra nice to each other because of a lot of bad things that have happened."

He still looked confused.

"My point is—"

"Thank God," he murmured.

"There's nothing to be sorry for," I said, ignoring his last comment. "You didn't do or say anything wrong."

"Well, thank you, I guess."

"No problem," I chirped. I lifted up the lever and hopped out of the car. Halfway up the driveway, I turned and waved. He was still in the car looking a little shell-shocked. Miraculously, I felt more lighthearted than I had all day.

Chapter Six

Ten minutes later I was sitting on a barstool trying to smooth the crumpled piece of paper I had "borrowed" from Joanne Riley's car. Somewhere in the rapidly shrinking, sensible corner of my mind, I knew I had committed a crime of some sort by taking the note without Baxter's knowledge. But discovering Jamie's number on Mrs. Riley's little tablet intrigued me. It was probably nothing more than a coincidence. Maybe she had heard about Jamie's catering service through Mark and decided to hire her for a fancy dinner she and her husband were hosting. There were a million rational explanations for finding the number there, but I just couldn't let it go. The other number on the sheet was one I didn't recognize. I'd never been to detective school, but I figured there was only one way to find out whom it belonged to. I reached for the phone.

I punched in the seven digits and nervously looked out the window for Villari's car. The guy had an uncanny knack for appearing at the most inopportune times. He had a sixth sense, a radar that beeped, flashed, and sent up flares whenever I was involved in something that might be considered a little questionable. Villari always managed to be at my side in no time at all, and always caught me elbow deep in the cookie jar.

"Sutherland Associates, Jack speaking."

The voice in the receiver made me jump. "Uh—Mr. Sutherland?" I stammered, searching frantically for something to say, when my eyes fell on the phone book.

"Yes," he replied. "Who is this?"

"I'm sorry, sir, I dropped the phone." This was certainly going well. "I'm calling from Qwest yellow pages," I said in my best operator voice. "We are in the process of updating our files and wanted to confirm your ad."

"I paid that bill two months ago," he said, irritated.

"Yes, sir, I know. Unfortunately, the computers went down and much of our information was lost. We are now reentering data and are personally calling our customers to confirm the information."

Nothing but silence.

"Would you like to continue your ad as it currently stands?"

"Yeah."

"Under what heading?"

"Private Investigators. Just like last year," he answered, a little suspiciously.

"Thank you, sir. I apologize for the inconvenience," I said.

"Have a nice day." Click. I didn't bother to wait for his good-bye. My palm was so clammy, I thought the receiver would slip out of my hand, and I didn't think Jack Sutherland would buy that story a second time.

Sutherland was a private eye? I don't know what I expected—maybe the coordinator for a large hotel ballroom where Jamie was catering a dinner. I thought the two numbers would be related somehow, although there was no real reason for my assumption. People randomly jot down numbers all the time. But still. Something nagged at me. Jamie's number at the top and a private eye's number right underneath. It didn't make sense.

I mulled it over while I called the towing service and made arrangements to have them pick up my Jeep and haul it back to Roy's Garage. I called Roy, but no one answered. I left a message so he wouldn't be surprised when my car, aka his children's college fund, was dropped off. I also added that I was none too pleased that I was practically stranded two hours after picking it up from his garage. "Doesn't anyone take pride in their work anymore?" I asked before hanging up. I felt a little guilty for my parting shot, but after having to endure his earlier lecture and disgusted looks, I figured he deserved it.

Once again, I picked up the phone and punched in a number I knew by heart.

"Hello?"

"Lisa?"

"Hey, Mag. What's going on?"

"Feel like a little adventure?"

"Sure . . . with anybody but you."

"And all this time I thought we were best friends."

"We are. But that doesn't make me stupid. Your idea of an adventure is: 'How close can we come to getting caught and landing in jail?' I've got a family now, you know. I can't just drop everything and run off on one of your idiotic escapades."

"What else are you going to do? Snip coupons and sew slipcovers for the sofa?"

"Cute, Maggie."

"Come on, Lisa," I wheedled. "There's no danger involved. I promise."

"You have no idea how *not* reassuring that is," she said, sighing. "Tell me what you want, what it's going to cost, and how much time I have before the black and whites are chasing me out of town."

"It's nothing that dramatic. I just want to take a little drive downtown."

"That's all, huh?" she said dryly. "You need me to tag along on an afternoon drive?"

"Yep. But we have to take your car. Mine's out of commission again."

"Again? I just dropped you off at the garage this morning. Some mechanic you've got there."

"Don't get me started," I warned.

"I won't say another word, as long as you come clean. What exactly are we looking for on this leisurely little road trip you have planned?"

"I don't really know," I said truthfully. "I found two numbers—"

"*Found?*" she asked suspiciously. "Found where?"

This was the sticky part. "In Riley's car."

"The guy that died?"

"Not his car, his wife's."

"Oh, thank God. That's so much better," she said dryly. "Do you want to explain what the hell you were doing in her car?"

"Nosing around, okay?" I admitted. "It was a Mercedes. One of those really expensive ones. It was all shiny and new and just sitting there practically begging me to climb in . . . and, well, what choice did I have?" I finished lamely.

"The same choice any rational human being has—walk on by," she responded emphatically. Any more emphatically and she would have blown out an eardrum.

"This is me we're talking about, Lisa. Be realistic."

"You're right. In your world, hopping into a car that belongs to the wife of a man now lying in a morgue with a tag hanging from his big toe is perfectly normal."

"Okay, maybe it wasn't the brightest thing I ever did, but there's no need to belabor the point," I said, feeling beyond dumb. "It's over and done with, and I'm stuck with two numbers." I recounted my phone call this afternoon. "Sutherland is a private eye. I'm just wondering how Jamie is connected to this guy."

"You realize there's a good chance that there is no connection."

"Yeah, I know, but there's more to the story." I described the strange man I saw Jamie with yesterday and how I tailed them halfway up the mountain before being forced to turn around, leaving out the part about the truck. "Don't say a word, Lisa," I said before she had a chance to launch Fit

Number Two. "I wouldn't have given the two of them a second glance if Mark hadn't been moping around one minute, and then ignoring her the next. When I saw her with another guy, I just punched the accelerator and followed."

To my surprise, Lisa started laughing. "God help you if Villari finds out."

"Believe me, I've thought about that," I said, wincing as I glanced out the window.

"Well, don't think about it too long, or we'll never have time to make that drive."

"Then you'll go?"

"Reluctantly, but yes, I'll go," she said. "By the way, Maggie, how do you propose to get information out of this guy? You can't just walk in and demand to know why his phone number is right below a local caterer's number."

"Don't worry. I have a plan."

Lisa groaned. "I was afraid of that."

"I think my husband is having an affair."

I patted Lisa's shoulder as she twisted the soggy tissue in her trembling hands and dabbed at the huge crocodile tears that had miraculously appeared. She was pushing for an Oscar with this dramatic performance, and I was worried she might be laying it on a bit too thick. But with tears swimming in her big hazel eyes, a quivering bottom lip, and a body that had grown men howling at the moon, Lisa could have kneed the guy in the groin and he would have begged for more.

Sutherland cleared his throat. "What makes you think . . . Has he done . . . I mean, has he said . . ."

The poor guy's mouth was so dry from salivating over poor Lisa, he could hardly spit out the words. The questions remained lodged in his throat. He kept swallowing and his Adam's apple kept bobbing until he finally choked out the word "water" and excused himself from the room.

When the door closed behind him, Lisa looked up at me and grinned. "This is a load of fun."

I barely had a chance to smile before Sutherland returned and I was relegated to more shoulder patting. He sort of ran in, half afraid that the stuff of his fantasies had up and disappeared while he was gone.

"Sorry about that," he said gruffly, taking a seat behind his desk. Tall and broad shouldered with long, lean legs, Sutherland wasn't exactly how I pictured a guy who needed to blend into the background. With a striped western shirt tucked into a pair of freshly creased, dark blue Wranglers, I'd spot this guy a mile off if he was following me around. Completing the outfit was a leather belt with a wide silver buckle and a money clip shaped like the star of Texas hanging from his back pocket. I don't know if this guy had ever even seen a horse, much less been on one, but he sure did like western wear. He was the opposite of nondescript, but I guess he knew more about PI-ing than I did. Sutherland grabbed a sheet of paper, plucked a pen from a chipped cup acting as a pencil holder, and stared at Lisa. He propped his forearms against the desk and leaned forward. "I'm going to need a few details from you."

Sutherland hadn't been gone long enough to take a cold shower, but he appeared significantly calmer and more relaxed. I didn't even want to think about what went on by the water cooler. He was all business now, taking Lisa through a whole list of questions about her husband's job, his finances, and friendships. Fortunately, on our way to his office, Lisa and I had decided that she should stick to the truth as much as possible. Although her first inclination was to lie through her teeth, we knew it wouldn't take Sutherland long to discover she was a fraud—no more than fifteen minutes on the Internet. And if that happened, he might decide to go digging and find out the real reason she was visiting his office.

So Lisa told Sutherland all about her husband, Joel, his job as a stockbroker, and their daughter, Mandy. She gave him Joel's work, license plate, and Social Security numbers. If Sutherland took the case and followed Joel around, the only thing he would uncover was a really nice man who was madly in love with his wife. Joel's only vice, if you could call it that, was the occasional drink with the boys after work in a local bar, about three blocks from his office. But Lisa grossly exaggerated this innocent stopover. What was in reality nothing more than a beer or two once in a while, turned into a nightly occurrence with Joel stumbling home drunk with a pair of panties stuffed in his coat pocket.

"Is there a ladies' room here?" I asked.

Without taking his eyes from Lisa, Sutherland cocked his head toward the side door. "Down the hall to your left."

"Thanks," I said, giving Lisa's shoulder one more reassuring squeeze. I left, but not before witnessing a few more strategic tears rolling down her face as she embellished the rest of her story. I held my breath, wondering whether Sutherland would buy her act or not. Personally, I thought he relished the idea of catching Joel slipping his hand down some woman's pants just so he could come back to Lisa and break the bad news. Once she broke down and sobbed over the fact that her suspicions were true, Sutherland could oust me out of my position as official shoulder patter. From there, it was only a hop, skip, and a jump to dinner and then to the bedroom, where he could pat something else.

Finding the bathroom, I closed and locked the door behind me. It was a small room, so it didn't take long to find what I was looking for. I glanced up and smiled. Above the sink was a window, an old-fashioned window with no screen. Putting the lid down, I stepped up on the toilet and then onto the freestanding sink, bracing both hands against the sides of the window. Once I had my balance, I reached up and unlocked the window, swiveling the lever counterclockwise, praying that a building as old as this one wouldn't have an alarm system. Slowly, I made my way back down, heaving a sigh of relief when my feet touched the ground. I flushed the toilet, washed my hands, and headed out the door.

Sutherland was helping Lisa out of her chair when I walked into the office. He was busily assuring her that he would get on this *problem* right away, possibly even tonight.

"Oh, I don't think that would do any good." She sniffed prettily. "We're going to his parents' for dinner, and he never misses that. They think their little boy can do no wrong."

"When does he usually go off on these little forays with the boys?" he asked, barely hiding the contempt in his voice. I wasn't surprised. Lisa had been holding men in the palm of her hand since I first roomed with her back in college. She knew it and she wasn't afraid to use it to her advantage.

"Almost every day. I'm sure he'll call or leave with some excuse tomorrow. He gets restless if he spends too much time at home." I had to bite my tongue to keep from laughing. The truth was, Joel was more of a homebody than any man I knew. The man was a gourmet chef, shared housekeeping chores, and absolutely adored his daughter. In fact, I often accused him of being a much better wife than Lisa.

"Tell you what. Call me at this number," Sutherland said, handing her his card, "and let me know when he leaves the house and where he's going. Don't worry about the time. Call me as soon as you know or suspect anything."

Two things were going on here. The guy wanted Lisa bad—and the guy wanted Lisa very bad.

But it worked. By the time we headed back to Monument, Lisa and I were doubled over with laughter. She kept batting her lashes at me, letting imaginary tears well up in her eyes and dabbing at them with a balled-up tissue. "Joel's going to kill me," she said.

"You're going to tell him?" I asked, surprised.

"Well, of course, Maggie. I don't hide anything from him. He's my husband."

"But he'll throw a fit, Lisa."

"True, but what can he do? It's a done deal," she replied, rolling her shoulders. "I tell him everything, just not necessarily in a timely fashion."

I had to grin. "I guess I don't understand this marriage thing."

"As long as I'm not in any danger, he'll get into the swing

of it all. Once he knows that Sutherland is tailing him, he'll take him all over the city. He'll love every minute of it."

"But we'll be breaking into Sutherland's office while Joel's being tailed."

"Joel doesn't need to know that, at least not right away."

"Apparently not," I replied. "But what excuse are you going to give Joel for sticking Sutherland on him in the first place?"

She lifted her shoulders. "I'm not sure yet, but I'll think of something."

I sighed. "It seems easier not to mention anything, but what do I know?"

"You know more than you're willing to admit."

I glanced over at Lisa and scowled. "What's that supposed to mean?"

"Villari. You'll tell Villari about it."

"Like hell. He'd kill me."

"It's that protective thing. You know he'll be angry, but in the end, you'll tell him."

"Not unless I'm suicidal."

She shook her head. "You love him, Maggie. You're scared to death to admit it, but the facts are still there. Trust me, you'll tell him."

"First off, love is a pretty strong word—way too strong for whatever it is that Villari and I have together. Besides, just because we enjoy each other, and even that's iffy half the time, I still don't see why I have to tell him anything. Having a boyfriend, if that's what he is, doesn't mean he's privy to all my secrets. It's nice that he knows I like pepperoni on my pizza, but I don't see why Villari needs to know how often I go to the bathroom. Whatever happened to keeping a little mystery in the relationship?"

"Do you want a partner?"

"Someday," I said vaguely. This whole relationship thing always threw me off course. The problem was that I wanted it all, and it embarrassed the hell out of me. I liked white picket fences and kids and dogs. I even liked apple pie. But there was also a part of me that was fiercely independent, and I didn't want to answer to anybody for any reason unless I wanted to. In fact, I had a rotten habit of getting really angry whenever I felt like someone was pushing to get too close. It made me claustrophobic and I tended to lash out with nasty retorts. At least that's what Villari tells me.

"If you want a partner, you've got to be willing to share."

"You like being an open book, Lisa. I don't. I've been a private person all my life. I'm not too keen on spilling my guts every time I run a red light or bounce a check."

"You're simplifying this, Maggie. I'm not telling you that you *have* to tell Villari, I'm just saying that you'll want to." She shifted in her seat and pushed harder on the accelerator. Lisa was no wilting flower when it came to speed. "Joel's the best friend I've ever had. I don't tell him everything because I have to, I tell him because I want to share my life with him. He's my partner. I didn't marry him so I could spend the next forty years holding secrets close to my chest."

"Maybe," I said, as close to conceding as I ever got. "But what you have with Joel is far beyond anything Villari and I have."

"Maybe," Lisa said.

I knew that was simply her way of telling me I was full of crap. We drove the rest of the way home in silence.

DURAN lived high up in the hills in a modest cabin-house that grabbed my heart and twisted it in envy. I've never been a big fan of cookie-cutter houses with identical floor plans, stamp-sized backyards, and built close enough to stick your arm out the window and shake hands with the neighbors. Tucked back into the trees and wedged into a crevice created by overlapping hills, Duran's home was built with such simple lines, it made me want to weep. Straight lines, large rectangular windows, and a wraparound porch completed the outside. It was difficult to believe that the owner of this house, a house built with such an affinity and understanding of nature, was a guy who wore enough checks and patterns to outfit the entire PGA senior tour.

Even Villari was surprised. As we drove up the mountain, carefully slowing down on the switchbacks, we exchanged glances and shrugged our shoulders in a sort of *Who would have guessed?* gesture. Certainly not me. I fully expected a lemon-yellow house with white shutters, a striped door, and a flock of pink flamingos mating in the front yard.

As we turned in the driveway, I double-checked the address on the mailbox. I still couldn't believe Duran lived in such a tasteful house. Villari pulled in slowly and parked between two other cars.

"We made a wrong turn somewhere," I said.

"What makes you say that?"

I rolled down the window and gestured toward the wide

panoramic view. "Natural beauty. Simplicity. Lack of clutter. These things do not add up to the guy dressed in the clown suit who liked my work."

"Speak of the devil," Villari said, nodding toward the short, squat guy standing on the porch wearing an eye-searing pair of pink-and-yellow plaid slacks topped off with a lime green polo shirt.

"My God, just when you thought it couldn't get any worse," I said in amazement, "the man comes up with a combination that would cause a peacock to pale in comparison."

Villari chuckled. "He does seem to have a certain flair for color."

"Well, let's get this over with," I said, opening the car door.

"You don't sound very excited about a potential client, even if it's a badly dressed one."

"I don't know what to think. Duran comes highly recommended. He and Mark are really old friends, and Mark would never push me toward someone disreputable, even for a large sale." I stopped and blew out a heavy breath. "But, Villari. Look at the guy. He looks like a walking flea market."

"And?"

I frowned. "And what?"

"And what difference does it make whether the guy wears purple socks and gold chains? He likes your art, he buys it and enjoys it. Who cares if he slips on a pair of pantyhose while he admires your work?"

I sighed. "I know you're right, and I don't have a good

answer for you. I just hoped that the first person who bought a sculpture of mine looked and acted a little more, well, refined."

"Since when did we become an Art Diva?" he asked, arching an eyebrow. "In my book, a sale is a sale."

"Probably," I admitted, slanting my eyes at him. "And how typical of you to be the one to bring me down a notch or two."

He grinned. "Just doing my job." Villari reached over and squeezed my hand. "Come on, honey, this will be fun." When I shot him a skeptical look, he hurried to reassure me. "First thing you learn at the police academy is that nothing is what it seems. People are never what they appear. My guess is that this guy is one shrewd bastard with a pot full of money. You get him on your side and you're set for life."

"You're kidding, right?"

"I've seen stranger things," he said, lifting his broad shoulders.

"You're a cop, Villari. Life's underbelly is familiar territory."

"Maggie?" he asked, a strange look slipping over his face.
"What?"

"Are you ever going to call me by my first name?"

Uh-oh. This was a conversation turn I didn't want to take.

"Take a deep breath, Maggie. I don't want you turning blue and passing out on me."

"I don't know what to say," I muttered lamely.

"Simple question. Simple yes or no."

"It's not that simple and you know it. Aren't you the guy

who just got through saying that things are never what they seem to be?"

Villari turned to stare at me. And he kept staring at me until I started to fidget. Without a word, he got out of the car and shut the door behind him. He leaned against the hood of the car and waited for me. Feeling like live scum, I crawled out of the car and slunk over to stand next to him. I felt horrible about my lack of response, but I didn't have enough guts to fix things. The man scared me. No. That's not true. He petrified me.

"Don't hate me, okay?"

He pivoted, grasped my upper arms, and pulled me upright. "Is that what you think?"

"I don't know what to think," I said, staring straight ahead, right into his chest. "I'm not good at this sort of thing."

"You're lousy at this sort of thing," he said gruffly.

I lifted my face and tried to stare him down. "I have it on the highest authority, your mother, that you don't happen to be too good yourself."

"What the hell does she know?"

"Considering the fact that she has God's number on her speed dial, I'd say a lot."

Fortunately, Villari laughed. In fact, he laughed hard enough to bring the twinkle back into his eyes. His lips fell easily into his lopsided grin. He pressed his lips against my forehead and trailed his index finger down the bridge of my nose. "Let's go, Maggie. Duran is waiting for us."

I'd completely forgotten. Swinging around, I scanned the

porch for that beacon of obnoxious color. He was nowhere to be found. "Where'd he go?"

Villari raised his shoulders. "Last time I looked, he was on the deck."

"You kids through fightin' or do you need some more time?" Duran called out as he stepped between the parked cars, carrying a cigar in his right hand and hitching up his pants with the left.

I shot a glance at Villari. "We're fine. Sorry about that," I said, not sure why I was apologizing when it was Duran who had watched us in the car and eavesdropped on our conversation.

"No reason to be sorry. At your age, emotions sit right on the surface, just ready to explode. Your man here has ants in his pants and you're running in the opposite direction like a bat out of hell," he said, puffing on his cigar. "You need some time to get accustomed to the idea of having a man around keeping your britches on fire . . . nothing wrong with that."

I stood there and gaped at the man. Did I have a choice?

After several very long seconds, I managed to gather my wits and respond. "I truly don't mean to sound disrespectful, Mr. Duran, but my business with Villari is personal," I said, clearing my throat and shifting from one foot to the other like someone who desperately needed to visit the little girls' room. "I do appreciate your concern, but I think we can handle it from here."

"She sure does get her dander up when someone steps foot in her pissin' area."

Villari smiled at that particular comment, started to

chuckle, and then he laughed out loud. I mean, he really laughed. At one point, he bent over, put his hands on top of his knees, and "busted a gut," as Duran would say. I stood there staring, not saying a word until he got himself under control. When he finally straightened and began breathing normally, I went from staring to glaring.

"Uh-oh. Looks like you dug yourself a little hole there, son," Duran said.

There was no missing the amusement in his voice.

"A hole doesn't begin to describe it," I said, a pinch of prissiness creeping into my voice.

"Ease up a little, Maggie," Villari said. I could tell by the way he was biting the inside of his cheek that he was trying hard to keep himself from laughing again. "You have to admit the guy has a certain way with words."

"No doubt," I responded. "If we still used burned sticks and wrote on cave walls, he would be a real stitch," I snapped, turning to Duran. "No offense intended."

"Don't you worry—my skin's tougher than an elephant's hide. You aren't the first woman to point out my lack of modern ideas. Probably won't be the last," he admitted. "I seem to have a particular knack for annoying pretty women. Part of my sex appeal, I guess."

Even I had to smile at that. I threw up my hands. "Okay, Mr. Duran—"

"Hank."

"Oh, yes, it's Hank, isn't it?" I said. "You're an old hand at instigating problems and then falling back on that 'Golly gee, shucks' act you've perfected to get yourself out of trouble."

Duran slanted an amused look at Villari. "Usually works like a charm, too."

"Maggie's a bit more prickly than most women," Villari said.

"She just needs a little extra attention. She'll fight it, of course, but the harder she fights, the more you got to give her."

Villari didn't respond immediately, but I did. "As much as I enjoy standing around, spitting and scratching our crotches while we discuss the womenfolk, maybe we could go inside and you could explain what you're looking for—in terms of art, that is."

Duran's laugh was as loud as his clothes. "You're absolutely right, Miss Maggie. Mary's probably madder than a wet hen right now, waiting for me to remember my manners and bring you in for supper." He turned to Villari and thrust out his hand. "We've howdied, but we ain't shook yet. I'm Hank Duran."

Villari took his hand and introduced himself. "I realize I wasn't invited to dinner, but—"

"But you were looking after Miss Maggie here," Duran finished for him. "Smart move. If I were in your position, I'd be worried about her hanging around an old coot like myself, too. I may be a little worn around the edges, but I can be a charming bastard when I put my mind to it."

"That's not exactly what—"

"If you want supper tonight, I suggest you let an old man believe what he wants."

"Lead the way, Hank."

Shaking my head in exasperation, I followed the two men

across the yard up to the front porch, where a small woman, brown hair pulled back in a thick ponytail and arms folded across her chest, stood impatiently tapping one foot against the floor. Duran stopped on the top step, introduced Villari, and then turned and pointed his finger at me as I reached the group.

"Maggie, this is Mary. She makes the finest steak this side of the Rockies. Thick and juicy, just melts in your mouth."

"Don't listen to him," she said, glaring at Duran. "He's late and he's trying to weasel on to my good side. It doesn't take any talent to cook a steak, although my mashed potatoes are above average and I make a lemon meringue pie that's to die for."

Just thinking about it was enough to make my stomach curdle. "That sounds wonderful," I lied.

She looked closely at me. "You don't like lemon meringue, do you?"

"I hate the stuff," I admitted, "but I wasn't born yesterday. I'm in no hurry to join Hank on your bad side. If you put a slice of that stuff in front of me, I'll dig right in. No complaints, no questions asked."

Mary fought off a smile and turned to Duran. "Are you going to stand out here all night dispensing your normal ration of bad advice or are you going to invite the two of them in?" She whipped open the screen door, stepped inside the house, and let the door slam behind her, leaving the three of us watching as she disappeared into the hallway.

"Way she acts, you'd think she owned this house instead of me," Duran mumbled as he reached for the door handle. "One of these days, the two of us are going to have a big sit down and I'm going to set a few things straight. If I want to have people over for dinner and have a conversation outside . . ."

Villari and I grinned at each other as Duran continued to rant and rave about Mary's bossiness, but all of his threats didn't stop him from dropping his voice to a low whisper as we followed him into the house. Apparently he was in no rush to have that little powwow. As his voice trailed off into another litany of complaints, I looked around the house and fell in love with what I saw.

The entryway flowed into the main room, a large, airy space. Soft maple paneling warmed the walls. Colorful rugs were thrown on top of glossy plank flooring, and a dark green couch with large pillows dominated the room. A huge bookshelf took up one entire wall, while large, single-paned windows offered unobstructed views of huge, jagged pink boulders that cracked the sky. I took in all the natural beauty, inhaled the scent of pine and freshly polished wood, and then forgot it all, because nothing, nothing could compete with the artwork Duran had in that room.

Large abstract paintings hung from the walls, sculptures stood in the corners, in the bookshelves, on the tables— everywhere. And every piece was obviously an original. The sheer diversity of the work was enough to boggle my mind. He had pieces in brass, rod iron, and porcelain; masterpieces of welded scrap metal sharing space with exaggerated female forms carved from black granite and realistic bronzed animal figures.

"I thought you'd like it," Duran said.

I swiveled around and stared at him. "It's unbelievable. It's like a museum."

"I told you I'd been collecting a long time." He swept his arm around the room. "I can look at each piece and tell you everything about my life . . . who I was married to, how much money I had in the bank . . . If I thought hard enough, I could probably figure out how much I weighed and what size pants I wore at the time."

I could hear Villari's soft chuckle next to me.

"That's probably more than I need to know," I said.

Duran laughed. "Believe me, it's more than I want to remember, too. Getting fat is not a particularly inspiring story, but the point is, everything here is a part of me. Some people like to paste pictures in a scrapbook, I like looking at something that makes me think. That's the good part about art. There's a lot of memories here, no doubt about that, but every time I look, I see something I didn't see before. I like that. Keep a man thinking and he has reason to get up in the morning. Nothing dies faster than a mind full of cobwebs."

This guy had enough homespun wisdom to fill a book.

"The point is, I liked what I saw the other night. But like I said, it's not raw enough for me."

It was hard to imagine that a man wearing Popsicle colors needed something more raw. But for once, I didn't say anything. As Villari said, a sale was a sale, and I needed this one. There was no telling how long it would be before The Outlook was open for business again, and even then, who knew whether or not I'd get another chance to show my work? Jeff Riley's murder was certainly more newsworthy than my art, and the critics never even filed a review. With no reviews, people would lose interest in my work in no time at all.

"Now, the stuff back in the storeroom was a little more to my liking, but I still think you're missing something. You're still hanging in the middle of the road where you can't get hurt."

Okay, I knew I was going to have to accept some criticism in this line of work, but the hairs on the back of my neck were standing straight up and my jaw was starting to tighten . . . just a little. I forced myself to take a deep calming breath and relax my muscles so I wouldn't strangle him, at least not right away.

"Do you think you could be a little more specific?"

Duran glanced up at the tone of my voice. "Uh-oh. I've offended you, haven't I?" He shrugged his shoulders. "Well, it can't be helped. Not if you want to get better. Artists, and I am including you under that label, don't have the luxury of sticking their head in the sand because their feelings are hurt. You might as well learn to face the bullet with a friendly firing squad—that being me."

One more folksy analogy and I was going to smack him.

Then Villari popped up with, "I don't think it would hurt to hear the guy out, Maggie."

Duran held up his hand and said, "Case in point. You're fighting mad right now. You're working overtime to keep it under control, but your face couldn't hide a feeling if it tried. That's a lousy thing in a poker game and a damned good thing for an artist."

This guy was talking country gibberish. Maybe Jed

Clampett and his hillbilly posse could unravel this line of reasoning, but I was lost.

"Don't get me wrong. Your work is good, otherwise I wouldn't bother inviting you over here, and I wouldn't be thinking of adding something of yours to my house. I sure as hell wouldn't put myself through the grief of listening to Mary holler about how late I was or how I didn't tell her we had an extra guest tonight, which, of course, I didn't know." He shook his head and rubbed his hand over his balding scalp. "But that's not the point. The point is, you could be a whole lot better if you quit holding in your fury like you're doing right now and let it explode."

Okay, I was listening.

"You got real sad eyes, honey, but there's no sadness in your art. You got a temper to beat the banshees, but your art is nice and proper like you just graduated from charm school. I know you're well-trained, Mark told me all about your history. But now you have to push everything you learned into the back of your mind, put your hands on the clay, and go for it without thinking about anything but you and that solid piece of earth you got underneath your fingers."

I didn't know what to say or how to respond. His words were simple enough, but what he was asking me to do was something I'd spent years trying to avoid. My emotions were loud and messy, but I learned to keep the deepest part of me under wraps. I had grown up in the shadow of my father's grief. Somehow I believed that if I exposed my real thoughts, I would lose control. And I just couldn't do that. Not with my father spending every minute of his life tying up his own feelings into a nice neat little package.

"I'm not sure I can do that."

Duran rubbed his jaw several times and studied me. "Well now, that's the real question, isn't it?"

Villari looked at Duran, then me, back to Duran, and then me again.

"You're scared, aren't you?" Duran said.

I frowned. "Don't be ridiculous. I'm just not sure it's what I want to do."

"No, that's not true. You're afraid to try, just like you're afraid to have a relationship."

I felt my cheeks get hot. "If you don't mind, my relationship with Villari is between the two of us."

"That's fair enough. I think we'd better table this conversation until after dinner. I can hear Mary banging the pots out there, and I'd just as soon not be on the receiving end of another lecture."

Now my jaw was set. "I think that's a good idea," I bit out. "I'm starving."

"Somehow I doubt that," Duran replied mildly, "but there's nothing like a good home-cooked meal to take the edge off of everybody's temper." And with that pronouncement, he led the way through a set of swinging doors into the bright kitchen, where Mary was tapping her foot again and vigorously stirring mashed potatoes.

"Where do you want us tonight, Mary?"

"Same place we always serve guests," she snapped. "Where else?"

"I thought so, but given the mood you're in, I thought I'd do you the courtesy of asking," he said, walking across to the other side of the kitchen and gesturing for us to follow him.

"A bucking bronco would break down and cry under that woman's hand," he commented as we moved to the dining room.

We sat around a small table set for four. I was glad to see that Mary was planning on joining us tonight. Watching her put Duran in his place was pretty amusing, and right now, I could use a good laugh. I didn't want to admit it, but everything Duran had observed about my work was true. His comments had stung, and the last thing I wanted was to sit and make polite conversation. I needed time to digest his words. Of course, I knew exactly what he was saying. Elizabeth was always trying to pull me out of myself, and Duran, in his loud and bumbling way, was doing the same thing. He wasn't criticizing my technique, he was merely pointing out the lack of strong feelings in my work.

"Mary, you've done it again."

I looked up to see Mary bringing in a bowl piled high with mashed potatoes. She left the room and came back with a platter of steaks. She shook her head at my offer to help, and I lost count of all the trips she took, but before long, the small table was even smaller, completely burdened with enough food to feed North Dakota. And dessert was still to come.

Mary finally sat down and started passing the bowls.

"I suppose you can't give out any details here," Duran said, "but is there any progress on the murder investigation?"

Villari looked up from a plate mounded high with artery-busting food and shook his head. "I can't say much more than there isn't much to say at this point. We're still interviewing people and waiting for different lab reports, but nothing solid has come out so far. Of course, I'm on the investigating team, but I'm not the lead on the case, so I don't always get the latest information until we meet in the morning."

"Who's the point man?"

"Lieutenant Baxter. I'm sure he questioned you that night."

"Lovely man," I said under my breath.

Villari's mouth twitched. "Maggie isn't exactly fond of Lieutenant Baxter."

Duran turned to me. "Why is that? Seemed like a decent enough fellow."

"He's all right," I granted. "I just don't enjoy being questioned."

Duran chuckled. "Somehow that doesn't surprise me."

"Did you see him at the memorial service?" Villari asked.

I nodded. "First at the service, and later on at the reception or wake or whatever you call a crowd of people eating a lot of food and toasting a dead person."

"I thought you weren't going to the reception," Villari said.

"I wasn't, but my car broke down at the church and Michaels gave me a ride home. He had to stop by Riley's house first, though, to pick up some files from his office. I didn't see Baxter until we left the house, but all he has to do is look at me and I feel guilty."

"And what would you have to feel guilty about, Miss Maggie?" Duran asked casually.

"Nothing," I mumbled before forking a bite of steak into my mouth.

"Why didn't you call me when your car broke down?" Villari asked.

My jealous detective was so intent on questioning me about my association with Michaels that he completely missed the contemplative look on Duran's face. But I didn't. Duran leaned forward, steepled his fingers, and studied me closely. Between Villari's narrowed eyes and Duran's suspicious expression, I felt like a cornered rat. I squirmed like a five-year-old and started shoveling food in my mouth and washing it down with unladylike gulps of water.

"The way you're packing that food down, I guess you really are starving," Duran said mildly.

"Hank," Mary chided. She turned to me. "Don't pay any attention to him. You eat as much as you want. There's plenty more where that came from."

"If we kill another cow," he noted.

"Why did Michaels drive you home?" Villari persisted. "Why didn't you just call me from the church?"

"The boy does have a one-track mind, doesn't he?" Duran commented. "Who is this Michaels fellow anyway?"

"Now, Hank, that's none of your business."

"The hell it isn't. This is my house and my table and my dinner she's putting away with an appetite that would shame a truck driver. Any conversation brought up under my roof is fair game for discussion."

I held up my hands. "Okay, that's it. Everyone stop."

Taking a deep breath, I plunged in. "First of all, Dylan Michaels is a member of a law firm that is closely affiliated with The Outlook. Mark has asked him to take over Riley's responsibilities until a more permanent arrangement can be found. As for—"

"Good-looking?" Duran asked.

"What?"

"You heard me. You planning on testing the bedsprings with this Michaels?"

At that comment, Mary groaned and put her face in her hands. Villari and I just stared speechlessly at our host.

"I don't know what everyone is so upset about," Duran said as he looked around the table. "All I did was save ourselves a bunch of time. Your young man here wants to know whether there's another bull in the pen. You were going to dodge the issue with a lot of long explanations and fancy footwork, and the poor guy was never going to get his answer. A man likes to know what he's facing. Then he's got a choice: Prepare to fight or pull the boots back on and start walking."

Villari cleared his throat. "I appreciate the help, Hank . . . I think."

"No problem." Duran glanced at Mary, who was shaking her head. "I was just helping the boy out, Mary. He understands that."

"We'll talk about it later," Mary said quietly.

Duran turned to me. "Now I'm in big trouble. The lower her voice, the bigger the argument. Between the whisper and the daggers she's shooting across the table, I might as well save her the trouble and jump in the grave myself."

I had to smile at his predicament. After being embarrassed by him several times already, I was more than happy to see that Duran had a fight on his hand with a formidable opponent. I didn't understand the exact nature of their relationship, but clearly, Mary was nobody's lap dog.

"Do you want to answer the question?" Villari asked in the ensuing silence.

"You're kidding, right?"

He shook his head. "As unorthodox as Hank's questions are, he's right. I do want to know what I'm facing." Villari then turned to Duran, who had folded his arms across his chest and was smiling smugly to himself. "But I'm warning you now, Hank, step across the line that's none of your business one more time and I'll break your nose."

Duran smile just got broader. "Understood."

Villari swung his gaze back to me and waited.

I shrugged. "He was there. He offered and I accepted. It was no big deal."

Villari seemed to accept my explanation and dropped the question . . . for the moment. "Baxter's not going to like the idea of any files being removed from Riley's office without his permission. Quite frankly, neither do I. It skims that edge of legality." He raised an eyebrow. "I'm assuming you didn't bother to ask before you removed anything."

If the files bothered him, Villari would have a coronary if I told him about the page I'd torn off the notepad. By the time he lectured me, paced the room, and threatened to throw me in jail, life as I knew it would be over. I wanted to confess, I really did, but the mere thought of dealing with all that anger was enough to keep my mouth shut.

Besides, if I thought Villari would be upset about the slip of paper I'd borrowed . . . well, stolen . . . he would be less than pleased with what Lisa and I were planning tomorrow. Just thinking about his reaction made me shudder.

"I was only along for the ride," I replied. "I don't know if Michaels talked to Baxter beforehand or not." Villari didn't look happy, but there wasn't much he could say. The truth was, this time it wasn't my fault. I was there by coincidence. If it hadn't been for my Jeep falling apart on me again, I would have been safe and sound in my own house when Michaels went foraging through Riley's office.

I looked up and met Duran's wary gaze. Intellectually, I realized that he didn't have a clue about the phone numbers, but that didn't stop my nerves from tingling and my heart from pounding. Duran was quite adept at reading my face, especially given how little we knew each other. But he had guessed right away that I was hiding something. The man's eyes were searching my face as thoroughly as a blind man's hands. I finally had to look away.

"Michaels did ask his wife—his widow, I mean, before he took anything," I said.

"Doesn't matter. I'll have to let Baxter know about this. He'll probably want to examine those files."

"I'm sure Michaels will cooperate. I mean, he's not hiding anything." *But I am,* I thought, dropping my gaze while I pushed the remaining food around the plate.

"Mmmm, suddenly lost your appetite, have you?" Duran asked.

"Leave the poor girl alone, Hank," Mary insisted, turning to me. "He's a questionable host in the very best of times, but I don't know what's gotten into him tonight."

"Nothing's gotten into me. Just because you get a burr under your saddle whenever there's a little straight talk at the dinner table, doesn't mean the rest of us can't enjoy a little lively conversation."

"I hardly think this is the time to discuss—"

"Well, hell, you brought it up."

And so it went. Mary and Hank bickered back and forth while Villari and I exchanged amused glances. Conversation was never a problem, not with Duran shooting little zingers at any available target. The man could be described as loud, obnoxious, coarse, and a whole host of negative adjectives but there was no doubt in my mind that he was nobody's fool. He had a way of zeroing in on the bottom line, and that's all he cared about.

"So, Maggie, I've wined and dined you, so to speak. Think you're ready to step up to the plate?"

"Yeah, I guess I am. At least I'm willing to try."

"Can't ask for more than that," he replied. "My guess is you're gonna surprise the hell out of yourself."

"I hope you're right."

"Honey, I've been right more often than I've been wrong. Picked out some good friends and stuck with them. Worked hard, made some good investments, and grabbed on to Mary here and held on fast. I have an eye for talent, and you've got it. Besides, I'm going to give you a fairly sizable amount of money up front, and I'm not in the habit of throwing my dollars out the window."

The man did have a way with words.

After his little speech, we all went into his office and

hammered out a deal, which essentially meant that he laid out the terms and I agreed to them. It wasn't difficult. He gave me a generous sum of money as a down payment and some rough ideas of what he was looking for. I tried to appear as businesslike as possible, but my insides were quaking like crazy and all I could do was squeak out a simple yes whenever he asked me a question. I'm sure I looked like an idiot and sounded even worse, but this was my first sale, and I was having a hard time containing my excitement.

On our way home, Villari and I replayed the whole evening, skipping over the dangerous parts that were bound to lead us into an argument, and laughed at all the "Hank-isms," as we now called them. When we arrived at my house, Villari reached over and took my hand.

"Are you ever going to answer my question?"

"What question?"

"My name, Maggie. Are you ever going to call me by my first name?"

I thought for a moment. "Maybe."

He smiled. "Looks like we're making progress."

Chapter Seven

The Catholic Church teaches that there are two different kinds of sins—venial and mortal. The first category covers the regular, run-of-the-mill transgressions we commit every day. All those little well-meaning lies we tell, like vigorously reassuring a very large woman that her purple plaid pants really are very slimming, fall under the venial sin umbrella. Or when we forget to inform our parents that the A we earned was not entirely on our own, that sitting behind the class genius who forgot to cover his paper might have helped a little—or a lot. These minor infractions are easily washed away and the gateway to heaven is still bright and shining. But the mortal sin umbrella is a whole other animal. Much more ominous, this sin is the one that has three major criteria: a) The act is wrong—very wrong.

b) You know it's wrong—very wrong. c) Knowing what you know, you do it anyway.

I was still debating how the saints would view my trip to Sutherland's office. On the one hand, it didn't seem all that bad. After all, Lisa and I had a very good, if not moral, purpose for carefully examining documents in the PI's office while he was busy doing other things. There was a murder investigation going on, and we were just doing our part as concerned citizens. The fact that our part was unsolicited, unknown, and unwanted by the police shouldn't deter us. Perhaps a priest would look at breaking and entering a man's office as a more serious sin than slipping away from my sixteenth birthday party and going to second base with Adam Crawford behind the juniper bushes, but it was for a greater good. Wasn't it?

In the end, I knew I was pursuing this because something fishy was going on and I had a strong hunch that the common thread could be found somewhere in Sutherland's office. Besides, there wasn't much I could do at this point—things were out of my hands. Lisa had already called Sutherland and told him that Joel had left the house this morning, giving her several flimsy excuses. Joel took Mandy along with him, but Lisa swore it was only to make his errands look legitimate. She begged him to tail her husband, and Sutherland could hardly contain his excitement.

"How did Joel react when you told him about our little excursion?" I asked as Lisa drove us toward the Springs.

"I didn't exactly tell him."

"Didn't tell him? What about that long speech you gave me about honesty and partnership?"

"What can I say?" Lisa said, raising her shoulders. "Joel was feeling especially amorous last night and I wasn't about to spoil the mood."

"You chickened out."

"I didn't 'chicken out,' as you so childishly put it. I just didn't see any reason to ruin a perfectly good evening explaining what we were doing. Besides, if things go smoothly, he'll never know he's being watched and everything will return to normal."

At which point I pursed my lips and let loose with my finest chicken cackle.

"Okay, you're right," Lisa admitted, a mischievous grin deepening her dimples. "I didn't have the heart, or guts, to tell Joel. What was I going to say? 'A private investigator is going to be following you around today while Maggie and I commit a felony and break into his office.'"

"I prefer to think of it as premeditated snooping."

"Call it what you want, but the result is the same. Judges don't look kindly on the old breaking and entering."

Okay, now I was getting worried. "We can always back out."

"Not on your life. Not with our secret weapon."

"What secret weapon?"

"Villari, you idiot. I figure it wouldn't take him long to convince any judge that you and I, especially you, are certifiably nuts. We'd be out in no time."

"How do you know he wouldn't recommend a lengthy stay in a mental institution?"

"You'll have to convince him otherwise, Maggie," she said suggestively.

I sighed. "You're putting an awful lot of weight on my sexual prowess."

"I'm not putting anything on your sexual abilities, but I am banking that Villari is a typical red-blooded American male who would hate limiting sex to conjugal visits behind bars."

"You're saying Villari's going to save my butt so he can get some?"

"The facts are indisputable, Maggie. He's seen the state of your lingerie, and he still wants you."

"Why does everyone keep coming back to my underwear?"

"You're missing my point."

"Which is?" I asked.

"The guy really cares about you. But you've hidden behind that wall of yours for so long, you don't know love when it pops you right between the eyes."

"There you go with that love word again. Don't you think you bandy that around a little too easily?"

"No, I don't. But we'll have to table that discussion for another time," Lisa said, stopping at the curb in front of a blue-and-white Victorian house we had found yesterday as we scouted the area on our way home. "We're here."

She parked in a spot approximately a quarter of a mile from Sutherland's place. His place was located on the outskirts of the downtown square, not too far from The Outlook. Fortunately for us, a wide alley ran parallel to the building. If we needed to make a quick exit, it would be easy to follow the alley downtown and blend into the crowds milling around Chinook Bookstore or slip into the coffee-house situated on the corner.

Lisa and I sat in the car gazing out the window for several minutes. The neighborhood on the north end of downtown was old and relatively quiet, especially away from Cascade and Nevada Street, the two main thoroughfares. A couple of bicyclists rode by and waved. Finally, almost simultane-ously, we unlocked our doors and hopped out. Without say-ing a word, we took off, our footsteps hitting the pavement in tandem. We strode down the alley until we reached the side of Sutherland's building, the front of which faced the street. Trying to look nonchalant, we kept moving until I spotted the window I had unlocked the day before. I tapped Lisa's shoulder and pointed up.

"It's okay to talk, Mag," she said dryly. "We're trying to look natural, remember?"

"And how do we accomplish that while we're climbing through the window?"

"I'm not sure. Shut up and let me think."

I was too nervous to stand still and be quiet. "I think we need—"

"What you need is a lookout person," a deep voice boomed. "A watchdog."

My heart jumped into my throat, a habit as of lately, and I swung around to see Duran standing behind us, his arms crossed against his chest. Judging by Lisa's startled gasp, she was as surprised as I was.

"Wha—what are you doing here?" I stuttered.

"Following you, of course."

"But why?"

"Because of what you said last night."

"You told him?" Lisa asked incredulously.

"I didn't say anything," I denied furiously. "I never said a word."

"She's right about that. It's more what she *didn't* say than what she did." Duran thrust his hand out in Lisa's direction. "I recognize you from the opening the other night, but I don't believe we were ever properly introduced. I'm Hank Duran."

Without skipping a beat, Lisa shook his hand. "Lisa. Lisa McKenna. It's nice to meet you. Maggie's told me a lot about you."

"Would you two knock it off? This isn't a social gathering."

"*That* is the million dollar question, isn't it? Exactly why are we gathered here?" Duran asked, gesturing widely at the alley.

I didn't know whether to involve Duran or not. I was already feeling guilty about dragging Lisa into this whole mess, and I wasn't sure I wanted to be responsible for including someone else.

Sensing my hesitation, Duran folded his arms and spoke quietly. "Go ahead and spit it out, Miss Maggie. And don't bother lying, because I can see right through you."

"I wasn't going to lie, I was just debating on whether I should say anything or not. This little errand we're running here sort of blurs the edges of legal activities."

"If you're thinking of climbing into that window up there, like I think you are, then you've gone way over the line of being neighborly. What you're mulling over is a crime, and I've got a feeling that boyfriend of yours wouldn't take too kindly to this morning activity you've got planned."

"No he wouldn't," I admitted morosely.

"Mind telling me why this building is so important?"

I glanced at Lisa, who shrugged her shoulders and murmured, "Might as well. Doesn't look like he's going anywhere."

"Okay, here's what happened." I then proceeded to outline the story of finding Sutherland's phone number and the hunch I had about discovering a connection somewhere in his office.

When I stopped talking, Duran, outfitted in another patented plaid and polka-dot ensemble, rubbed his chin with his thumb and index finger. "The story sounds a little sketchy in parts, like how you happened to trip over this particular number, but I don't think we have time to quibble about that right now. Seems to me that what we need first is a plan."

"Are you sure you want to do this?" I asked. "I mean, we could get caught and even go to jail."

"That possibility increases the longer we stand here yakking. Don't worry, Miss Maggie. I've been making my own decisions for a long time now. If I didn't want to be here, I'd just stroll on by."

"How'd you find us, anyway?"

"Piece of luck. I drove over to your house intending to have a sit down with you and find out what you were hiding when you kept averting your eyes during dinner. The minute I turned onto your street, you and Lisa here were pulling out of your driveway. I just hunkered down as you drove past, pulled a fast U-turn, and followed you downtown. Course, you almost lost me when you started walking. You girls set quite pace for an old guy like me."

"I think he's right. Let's get a plan together and go with it. The longer we stand here, the better the odds are that someone is going to spot us." Lisa eyed Duran's outfit. "To be honest, Mr. Duran—"

"Call me Hank. If we're going to jail together, we ought to be on a first-name basis."

Lisa smiled. "I have to admit, I'm a little nervous about the, uh, bright colors you're wearing. We were hoping to get in and out without attracting a lot of attention. I'm afraid your clothing is a little hard to ignore."

"Isn't that the truth," Duran agreed. "Course, I see that as a positive thing. I sure don't dress like a regular thief or look like someone capable of crawling up a wall. That window is half the size of my belly—not to mention my rather expansive behind."

I forced myself to stay calm, knowing he would eventually get to the point.

"I look like someone who got lost or like some old geezer taking a walk to lower his cholesterol count. If anybody comes around, they'll take one look and keep right on looking—at me, that is, and nowhere else. And that's what we want. If a cop drives by and stops, I divert him with friendly conversation and send him on his way with nobody the wiser."

The guy made sense.

Lisa and I looked at each other and nodded. "Let's do it."

Luckily, the window wasn't that far off the ground, but we still couldn't have done it without Duran's help. I stepped into Lisa's and Duran's interlocked fingers and they hoisted me up a couple of feet, holding me there while I struggled to open the heavily painted window. When it finally moved, I wiggled through the opening—face first—missed the sink, and crashed onto the floor, narrowly missing my nose, but skinning my elbows in the process. Groaning, I got up, dusted my hands and knees, checked for broken bones, and limped over to help Lisa. Duran's face was beet-red by this time, and beads of sweat were popping out like a rash of pimples, but with one last grunt, he boosted Lisa high enough to get her through the window. She slid through, caught the sink's edge, swiveled her body around, and lowered her feet. I gave her a 10 for the dismount. I leaned out and sent Duran a thumbs-up. So far, so good.

Lisa and I didn't waste any time. We headed down the hallway into Sutherland's office. Lisa started with the file cabinets and I went to his desk, experiencing a feeling of déjà vu—of the time when Michaels and I were scrounging around in Riley's office. My hands were shaking as I sat in Sutherland's chair, but I managed to hold on to my composure and the contents of my stomach. I pulled out the bottom right drawer and started thumbing haphazardly through the files. Midway through, my breath caught when I stumbled across a file labeled *Jamie's Café*. With shaking hands, I pulled out the file and flipped it open.

"Lisa," I said, my voice dry and raspy.

"What?"

"I think I found something."

The rollers squeaked as she slammed the cabinet closed and rushed to the desk where I had laid open the file. She leaned over my shoulder and stared. Several silent moments ticked by.

"Why is Kevin's picture in a file in a PI's office?" Lisa asked.

I shook my head. "I'm not sure. Maybe it's nothing. Maybe Jamie was doing a typical background check before hiring him as an employee."

"By going to a private investigator? Isn't that a little extreme? Wouldn't it be easier to ask for references?"

"I don't know. I'm just throwing out ideas—"

Something crashed against a wall. Working on autopilot, I shoved the file somewhere in the middle of all the other folders and threw the drawer shut. My only thought was that Duran had to be warning us to get the hell out of there. Lisa grabbed my arm and yanked me toward the bathroom. Running through the doorway, I saw a small rock lying on the floor where it had landed after hitting the bathroom wall. I picked up the rock, stuck it into my pocket, and raced to the window. Duran was strolling across the alley as casually as you please, whistling a tune I didn't recognize, but behind his back, his right hand was flapping like crazy, waving us down. Lisa began shoving me toward the window, urging me to get out, and I shoved her right back, insisting she climb down. We wasted several precious seconds pushing and pulling and arguing over who should go first. Fortunately, the ludicrousness of what we were doing hit us both at the same time. Lisa scrambled on top of the sink and backed out of the window feetfirst, until she was hanging from the ledge by her fingertips with her shoes dangling a couple of yards off the ground. Suddenly, she let go and dropped, slipping a little on the loose gravel. I followed quickly behind, although this time Lisa and Duran grabbed my legs and held me aloft long enough for me to close the window before dropping me none too gently onto the road.

We were all breathing pretty heavily at this point, more from the adrenaline surge than any real physical exertion. Without saying a word, Duran and I caught up with Lisa, who had taken the lead and started walking down the alley just as we had planned. The three of us took a right at the end of the building and headed south. The hardest part was staying calm and not sprinting down the road—a good thing, too, because my heart was pounding so hard, I wasn't sure it could work any harder without causing a massive heart attack. Lisa was on my right, staring straight ahead and marching forward. She looked a little sweaty but very determined, sort of a nonchalant power walk. We were moving as fast as we could without drawing attention to ourselves and not leaving Duran, who was ambling down the road like an old horse put out to pasture, in the dust.

It took only a few minutes to reach the square, minutes that lasted longer than my entire childhood. We stopped in front of a store and pretended to look at the shoe display.

"Now, that was a helluva good time," Duran groused out of the side of his mouth.

"Your little signal scared me half to death, Hank."

"I had to warn you somehow. Just be thankful my pitching arm still works."

"Did you see Sutherland?" Lisa asked.

"Don't know. I've never met the man, but a car passed me in the alley and turned toward the front of the building. I don't know if it was him or not, but I figured it was better to be cautious than stupid."

"Probably," I said, a little frustrated, "but it didn't give us much time to search the place."

"Next time you girls want to break into an office, I suggest you spend some time on alternative plans."

"Why would Sutherland come back so quickly?" I wondered aloud.

"Who knows?" Lisa responded. "Maybe he forgot his camera or a file, or maybe Joel went home early and there was nothing left for him to do. Maybe he wanted to go to the bathroom. Who knows?" She turned to Duran. "I, for one, thank you for throwing that rock. Prison jumpsuits make a lousy fashion statement."

"My pleasure. Now, tell me, did you find anything at all?"

"What we found doesn't make any sense," I replied, telling Duran about the file. "I didn't have time to see what was under the picture."

"You know this boy?" Duran asked, slipping his hand to my elbow and guiding me away from the store and down the street. "Ladies, if we're going to pretend to window-shop let's keep moving, otherwise the owners are going to come out and start pressuring for a sale."

He was right, of course, so we meandered from store to

store, stopping now and then to look through a window and slip in a little conversation.

"I still don't see why Sutherland would have Kevin's picture," I said.

Lisa shrugged. "Maybe Kevin admitted to having a checkered past and Jamie wanted someone to check up on him, find out what really happened. If I knew how, I'd get on the Internet and do some tracking myself, but I'm computer illiterate."

I rubbed both hands over my face. "I don't think we have any choice, then."

Duran shook his head. "I was afraid you'd say that."

"Say what?" Lisa asked.

"Your friend here thinks we ought to go another round with breaking and entering."

Lisa whirled around and stared at me. "Tell me you're not thinking what he thinks you're thinking."

"It's the only way," I insisted. "We've gone this far, we can't just quit."

"Why not? We've got nothing except a picture in a file we weren't supposed to see. Other than becoming a card-carrying member of the criminal element, I don't see that we've accomplished anything."

"And we won't if we drop this thing right now. I know there's a thread somewhere. We just have to find it."

"Don't tell me—Kevin's place, right?"

"Where else?"

Lisa shut her eyes and groaned while Duran and I grinned at each other. At some point in this escapade, he and I had become comrades in arms, buddies in crime or something like that. There was no way I could stop now, not with a dead body looming in my head like a resurrected ghost. I couldn't sit back and let things roll along. Little bits and pieces of information were floating around out there, and I was determined to find out how they all fit together.

And judging by the gleam in Duran's eye, he felt the same way.

"When? Where?" Lisa demanded.

"You don't have to be part of this. In fact, I'd feel a lot less guilty if you weren't," I said. "I don't want to be responsible for getting Mandy's mom sent to the Big House. I can do this on my own."

"Maybe you can, but you won't," Duran interjected. "We're partners now, like it or not." He held up his hand when I started to speak. "Don't give me any trouble about this, Miss Maggie. If you do, I might accidentally let something slip around that boyfriend of yours, and he's already a tough dog to keep on the porch."

"Fine," I said, surrendering. "You can come—but do you think you could find something a little more sedate to wear? If Kevin lives in an apartment complex, which would be normal for a guy his age, we might not have the opportunity to make a quick get away. It'd be nice if you weren't so, uh, *visible*."

"Honey, as they say, a barn is a barn no matter what color you paint it. All black makes me look like a giant Hostess cupcake, and if I dressed in nothing but brown, I'd be mistaken for a mud slide. I think these colors keep me looking rather jaunty."

"They also make you recognizable."

"That's where you're wrong," he said, patting his expansive stomach. *"This* is what makes me recognizable, and at this point in the game, we're stuck with it."

I sighed and gave up. He was probably right after all. Nothing about this man blended into the background, so there was no reason to waste time trying.

"When and where?"

"No way, Lisa. You're out of this. It was bad enough that I dragged you into the first break-in. You don't need to be involved anymore. Duran and I can handle this."

"First of all, you didn't drag me anywhere," she insisted. "It was my choice to come along, and if you're determined to go through with this, then I'm not going to bail out now. What kind of best friend would I be? Second, we've already seen that Hank is a perfect point guard but—no offense to Hank—he's not going to be a big help sneaking into Kevin's place."

Duran nodded his head. "I don't like to admit it, but she's right. You need to get in and out quickly, and I'm not exactly limber on my feet. I'd be lumbering around and making more noise than a herd of cattle at feedin' time."

"You heard him," Lisa said, clapping her hands. "You need me."

I gave up. "Don't blame me if we get caught and you're stuck wearing those hideous jumpsuits you were complaining about earlier."

"Wouldn't bother me none," Duran said. "Orange is my best color—brings out the green in my eyes."

Lisa and I didn't say much on the way home. The three of us had finally decided to meet for lunch the next day at

Jamie's Café. Our plan was to skillfully manipulate Kevin into slipping us his address through a lot of seemingly innocent questions and conversation. Duran insisted he could handle this blindfolded with one arm tied behind his back, but I had my doubts. Subtle maneuverings just didn't seem to fit in with Hank's personality. Once we had Kevin's address in hand, though, we were going to drive by, check out his place, and firm up Step Two. I was so lost in my own thoughts that I was actually surprised when Lisa turned down my street. The one thing that didn't surprise me was seeing Villari's car parked in my driveway. Whether I was actually in trouble or just contemplating trouble, he knew it.

I hopped out of Lisa's car and waved good-bye as she pulled away. Villari was sitting on my front porch smoking. I didn't like that he smoked—in fact, we'd had a few heated words about the subject, but I had to admit, he could have been the Marlboro Man's twin sitting there in worn jeans and taking a drag off his cigarette. The man had probably never ridden a horse, rustled a cow, or straightened a barb-wire fence, but he was the kind of rugged, manly man who could do all those things . . . and a whole lot more where it counted the most. Just watching the way his muscles bunched under his T-shirt was enough to make me blush.

"Hey," I said as I walked up the driveway.

"Hey, yourself," he said, tossing the cigarette down on the front lawn.

"Villari," I warned, stamping it out with the toe of my shoe.

"Don't worry. I came prepared this time." He straightened and walked down the steps. From his back pocket, he pulled out a plastic bag, picked up the mashed cigarette butt, and dropped it in.

I smiled. "Looks like I've got you trained after all."

He smiled back. "My mother always said, 'A well-trained man is the secret to a successful relationship.' "

"That's a little like asking for moist turkey—sounds good in theory, but it doesn't ever happen in real life."

Villari reached out and pulled me toward him. "I bet if you asked really nicely, I'd learn to heel," he whispered against my forehead.

"In your dreams, Detective. The first time I whistled for you, you'd break my neck."

He trailed his lips down the side of my face, sending pleasant little tingles through my body. "Wouldn't happen . . . not with such a pretty little neck."

"Remember that thought the next time you get angry, okay?" I murmured, wrapping my arms around his waist and pulling him closer.

He leaned back and gazed at me. "You sound like you expect me to angry."

"With our track record, don't you?" I said, thinking it might happen sooner than he expected.

Villari fingered a loose curl and pushed it behind my ear. "It could be different, Maggie, if that's what we wanted," he whispered, right before claiming my lips for his own.

He's talking about the relationship, I thought, before succumbing to his slow, drugging kisses. *Mrs. Peterson is probably craning her neck and getting quite an eyeful,* was my last coherent thought before I finally gave up thinking and let

Villari hustle me right up to sensation heaven.

Time stood still while my detective ruffled every possible nerve ending without removing a stitch of clothing or getting us arrested. He had wonderfully demanding lips and strong, suggestive hands that effortlessly coaxed all sorts of shivers and trembles from my body. My natural defense mechanism flipped into paralysis mode whenever he came near me, and in the end, no matter how I fought it, my body turned to his in reckless abandon. I knew he wanted more intimacy, a firmer commitment, and even though my head and heart had questions, my body sure as hell didn't.

The taste of his lips was still warm and sweet on mine when we broke apart. He raised his head and gazed down at me, letting that lazy, crooked grin of his stretch across his face.

"Damn, you're good."

"I bet you say that to all the girls," I replied, laying my cheek against his chest.

"Nope. Just you and Amanda."

He held me captive as I tried to wiggle away. "And who is this Amanda?"

"Amanda, light of my life," he sang softly over the top of my head, *"God should have made you a gentleman's wife."*

"Sounds like a bad line from country music."

"Actually, it's a good line from *The Best of Willie Nelson.*"

"Shouldn't you be wooing me with songs about *amore* or *Volare* or something from that romance language you're always pounding your chest about?"

"But you don't like Italians."

I snuggled closer. "I like *one* Italian."

"You damn well better, *mi'ja*."

"Is that Italian?"

"No, I think it's Spanish."

"Just my luck to get a disabled Italian."

"Not where it counts, *cherie.*"

"Italian?"

"French."

WE kissed again, interrupted only by the sounds of wrens chatting in the trees and black-capped chickadees cracking birdseed. Nuthatches perched upside down on the tubular mesh feeder suspended from the evergreen firmly rooted in the middle of the front lawn. Battling hummingbirds, like kamikaze pilots, dove straight and fast toward the jars of sugar water hanging from the roof, reminding me to remove the bottles before too long to encourage the birds to continue their migration.

The deep cobalt blue of summer had faded and the air was cooler, crisper now. Before long, the sun would weaken, the sky would pale, and the snow would begin to fall. But today, the air was still and only the hint of winter wafted on the air.

We separated slowly, a little dazed and unsteady, like drinking that first glass of wine and feeling the edges begin to soften. Villari raked his fingers through his hair and draped his arm loosely about my shoulder. We moved to the front porch and sat down, a little shaken by the heat that existed between us. It wasn't the heat so much as the intensity. The man sitting next to me, with his strong face and uneven smile, had enough sex appeal to turn a woman into jelly without moving a muscle. It didn't take a genius to understand why my body shamelessly flopped on its back whenever he crooked a finger. But the problem, the part that scared me, was that it didn't end there. Our attraction didn't stop after diving under the blankets. By the time we resurfaced, I wanted him even more. And that scared the hell out of me.

"Sorry, Maggie. I've got to get back."

"Nice of you to get me all hot and bothered and then take off," I said lightly.

"I don't have much choice this time. The coroner's report came back today."

"And?"

"And what?"

"Well, what did it say?" I asked, exasperated.

"Now, why would I tell you that?"

Because I'm already knee deep into this case, I thought, but wisely bit back the words. "Because I found the guy, Villari. I'm curious, that's all," I explained innocently.

He studied me for several long seconds before grudgingly giving in. "Obviously, I can't give you a lot of details, but the report basically confirmed what we suspected all along. Riley was murdered on the premises. He wasn't killed and then brought to the gallery.

My eyes widened at the thought. "You mean he was killed at The Outlook?"

"Yep. We're not exactly sure when, but that's the report in a sound bite."

"So while we were drinking champagne and mingling with the beautiful people, a guy was being prepped and baked in the other room?"

Villari looked at me wordlessly. "Is that some kind of nervous tic you have?"

"What are you talking about?"

"This compulsion you have to describe Riley's death in graphic details."

"I'm just saying what happened."

"No, you're not, Maggie. You're turning it into some kind of black humor scenario. Riley wasn't baked, broiled, or barbecued. He was knocked unconscious and thrown into a kiln, where he burned to death. I guess I don't see the humor in it."

I caught my breath as the meaning sunk in. "He was still alive when they put him in the kiln?"

"Yes, that's exactly what I'm saying."

I dropped my forehead to my knees. My stomach felt sick and queasy, and I was having hard time pulling air into my lungs.

Villari took pity on me, I guess, and laid his broad hand on my back and started kneading the tightened muscles up and down my spine. "Me and my big mouth. I didn't mean to let that last part slip out. I know your flippancy or sarcasm is your way of protecting yourself, but once in a while it rubs me the wrong way. I guess this is one of those days."

I raised my head and smiled weakly. "Well, that's bound to happen now and then."

He turned toward me and cupped my chin in the palm of his hand. "Listen to me, Maggie. Forget what I said. You do what you need to do to survive. I mean that. Cops bump into the vilest part of human nature on a daily basis, and most of us do a lousy job of handling it. Some of us get angry, some drown themselves in the bottle, and some don't say a word—until one day they explode because they simply don't have the room for one more tragedy. Truth be told, most cops have a morbid sense of humor and handle it much like you're doing."

"Then why were you upset?"

"Because you sounded too much like the world I work in. I don't want you to be a part of that, see the things I have," he said sadly. "I'm human, Maggie. And I'm in love."

There it was. Out in the open.

Villari took one look at my expression and grinned. "Get used to it, honey, because I'm going to say it again and again. And if you keep running from me, I'll hunt you down like a dog and bring you right back."

"What a lovely proposal," I choked out.

"Yeah, well, we Villari men have a certain something women can't resist."

"What you have is a swagger."

"Charming, isn't it?"

"Get out of here, Villari, before you pass cute and plow right into arrogant."

He laughed and stood. "I'll call you later. If it's not too late, maybe we can grab a bite to eat or I can pick up a pizza on my way over."

"You're coming over?"

"Didn't I tell you?" he asked, pulling me up. The detective leaned over and pecked me on the cheek. "I'm tucking you into bed tonight."

He sauntered off then, glancing over his shoulder and grinning when he saw me checking out that delectable little swagger of his. Villari got into his car, slipped on his sunglasses, and backed out of the driveway. I walked up the steps and was reaching for the doorknob when I remembered. Spinning around, I faced Mrs. Peterson's house and waved. One nosy neighbor to another.

Chapter Eight

"It's dead, Maggie."

"Tell me something I don't know."

Andy had come by with the latest news. The Jeep couldn't be revived and was now slotted for the car morgue.

"He blames you."

"He's just lashing out. It's the first step in the grieving process."

"Don't make jokes, Maggie," Andy said, barely hiding a smile. "He's threatening to take action."

"What's he going to do, report me to NANCO?"

"And that would be . . . ?"

"The National Association of Negligent Car Owners. My guess is that Roy is the president of the Rocky Mountain chapter. Every year the members confiscate ignored, unwanted vehicles and tow them, caravan style, to a used car lot. They dismantle the engines, lament over mistreated car parts, and shed tears for the dearly departed junk heaps before flashing headlights in memoriam." By the time I was finished, Andy had flopped down on the couch, put his feet up on the coffee table, and was grinning from ear to ear.

"If Roy heard you talking right now, he'd clutch his wounded heart at your complete lack of remorse."

"It was just a car!" I exclaimed.

Andy laced his hands behind his head and chuckled. "I admit that Roy is a little fanatical, but he does have a point, Maggie. You're a terrible car owner. You never change the oil or tune the thing up. You are queen of the 'Bare Minimum to Survive.' Roy thinks he might have been able to save the car if he'd gotten his hands on it a little earlier."

I sighed and dropped into the large easy chair next to the sofa. "Okay, I give up. You're probably right, I could have been a little more conscientious, but it's never been high on my list of priorities."

"Until the thing breaks down."

"So rub it in while you're at it. I'm actually starting to feel like I've broken one of the Ten Commandments."

"According to Roy, you have."

"He probably oils the wheels on St. Peter's chariot," I said dryly. "So what do I do?"

"You and I have an appointment with Roy tomorrow afternoon. You're going to grovel until Roy takes pity on you and then he's going to set you up with a line on a new car."

"I suppose I'll have to sign in blood that I'll rotate the tires on time."

Andy chuckled. "I do believe old Roy will force you to sign a maintenance schedule giving him the power to repossess the car if you fail to comply."

"You know this guy is a real nutcase, don't you?"

"Yeah, but he's a damn good mechanic. If you manage to get on his good side, your next car should last longer than you do."

"How much is this little investment going to cost me?"

"I gave Roy a general figure, Maggie, but you're going to have to loosen the purse strings a little. Use some of that money you make from taking care of Elizabeth's estate."

"I've been putting that aside for a rainy day," I said.

"You've been hoarding it," Andy said flatly. "Normally, that wouldn't be a problem, but the fact is, unless you plan on having your groceries delivered and hiding out in your house, you're going to need something with four wheels. I'm sure as hell not going to chauffeur you around while you're socking away interest on money I'll never see."

"Aren't you full of warm brotherly support."

"You wouldn't recognize me any other way."

I threw my hands up. "Fine. I give up." He was right. I couldn't live without transportation, and since the only car parts I recognized were tires and the steering wheel, I didn't have any choice but to swallow my pride and face Roy. "But I can't meet you until after three," I said, thinking about my potential trip to Kevin's the next day.

"Works for me. I'll set it up with Roy." Then Andy cleared his throat and threw a bomb. "Now comes the hard part."

"What are you talking about?"

"Dad and Sherri want you and Sam to come to dinner on Friday night."

"Why?"

Andy raised his eyebrow. "Well, let's see. You glide into the biggest night of your life escorted by this 'ruggedly handsome' guy, Sherri's words, not mine, someone your father and stepmother have never met before, even though you've been dating for at least a year. Then, while you have a heart-to-heart with Dad, you don't bother to introduce him to the family."

"You've met Villari lots of times."

"You're being deliberately obtuse, Maggie, and you know it."

"So I'm on a date with a guy that Dad's never met. I don't see what the big deal is."

"You know exactly why it's a big deal, and that's why your IQ just dropped below your bra size."

I couldn't sit still then, not with my nerves jangling and Andy waiting expectantly. Jumping up, I began to pace the room, running my hands through my hair, a little habit I picked up from Villari—a habit that looked a lot better on him than me. Whenever he jammed his fingers through his thick black hair, it ended up looking tousled and, well, deliciously male. I ended up looking like a mushroom cloud. It really was ironic how women primp, preen, and spend large chunks of money trying to look good, while, in direct contrast, unless they're on the cover of *Hunk* magazine, men couldn't care less. I mean, how often does a man turn down a second beer because he might gain a pound? The average man does next to nothing to stem the tide of a burgeoning beer belly, and the worst part—they feel absolutely no guilt for that extra dollop of butter on the mashed potatoes. Chalk up another reason to believe God is a male.

"Tell me why you're upset," Andy asked.

"I'm not upset, I'm just a little . . . I don't know . . . agitated."

"Why would a simple dinner throw you off your game?"

I stopped in front of the coffee table. "Come on, Andy. You accuse me of being obtuse, don't return the favor, okay? Otherwise I have to find a comparative IQ analogy, and I don't know if jock straps come in different sizes."

Andy grinned. "Extra-large fits.

I rolled my eyes.

"Snugly."

"Oh, brother. It never changes. Men obsess over their, uh, physical components, while women flail around in a quagmire of emotions."

"Maggie, do me a favor and stick with one topic for a change. We can discuss the dueling dynamics of men and women anytime you want, but for right now, I just want to know why you're so upset over a little dinner invitation."

"It's not simple, and you know it," I said, propping my hands on my hips. "Dad and Sherri invite me to dinner about once every three or four months—"

"They'd invite you more if you accepted once in a while," Andy argued, "which is why I'm the messenger today. If they called, you'd turn them down flat, saying you didn't want to miss the latest rerun of *Leave It to Beaver*."

"That's a bit of an exaggeration."

"Not much, you idiot. I'm just showing you how transparent your excuses are." Leaning forward, Andy planted his elbows on his knees and rested his chin in the palms of both hands. "Maggie, how long are you going to hold this grudge against Dad?"

I stopped my pacing and swiveled around. "I'm not holding anything against him."

"Sure you are. You've been punishing him ever since you were old enough to think for yourself."

"And what is that supposed to mean?" I asked, glaring at my brother.

"It means that people do the best they can, Maggie," he said quietly. "I admit, the man isn't an emotional giant. Once Mom died, he was incapable of giving you, or me, what we needed when we were kids. It happens."

"That's a great theory, Andy," I said, tears welling up in my eyes, "and I think that for the most part, I agree with you. But the fact remains that he was cold and distant while I was growing up, and now, suddenly out of nowhere, he wants to be part of my life."

"But that's only part of the problem, isn't it?"

"Don't tell me you're going to analyze my life now."

Andy shrugged. "Villari wants to be part of your life, and you're repeating an old pattern by running away like a crazed woman."

I flung myself back on the sofa chair. "Isn't that just a little too Freudian? 'Broken relationship with father leads to unsatisfying relationship with boyfriend'?"

"No offense, Mag," Andy said, shaking his head, "but you're not that hard to figure out. First off, you're pissed at Dad, and hiding your boyfriend is a nice convenient way to let him know you plan on staying mad. And second, my guess is that you're holding Villari at arm's length because the only male figure you're comfortable with is me . . . but then again, who wouldn't be?"

I smiled for the first time in what seemed a long while. "I'd be more comfortable if you'd deflate that ego of yours a bit to make room for the rest of us. It's getting a little cramped in here."

"You say that now, but you'd hate it if I didn't hit you with the truth now and then."

"Funny how the truth is always punctuated with a caveat on how wonderful you are."

"I can't dodge the facts, Maggie," Andy said, leaning back on the couch and plopping his feet back on my table. "But back to the question at hand. Sherri and Dad would like you and Sam to come to dinner on Friday night. That's two days from now. That gives you plenty of time to run through your gamut of emotions and then to come to your senses and be there."

"What makes you so sure I'm coming?"

"That's easy," he continued smugly. "I'm going to be there, dateless, which means I can help carry the conversation for you, although with Sherri around, that's not the problem it used to be. And because, in the end, you always do the right thing. Reluctantly, maybe. Whining, absolutely. But you've got a Catholic backbone, and guilt always pushes you in the direction you need to go."

"Why is it that guilt rolls off your back?"

"Lucky, I guess."

I sighed. "Okay, I'll ask Villari. If he can get away, we'll be there, but I can't promise anything. He's pretty busy right now."

"The murder?"

I nodded. "He's fairly closemouthed about most of it, so I can't tell you much, but it looks like things are breaking open a little."

"Good." He sat up and pinned me with one of his "I'm really serious" looks. "How are you handling all of this?"

"Okay, I guess. Villari says I hide my feelings behind humor and sarcasm. He's probably right."

"I'm guessing you hide your feelings from him, too."

I cocked my head. "My, aren't you the little brain doctor today?"

He grinned and stood up. "But I'm right on the money, aren't I?

"Maybe," I mumbled.

Andy lightly punched my arm in that annoying big brother way of his. "See you on Friday, okay? Six o'clock."

"What about penance with Roy tomorrow?"

"That's right, I almost forgot. I'll call you after I set up the appointment. After three, right?"

"Yeah, yeah," I muttered as Andy squeezed my sagging shoulders and left.

I rested my head against the chair and closed my eyes. A thousand jumbled thoughts ricocheted against my skull until I didn't have an ounce of energy left in my body. This thing with Villari was growing into something I couldn't ignore for much longer, and yet I still didn't feel any closer to understanding what existed between the two of us. After all, it was just yesterday when I was flirting with Michaels and felt disappointed when he appeared oblivious to my girlie charms. Why was I batting my eyes at other men if Villari was The One?

Despite my own mixed emotions about my relationship with the detective, no one else seemed to share my confusion. Every person close to me waved away my concerns like pesky mosquitoes, totally convinced that I was simply afraid to acknowledge my true feelings—an assertion I couldn't completely dismiss. I was never really adept at dissecting my own emotions. I never took a hard look at the feelings that drove everything I did, never laid them bare under an unflinching light, like those set up in dressing rooms to spotlight every extra pound, wart, and dimpled bottom. Introspection was not my strong suit. If things had been different, maybe I would have confronted my father years ago instead of playing this passive aggressive game that led nowhere but backwards. Our relationship was still mired in unresolved anger and disappointment that was swept under a rug . . . a mighty lumpy rug.

The rest of the day passed strangely, a blur in slow motion. Minutes begrudgingly ticked by, but then I'd check the clock and realize that an hour had passed and I couldn't remember a thing I had done. By nightfall, I stopped, looked around, and was surprised to see a freshly vacuumed floor, clean dishes, laundry swirling in the spin cycle, and little memory of this housekeeping jaunt. Obviously, I was suffering from a split personality. Merry Maid must have taken over for a few hours while Sarah Sloth was zoned out.

I fell asleep watching TV and didn't wake up until I heard a familiar tap on the front door. Only one person could make my heart beat a little faster just by the sound of his knock. I hurried to let him in. After all, he promised to put me in bed. The least I could do was return the favor.

DAWN tumbled through the soot-colored sky spilling pink and orange ribbons of light. I tucked my hands under my head and stared out the window, smiling to myself. Villari was already up and gone, brewing coffee and bringing me a cup before he left. There were some definite advantages to having a boyfriend . . . the coffee was a nice touch . . . the sex was even better.

I stretched out like a cat, a well-satisfied, completely relaxed cat. Villari could ease me right out of myself. My brain emptied itself of any doubts or worries until there was nothing but him and me and the places we touched. Afterward we slid right into slumber as smoothly as a hand slipping into a glove.

I would have slept through the morning if Villari hadn't gotten up to shower. By the time he leaned down to kiss me good-bye, I could see the stress etched in the lines around his eyes. Being a cop was a hard thing. I was beginning to learn about the isolation of classified information. Not only did Villari want to shield me from the darker side of life, the nature of his job demanded confidentiality. The case was wearing on him and I felt bad that I couldn't do more to relieve him of his burden.

Of course, that didn't change my plans for the day. I was going to break the law for the second time for reasons I couldn't really explain. My best friend and my . . . well, I wasn't sure what Duran was . . . were both involved now, and we were marching onward, never questioning, never looking back . . . three horses wearing blinders.

I threw off the covers and climbed out of bed, determined to go through with this obviously half-baked idea. A dead man had practically fallen in my lap, along with several pieces of information that were somehow related to his death. At least, that was my theory.

I spent most of the morning in my studio, sketching preliminary ideas for Duran's sculpture. Nothing really came together, but I made myself sit and draw even though it felt more like doodling. Inspiration didn't come like a flash of lightning. It sort of tiptoed behind me and tapped me on the shoulder. My life was nothing like what I saw in the movies—an artist stepping confidently to face a blank canvas. An immediate vision flashes in his brain and, like instant oatmeal, the entire work is completed in less than five minutes. On the screen, there was no need to think or rethink, no need to step back and examine the progress. In negligible time, and with Chopin blaring in the back-ground, a grand masterpiece magically appears in the middle of a clay-strewn floor or on a canvas surrounded by eighteen paint-sloshed cans.

Inspiration was much more subtle with me. It arrived after hours of plodding through pages of drawings until some little something, some little flicker caught my attention. Then like a timid lover, a gentle nudge would move me in some particular direction where I could touch the edges of a spark.

There were times when I thought I would go crazy waiting for that little push, but over the years I'd become more patient, more willing to discipline myself to start at the beginning. I was prepared to work, to work hard, until that little tap urged me forward to where I wanted, and needed, to go.

After putting away my pencils and sketchpad, I took a quick shower and got dressed. I ran a brush through my short hair, slipped into my tennis shoes, and headed toward the kitchen for a quick glass of water and a bite to eat. I had skipped breakfast and I was starving. I was in the middle of making a tuna sandwich when I heard Lisa honking from my driveway.

"You couldn't wait? We'll be eating in twenty minutes," Lisa complained when I climbed into her car with my food. "Try not to drop tuna all over the seat."

"Aren't you in a great mood this afternoon," I said between bites.

"Actually, I'm not. I got a call from Sutherland this morning. You know, 'reporting in.' He said he followed Joel all over town yesterday as he ran errands with Mandy. Obviously, it wasn't Sutherland that Duran saw turning the corner. As far as Mr. PI knew, Joel did not make contact with a woman or make any suspicious moves."

"Of course he didn't," I said around a mouthful of food while dropping a mess of crumbs on my pants. I didn't make a move to brush myself off for fear that Miss Bad Mood would whip out a Dustbuster and start vacuuming my lap. "So what's bothering you?"

"Nothing more than some major guilt pains," she said, shooting me a thin smile that fell an inch short of a grimace. "It's bad enough that my husband doesn't have any idea he's being stalked by a private investigator, but to make it worse, Joel was a little, uh, amorous, and—"

"Again? I thought sex was supposed to taper off when you got married. You guys hit the sack this morning?"

"I had a more delicate phrase in my mind, but yes, we made love this morning. I felt lousy afterward, knowing I was heading off somewhere behind his back."

"Drop me off at the café, Lisa, and then turn around and go back home. I told you yesterday not to come along. Duran and I can take it from here."

"Sure you can," Lisa said dryly. "Duran is older than the hills and a whole lot broader, and not exactly light on his feet. How much help would he be if you needed a quick getaway? And your idea of thinking ahead is three minutes after the fact."

"Gee, thanks for the morale boost," I said, pushing my hair behind my ears. "But I mean it—I don't want you there if you're having second thoughts."

Lisa shook her head. "Just because I experienced a little guilt doesn't mean I'm backing out. We've come too far, Maggie. Something's not right about this whole thing, and since I've already jumped off the cliff once, I can't turn back now. Like I told you yesterday," she said, glancing in my direction, "what kind of best friend would I be if I abandoned you in the middle of an adventure?"

"Lucy and Ethel, right?"

She smiled in agreement. "Someone has to look after Lucy."

"I knew I'd get the red hair," I grumbled.

"Consider yourself lucky," she said, chuckling. "I get Fred, remember?"

MINUTES later we arrived at Jamie's Café. Surveying the restaurant, I spotted Duran sitting at a booth in the back. He was sipping coffee and scanning a menu. Two days ago I was having breakfast with Mark, and now here I was meeting Duran, only it was lunch this time. I spent more time eating in this little bistro than I did working in my studio.

Duran looked up and waved Lisa and me over.

"Hi, Hank," I said, sliding into the opposite end of the booth, scooting over to give Lisa room.

"Hi, back." He glanced at Lisa and smiled. "You look good today."

"Well, thanks, Mr. Partner in Crime."

Then he checked me out. "You look like you borrowed clothes from your big brother's Goodwill bag."

"That's a pretty funny comment coming from the guy who could stand in for a Christmas tree."

Lisa grinned. "I don't know, Maggie. He looks a little less, uh, exuberant today, don't you think?"

"Thank you, pretty lady," Duran responded, pleased as punch by the semi-compliment. "I tried to tone down my natural fondness for color so I wouldn't stand out like a festering sore during our little escapade this afternoon. Apparently," he said, eyeing my wardrobe, "you didn't have the same thought."

"But I don't have a tendency to wear every color of the rainbow simultaneously."

"True enough, but skinny as you are, you could be mistaken for a curtain rod with all that material hanging from your shoulders." He shook his head. "By God, it's a wonder that boyfriend of yours can find you under all that cotton."

"Why is everyone so concerned about what I wear?" I demanded, narrowing my eyes at Lisa, who was practically rolling in the aisle with laughter.

"Hell, I don't care what you wear, little darling," Duran said, his eyes twinkling with amusement, "but I thought I'd give you a shot of of your own medicine. You spent a lot of time tearing down my taste in clothes yesterday."

"Maybe so," I admitted, "but why pick on me? I wasn't alone, you know. Old Pretty Lady was there, too, remember?"

Duran's face split into a wide grin. "Sure is easy to rile you up, isn't it?"

"It sure is," Lisa piped in happily. "This gal's got a trigger temper."

I scowled. "Let me guess—you suddenly rode in from Amarillo, Texas."

Lisa shrugged. "I couldn't help myself. I've always wanted to be a good ol' boy."

"Honey, we got more than enough boys on this earth— sure as hell don't need another. The Good Lord blessed you with some mighty fine attributes and you're doing all of us a favor just sitting there and letting us enjoy the view. On top of that, you've got a good brain and you could charm the rattle off a cornered diamondback."

I sighed. "Do you think you two could put a lid on this

mutual admiration society and help me figure out how we're going to get Kevin's address?"

"Now don't get your dander up, Miss Maggie. You're awfully pretty in your own right. You've got good bones, good teeth, and strong legs, even if they are too skinny for my taste—you're just a little short in the charm department," he said, pausing to share a conspiratorial smile with Lisa before turning back to me. "One nasty comment from you and a man would be smart to zip his pleasure back in his pants and run like hell."

By this time, even I was smiling. It was hard to stay angry at a guy who compared you favorably to a fine quarter horse. "Okay, the party's over. Let's order and map out a plan." I flipped open a menu. "What looks good?"

"Don't have a clue. I was just pretending to look it over."

I frowned. "Why were you pretending?"

He smiled easily. "I thought I might ask young Kevin for some help."

"Good idea, Hank," I said, craning my neck to see over the high-backed booth and spotting Jamie in the back cooking. "It looks like Kevin is manning the front right now, so you'll be able to talk to him alone."

"I thought so," he said proudly, leaning back. "You girls go first and order a sandwich or whatever you want and I'll ask a couple of questions about the food and see if I can't pull him into a conversation. If you see an opening, feel free to jump right in. Just be gentle and don't appear too nosy. Last thing we need is to scare him off."

It didn't seem like a surefire plan, but it was all we had. Jamie had to have Kevin's address somewhere—he was an employee, after all, but I didn't think we'd have much success at sneaking back to her office undetected. Besides, if everything went well, the three of us would be visiting Kevin's residence a little later, and I wasn't sure how many times I could slip in somewhere uninvited without being caught. My luck was going to run out sooner or later.

Duran caught Kevin's eye. He shuffled across the room, the soles of his shoes polishing the linoleum. Eventually he reached our table, pulled out his pad and pencil, and stood ready to take our orders. Lisa ordered the turkey avocado sandwich and I ordered a bowl of soup. As Lisa had predicted, the tuna didn't leave much room for anything else. Then, as if by mutual consent, we sat back and watched Duran go to work.

"And you, sir?"

"Well, son, I've got myself a little problem. Everything's lookin' awful good and I'm having a hard time deciding. Maybe you could help me out a little." Duran pointed to the menu. "I'm guessing there are a few lunch specials running today?"

"Yessir." We all listened patiently while Kevin proceeded to rattle off the list of food choices.

"Now, that just makes the decision all the more difficult. In the old days, things sure were a lot simpler. You had two choices: meatloaf sandwich or barbecued ribs. Nowadays you got so many fancy dishes, it makes a man plumb dizzy."

Duran's accent was growing thicker by the second, and his country talk was now less of a proud, savvy Texan and more like a man whose lineage included a long line of first cousins. The way he was twanging on, I'm surprised he wasn't barefoot, wearing cutoffs, and "chawing" on a piece of straw.

Lisa and I managed to avoid looking at each other during this performance. One glance and I knew I would lose the thin hold I had on my composure. Duran was always throwing out little Southern colloquialisms, but there was never any doubt about his intelligence.

To Kevin's credit, he managed to keep his face blank and expressionless during the whole discourse, even as Duran waxed eloquent about his mother's famous pecan pie.

". . . a crust so flaky, it melted in your mouth faster than you could swallow."

I cleared my throat as delicately as possible. "Hank, I'm sure Kevin has other customers he has to wait on. Maybe you could order?"

"I'm sure you're right, Maggie, but now we're right back where we started. I don't know what to pick. Like I said . . ." Duran started, then stopped. His gaze swept over Kevin like he didn't recognize him, like he hadn't been standing there for the last five minutes. "Now son, maybe you could lend an old fellow like me a hand. When I was your age, my appetite was big enough to choke a cow. And still I was hungry, hungrier than a pig pawin' an empty trough. No matter how much I ate, I was skinny." He patted his stomach. "Course, things changed when the years started piling on, but back then, I could eat a horse and still squeeze through the rails in a picket fence without holding my breath."

"Uh, Duran?" For the life of me I couldn't see where he was going with this slice of country life.

"I know, honey, I know. It just takes me a while to get around to my point. My mama used to say molasses could outrun me, and I 'spect she was right. Anyways, I thought maybe young Kevin here could tell me what he eats—I figure if it fills him up, it ought to work for me. We both got some growing to do, just in different directions."

"I don't usually eat here, sir."

"Why's that? Don't like the food?" Duran turned to us. "Maybe we ought to go elsewhere if the help doesn't like the food comin' off the griddle."

"No, sir," Kevin interrupted hurriedly. "The food here is great. All of it. I just can't afford it."

"Well, I sure can understand that. Truth be told, when I was your age, it didn't much matter what I put in my belly just as long as it was warm and it didn't cost too much. Money doesn't stretch as far as it did when I was a boy. I'm guessin' you got to work long hours to pay off the bills, am I right?"

Kevin nodded his head. "Sure do," he said, obviously relieved he hadn't scared us off.

Duran studied him. "You going to school?"

"Yes, sir. In the Springs. UCCS."

"Someone helpin' you with the tuition?"

"No. I'm doing it myself."

"You livin' on campus or sharin' a room with some buddies?"

I let out a long, low breath. It had taken me a while to figure out where he was going with all this "by golly" routine, but it was becoming clear now. By appearing to be about as intimidating as a newborn puppy, he had slowly and completely disarmed Kevin. Male teenagers don't have a lot of communication skills beyond a series of grunts, so I was pretty impressed that Kevin was talking at all. I crossed my fingers and hoped that Duran could coax more information out of the boy, because if this failed, I didn't know what to do next—I was fresh out of ideas.

"I'm living with a roommate in an apartment."

"That's good. Sharin' the expenses has to help."

"Sure does. I couldn't do it by myself. It's hard enough paying for college."

"What about a car? In my day, you could walk most everyplace you wanted. Can't do that now. 'Sides, if you want to take out a pretty lady, you got to have something to roll around in."

Kevin smiled. He had a really nice smile—straight teeth, strong jaw. It transformed his face, erasing the quiet, almost timid expression he wore most of the time. His blue eyes softened and the hint of dimples deepened the sides of his mouth. Some girl was going to fall madly in love with that smile someday.

"I've got an old Chevy Nova my parents gave me years ago. It's already paid for. It's not pretty, but it gets me to work, and I live right across from the college, so I can walk to class—like when you were young," he added helpfully.

"Hell no, son. I lived at home. We couldn't afford apartments across the street. Must be hard to get into, everybody wanting a place close by."

"Yeah, but I was lucky. Mountain Ridge was filled up, but a guy dropped out of school, so there was a vacancy and

I was the next person on the list. I packed up and moved in."

"Things have a way of working out, don't they?" Duran said, surreptitiously winking at Lisa and me before turning back to Kevin. "Now, young man, with all this visiting, I've worked up quite an appetite. I'd be appreciative if you could pick something out for me, something plain and simple, not too spicy. I don't want to spend the rest of the afternoon visiting the john, if you catch my drift."

"Uh, I don't know—"

"Just give him a ham and cheese on white bread, Kevin," I said reassuringly. "He'll be fine."

Duran raised his eyebrows. "Throw a salad on the side and I'll be a happy man."

All three of us waited while Kevin shuffled out of earshot.

"I've got to hand it to you, Duran. You were brilliant."

"I've never heard so much Southern blarney in my life, Hank, but the boy just fell right into your lap." Lisa stood up, leaned over the table, and kissed him on the forehead.

A huge smile split Duran's face. "You two were getting pretty worried there, weren't you?"

"*Worried* doesn't begin to describe it. I had no idea where you were going with all that 'back in my day' stuff you were pulling out of the air."

"To tell you the truth, I wasn't totally sure myself, but I knew I needed to make Kevin feel comfortable enough to open up some. There's nothing like a little Southern hospitality to make a person hang over the fence and start gossiping."

We talked a little among ourselves about inconsequential

things, but it was obvious that we were all a little excited and nervous about what was coming. Jamie finally came out of the back for a few minutes, just long enough to drop off our food and apologize for being too busy to sit and chat. I introduced her to Duran before she ran back to the kitchen. After she left, the three of us hurried through our lunch, anxious to pay the bill and be on our way to Kevin's place.

Kevin wasn't exaggerating when he said he lived close to UCCS. Fifteen minutes later, we drove into the parking lot of the Mountain Ridge Apartments, situated directly across the street from the university. It was easy enough to recognize the building as residential housing for college students. A four-story redbrick structure with cheap aluminum windows, it looked like a typical dormitory, only off-campus. Following Duran, we drove around to the back and parked in a semi-secluded corner under a huge oak tree. Getting out of our respective cars, we huddled together in the middle of the lot.

"Now what do we do?" I asked.

Duran said wryly, "I expected more from a crime expert like you, Miss Maggie."

I spread out my hands. "Sorry, Hank—it's been a little while. I'm a bit rusty."

"Okay, you two, knock it off. Let's do whatever we're going to do," Lisa demanded. "The longer we stand out here, the better chance of someone seeing or remembering us. We don't exactly look like the college crowd."

"Don't worry, Lisa. They'll just assume we're somebody's parent here for a visit. These kids are so oblivious to everything except the opposite sex, they won't even notice we're here."

"Maybe so, but I'd just as soon not chance it."

Duran nodded his head. "Fair enough."

"So, Mr. Just Sprung From Alcatraz, back to my original question, what next?" I prodded.

"We start with the obvious. My guess is there's a list of names on a mailbox of some sort—hopefully there's an apartment number, too."

"If not?"

"Let's just take one step at a time. No need to borrow trouble."

"All right, let's say we find the apartment. Any ideas on how to get in?"

"As a matter of fact, I do. Start with the simplest choice first. A credit card."

"A credit card?" Lisa asked. "I didn't think that worked except in the movies."

"Mind you, I'm not guaranteeing anything, but we've got a couple of things on our side here. First off, this is a fairly cheap building, prefabbed track apartment housing. Nothing customized here. In other words," he said by way of explanation, "whoever built this threw it up as quickly and efficiently as possible, with no reinforcements or added luxuries. Strictly utilitarian. If we're lucky, the doorjambs will be flat, no extra trim on the inside, making it a cinch to slip in a plastic card. Judging by the looks of this place, the developer didn't waste a lot of time worrying about airtight security."

"You're in construction?" Lisa asked.

"Honey, I've dabbled in just about everything," he replied vaguely.

"And the second advantage?" I pressed.

"We're dealing with a young man here."

"You've lost me."

"Teenage boys aren't real worried about safety or security. A girl has a lot more to worry about in that area. It's sad, but it's a fact of life. The scum in this world tends to prey on women, not men. The only thing boys are concerned about is losing their stereo system or speakers. Maybe a bike or some other kind of toy. Other than that, they don't spend a lot of time thinking about or protecting themselves from the criminal element."

"There's a point to this, right?"

"You can bet your last dollar there is. The point is, I'm betting that Kevin's door will pop right open, like a knife cutting butter, because he's never spent a minute shoring up the locks. Unless he's got some fancy gadget in there, which I doubt, seeing as how he's putting himself through school, I wouldn't be surprised if he didn't even lock his door."

"You expect to just waltz right into the building and open up his door?"

"No, I expect you to waltz right in. I believe that I'm the designated sentry for this group. As you might have noticed, my tongue wags at both ends, which means I have a gift for gab. I have a talent, you might say, for engaging people in conversation, which, I might add, you do not. You tend to annoy people," he said wryly. "If anyone suspicious comes along, and by that I mean anyone walking on two legs, I can easily stall them until you return."

"What if I can't get in?"

"Then come back down and we'll move on to Step Two."

"Which is?"

"I might happen to have some tools we can use, but we'll worry about that if and when we need to."

"And how do I fit in?" Lisa interjected. "Do I go in with Mag?"

"Not a chance," Duran said firmly. "You're the one with the family, you take the least risk. I want you in the car, ready to pull out at a moment's notice. Keep your head down, and if Miss Maggie is in trouble and jumps in your car, remember to pull out as calmly as possible. Don't bring any attention to yourself." Duran held up his palm when Lisa started to object. "Don't bother. You've got a little girl at home who needs her mama. I'm not taking any chances with you."

"Why is it that pretty women get all the cushy jobs?" I complained.

Duran laughed. "Everybody ready?"

"Wait," I said, digging through my purse for my wallet. I extracted my one and only credit card and shoved it into my back pocket. Handing over my purse for Lisa to hold, I nodded to my partners. "Okay, let's go."

While Lisa begrudgingly headed toward the car, Duran and I ignored the back exit and walked around to the front of the building, where we hoped to find a mailbox or buzzer with Kevin's name on it. My stomach cramped into a nervous knot as I took one more step down the path to hardened criminal. Duran, in direct contrast, looked like he was doing nothing more serious than walking through the produce department of the grocery store thumping for ripe watermelon. Even though there were several cars in the parking lot, the building itself appeared fairly deserted. Without planning it, our timing seemed perfect. It looked like students had eaten lunch and left for afternoon classes. If our luck held just a little longer, we might be able to sneak in and out unnoticed.

Duran pulled the door open for me and we slipped inside. Just as we had hoped, along the right side of the wall was a long row of bronze mail slots, each one labeled with a name at the top. Right smack in the center of each box was the apartment number. I turned and grinned at Duran, and then started scanning the names on top. The fourth one over was Brooks. Apartment 2C. K. Brooks. Bingo.

"Okay, Miss Maggie. Take your time and try to stay calm," he instructed. "Getting nervous doesn't do anything but make you work harder to get it right. Slow and easy, that's the ticket. If the card trick doesn't work, just come on down and we'll start back at square one with a new idea."

I studied my partner closely. "You've done this before, haven't you?"

"Hell, this is child's play, honey," he said drolly. "The stories I could tell you would straighten that mess of curls you got scattered on your head. But we don't have time to go into that now. Go on while nobody's here."

With one last glance around, I turned and walked up the stairs as calmly as I could, although my legs were begging to bolt. But Duran was right. I needed to stay relaxed and clearheaded so that I did everything once and only once. Fortunately, it was easy enough to find Kevin's apartment, second floor, third door on the right. I breathed a sigh of relief when I saw that the hallway was empty. Retrieving my credit card, I walked right up to Kevin's door and knocked quietly. I didn't want to take a chance of running into his roommate by surprise. After a few tense moments waiting for someone to answer, I realized that no one was home. Grabbing the doorknob in my left hand, I tried to turn it, hoping like hell that it was unlocked. No such luck. Using my right hand, and still holding the doorknob with my left, I slipped the credit card into the small gap between the jamb and the door itself. Starting several inches above the handle, I slid the card down very slowly until it reached the doorknob. Pressing down firmly, I felt the latch give, and the door pushed open. Looking up and down the hallway one last time, I nudged the door and slipped inside.

The apartment was nothing more than a box lined with cheap sand-colored carpeting. There was a large stained couch in the middle of the room, with an old television sitting against the wall on a makeshift stand of cinder blocks and plywood. Books and papers were strewn haphazardly on a coffee table placed in front of the sofa. Two crumpled beanbags, repaired with long strips of duct tape, were thrown on the floor, completing the living room decor. The kitchen was off to the side, enclosed by a small counter, two barstools, and a mess of dishes sitting in the sink and on the Formica counter. A small hallway forked into two bedrooms, one of which had to be Kevin's. Reciting a quick eeny-meeny-miney-mo, I chose the room on the left.

239

Seconds later, stepping on clothes that littered the floor and nearly tripping over a pair of tennis shoes the size of ski boots, I stood facing an unmade bed. Against the opposite wall was a desk, a chair with a long gash across the seat, and foam rubber poking through the vinyl. The room was stuffy, smelling faintly of sweat and dirty laundry. I kicked aside a pair of gym shorts with the toe of my shoe and wondered where to start. Not only did I not know what I was looking for, I couldn't help but wonder about the germs lurking underneath the layers of teenage grime.

If Kevin had something to hide, he wouldn't want it out in the open, not where any passerby, or trespasser, could take a peek. Unless there was a hidden door somewhere in the room, his hiding places were pretty limited. He had the desk, under the mattress, and beneath his unwashed clothes. His desk seemed the most logical, and most sanitary, place to begin looking.

I started across the room when a blinking light in the corner of my eye caught my attention. On the nightstand, half hidden by a notebook and a pile of papers tilting dangerously toward the floor, sat a telephone. I would have missed it completely without that red number "1" flashing in the corner. *It's a place to start,* I thought as I moved across the room to press the Play button.

A loud *Beep!* pierced the silence in the room. My heart slammed so hard against my chest, I thought it would come crashing through my ribs. Clutching the edge of the table, I tried first to stay upright and second to control the trembling that now threatened to wrack my body and send it sliding to the ground. With great effort, I forced my breathing to steady itself. I was so involved in trying to regain my equilibrium that I almost missed the message.

"Hey, Kev. It's Chris. Just calling to check in, see how things were going in Colorado. Nothing much happening down here. How are things up there? Have you told your mother anything yet? Must be pretty weird working for her without saying anything. Give me a call when you get in, doesn't matter how late. I've got a biology test tomorrow so I'll be up. Later."

Kevin's mother? Kevin worked for Jamie, and Jamie didn't have any children. At least, none that I knew of. She'd hinted at a wild past, but it was all in fun. She talked about sowing her wild oats, the crazy nights of staying up until all hours of the morning and the horrific hangovers she suffered through the next day. Nothing unusual or different than a hundred other people I knew—a few facts, a great deal of exaggerations, and a lot of laughter thrown in. Besides, if there was anything dark and murky about her past, Mark would know about it. And once he knew about a kid, he'd want to meet him, or her, and be involved in any way he could. He had a strong sense of right and wrong that way, especially give his own rotten childhood. He could never ignore something that was staring him in the face.

Lately, though, Mark and Jamie had been on a slippery road, and maybe Kevin was part of the reason. As I mulled that thought over, I could see all sorts of problems with it. According to the message, Jamie didn't know anything about Kevin. At least, she didn't know her waiter was quite possibly her son. But if he were her son, why didn't he introduce himself to Jamie? A hundred questions bombarded my brain, and as much as I wanted to sit down and sort through them, I didn't have the time. I wasn't sure how long I'd been in Kevin's room, standing there twiddling my thumbs as my mind meandered through a maze of thoughts, but I was getting increasingly nervous. With no place to hide except under a pile of dirty, sweaty clothes, I was a sitting duck. I took a quick look around the room and figured that I was lucky to get what I got. If Chris hadn't called and left a message, my only resort would be to dig through his desk and the piles of papers thrown on the bed and spilling off the rest of the furniture. As I looked around the room, I decided to chuck that idea. It would take me a year to wade through this garbage, and unless I bumped into a miracle, there was no way I was going to find anything, and time was running on short legs.

I didn't know how to reset the message, so I just left it off, assuming that sooner or later Chris would call again when he didn't hear back from Kevin. Surveying the room one last time, I moved quickly down the hall, through the living room, and to the front door. I looked through the peephole, and although I couldn't see much, I was at least assured that there was no one on the other side of the door. Turning the knob, I opened the door just wide enough to look down one side of the hallway. Seeing that it was empty, I stuck my head out a little further and checked the opposite end. Everything was clear. For the moment.

Chapter Nine

I hurried down the steps and through the front door, where Duran was strolling along the front walkway. Tucking my arm through his elbow, I steered him around the side of the building back to where we had parked and Lisa was still waiting. By the time we were halfway there, Lisa was already running to meet us.

"Everything okay?" Lisa asked worriedly.

"What happened to being the silent partner—the hidden one? You weren't supposed to hop out of the car and meet us in broad daylight so the neighbors three miles down the road could take a clear photo of you."

"So sue me," she said. "I'm not real well-versed in the art of subterfuge."

"Okay, girls, let's all calm down," Duran said soothingly,

directing us back to our cars. "Everyone's okay, no one got hurt, nobody got caught . . ."

Famous last words. As soon as he uttered them, an old, beat-up navy blue car with a peeling white vinyl top sputtered its way into the space next to us. We froze then, all three of us, listening to the muffler as it popped one last time and then went silent. We'd been so busy talking, no one had noticed someone pulling into the parking lot and driving around back. Toward us.

The door creaked open and a young, thin boy emerged. Turning around, I was frozen in place by two bright blue eyes staring into mine.

"Hi, Kevin."

"Uh, hey," he answered, confusion clouding his face.

"Why aren't you at the café?" I asked, figuring the only thing I could do was ask questions. The best defense was an overactive offense.

"I've got a class at two. I always leave early on Tuesdays and Thursdays. Marianne takes over."

"Hmmm," I said, scratching my head like I was trying to remember something important, "I don't think I've ever met her." *Keep him talking,* I thought, *so he doesn't wonder why in the hell the three of us are standing in the middle of the parking lot outside his apartment.*

"She's new," Kevin explained. "Ms. McGuire just hired her."

"Oh, well, that's good. I hope it works out. She was just telling me the other day how hard it was to find teenagers who were willing to work." Sweat was breaking out on my forehead and dampening my armpits. If this inane conversation went on much longer, I was going to be one soggy dishrag. I glanced sideways at Duran, silently pleading for help.

"Well, son, you'd better get going to class," Duran said smoothly, picking up the slack. "I'm sure teachers don't cotton to kids dragging their feet like a couple of turtles caught in a head wind. A good education's worth putting a little fire in your step." He took my forearm and started to turn toward the car. "Come on, ladies. Kevin here doesn't have time to flap his gums. Let the boy go about his business."

I think it was the extra-hearty good-bye waves that did it.

"This is where I live. Why are you here?" he asked. Like a spinning top, the three of us slowly and simultaneously turned around and stopped.

"Well, Kevin," I began, searching for some plausible explanation. "I . . ."

He paused for a second, thinking. "I told you where I lived at the café . . ." he said, the light slowly dawning.

"Yes, but—"

"You came to my apartment. But why?"

I shifted uncomfortably from one foot to the next, and I could feel my partners doing the same thing. "I . . . well . . . the thing is . . ." I looked helplessly from Duran to Lisa and back again. What a great trio we were. Three bright adults and not one of us could fabricate a decent enough lie to pull the wool over the eyes of a teenage boy.

"Why did you come here—you knew I was working," Kevin persisted, his suspicions growing by the minute. No doubt the guilt was written all over our faces, because his voice kept climbing higher and higher as he shot questions at us. "What could you possibly want? I've got nothing in there but a broken down television set and crappy furniture!" He took a step toward us and jabbed his finger in the air. "But you know that already, don't you? You've been in my place and in my stuff!"

Like a line of Rockettes, we all backed up at the same time. I glanced worriedly at Lisa, trying to catch her eye. I wanted her to break rank and take off for the car. She didn't need to be a part of whatever happened next. But my best friend hadn't taken her eyes off Kevin, who was now belligerently thrusting his chin at us and threatening to call the cops.

It was Kevin or the cops. I'd rather take my chance with an eighteen-year-old. I stepped forward. "Okay, that's enough, Kevin. If you want to bring in the police, I can't stop you. But you'd better think twice before you make that call." I rubbed clammy palms against my thighs. "I'm not in the position to explain what we've done, if anything, or the reason why. But I happen to know that you're not on the up and up, either." Both my partners looked at me quizzically, but I ignored them and pinned Kevin with my sternest glare. "You and I both know you're hiding something that you'd just as soon keep hidden."

"You really *were* in my apartment!" Kevin shouted incredulously. "I can't believe it! What the f—"

I held up my hands, palms out. "I'm not saying one way or the other, Kevin, but if you would calm down a little,

I'm sure we could work this out. You don't call the police, we keep our mouths shut about Jamie."

The shock that registered on his face was enough to convince me that my hunch was right. Jamie was this boy's mother. I didn't know all the details, but two things were obvious. First, Jamie didn't know who Kevin really was. And second, he didn't want her to know.

"How did you find out?" he asked in a stunned whisper, the blood leaving his face. "I was very careful . . . I didn't leave anything around. My roommate . . . he didn't know anything."

"It doesn't matter how I found out, Kevin," I said, feeling sort of bad for the kid now. His skin look pale and waxy, with a smattering of red pimples across his chin. "But I know that Jamie's your mother and you've been hiding it from her," I said authoritatively. From here on out, I was shooting from the hip.

"Jamie's his—" Lisa began.

I shot her a "play along with me" look. Lisa and Duran needed to pretend they knew exactly what I knew, otherwise, it was pretty damned obvious who'd been rooting around in Kevin's room. Fortunately, my best friend is no dummy. She caught on and started shooting from the other hip.

"Why haven't you told your mother that you're here in town? Why are you working for her?"

"What's the big secret?" Duran asked. His hips were too big to shoot from either side, but it didn't stop the man from adding his two cents.

"Look, you don't know what you're talking about. I don't know how you found out, but—"

"But, Kevin," I said, butting in where I definitely did not belong, "shouldn't you give her a chance? If you're her son, which you obviously are, then I'm assuming that Jamie gave you up for adoption when you were a baby. I'm sure she had her reasons. Maybe she was too young, or her parents kicked her out of the house and she knew she wouldn't be able to give you the home that you deserved." I was falling back on a lot of movie of the week plots here. Apparently, Kevin thought so, too.

"This isn't a soap opera, you know. I did tell her."

I was confused. "Then she does know who you are?"

"No, I wrote her a letter. I asked her to meet me, but she refused."

"Jamie didn't want to meet with you?" I asked, completely taken by surprise. It just didn't sound like the Jamie I knew, the one who preferred to face everything head-on— it was hard to imagine her shirking any situation, even one that was potentially painful. But then, who was I to judge? I didn't know what happened eighteen years ago, didn't know the situation or why Jamie decided to give Kevin up for adoption. "Maybe she's ashamed of what happened," I mused aloud. "Maybe it's haunted her for years, but the decision was right for the time." I looked at Kevin. "Whatever she did, Kevin, she did because she thought it was the best thing for you. I don't know what your childhood was like or what kind of parents adopted you, if anyone did, but I'm sure that her first thought was about giving you the best chance in life."

"Then why won't she see me? I'm not asking anything from her."

"I don't know, Kevin. I could probably come up with ten or twenty different reasons, but you wouldn't be any closer to the truth than you are now."

"How did you find your mother, Kevin?" Lisa asked.

"I started out on the Internet, but I didn't get too far. I finally went to an investigator who tracked her down here. That's when I wrote the letter. When she refused to meet, I decided to move here and face her in person."

"Even though she turned you down in the letter?" Lisa persisted.

"Look, my adoptive parents were—are great," he said, his eyes reddening. "They did everything they could for me, and I've got no complaints."

"Then why show up, son?"

"I can't really explain it," he said, dropping his gaze to the ground and kicking at an imaginary pebble.

"Give it a try, Kevin," Lisa encouraged.

I had to hand it to her. She had a way with men. Kevin looked up, read something in her expression, and the words just spilled forward. "I wanted to see if someone else had blonde hair and blue eyes and skinny legs like me. My adoptive parents are part Spanish. I look at them and all I see are brown eyes and brown hair and dark skin, and then out of nowhere, there's me."

"And that's how you've always felt—out of nowhere?"

Kevin let out a sad breath and nodded. "Yeah."

"So you went searching—"

"To find out where I came from," Kevin said, completing

her sentence. "I know it sounds like every other adoptive kid, but it's the truth. It's like someone kidnapped you from another planet and dropped you into some alien family."

I must have frowned, because he hurried on to explain. "I mean, all my friends talked the same, went to the same school, and all that stuff, but inside, somewhere deep inside, I knew I belonged somewhere else—and I just wanted to see that place for myself."

I put my hand out and lightly touched his forearm, surprised that he didn't flinch. "Kevin, I can't begin to pretend to know exactly how you feel, but I think I can sympathize. My mother died when I was very young, and there are times I can remember missing her so badly, I literally ached inside."

"Sort of like that," he mumbled.

I took his response for a "close enough," figuring that was pretty much all we were going to get from him. "So, what are you going to do now?"

"Just what I've been doing."

"Are you going to tell her someday?" Lisa asked.

"Maybe. I wanted to wait until I was sure she liked me— that she wouldn't send me away."

"But you've already gotten some of what you came for, haven't you?" Duran interjected.

"Yeah. It's not everything," Kevin said, switching his gaze to Duran, "but it helps."

"Sometimes that's all you can hope for," he replied. Turning to Lisa and me, Duran cleared his throat. "Well, girls, I guess we're done here. Why don't we all leave and let the young man go to class."

"But you still haven't answered my question," Kevin insisted. "I know you were in my apartment, even if you won't admit it. What the hell for? A lousy stereo?"

Now it was our turn to shift and mutter and fidget. But not for long. Just when I started to spin a yarn, as Duran would say, a blaring siren and flashing red light awkwardly perched on top of a black Bronco came flying across the parking lot, spewing gravel as it fishtailed to a stop.

A lean man wearing a rumpled coat and an awesome mane of black hair climbed out of the car. Draping one hand over the top of the car door, he simply stood and stared at the four of us. Well, that's not exactly true. What really happened was that his gaze swept over the clan and zeroed in on me like a laser beam, and it wasn't because I was one hot babe.

He leaned into the car and flipped a switch. The siren died. The light stopped flashing.

"Tell me I'm not seeing what I'm seeing," Villari said as he shut the door and walked over to stand directly in front of me.

"Well . . ." I fumbled, starting a little verbal soft-shoe. I felt like I was eight years old again and my father was passing a parental hairy-eyeball look between Andy and me, trying to sweat out the kid who had pitched another baseball through the bathroom window.

"Don't be too hard on the girl," Duran said, coming to my rescue. "She's not the only one involved here. I suppose we're all a little guilty."

Villari didn't even look up. "A call goes out on the radio that a group of unfamiliar, possibly suspicious people are loitering around the apartment complex. Being right down the street, I say I'll check it out, thinking it's probably nothing." He fixed me with a glare I could feel burning right through my scalp as I stared down at my toes. "Tell me it's nothing. Tell me you're here because you ran out of gas or you stopped to ask for directions."

"Not exactly," I said, my voice barely audible.

Then Kevin piped up. "They're friends of mine, sir."

I pulled my chin off my chest and stared incredulously at the teenage boy who was defending me.

"And who are you?" Villari asked, finally shifting his scorching gaze.

"Kevin Brooks. I live here," he said, waving in the direction of the building.

"These friends of yours," he said suspiciously, "how exactly do you know them? They seem a little old to be hanging with a college crowd."

"From the restaurant," Kevin said meekly, starting to wilt under Villari's stare. "I'm a waiter."

"Do you always invite your customers home with you?" Villari asked dryly.

"Last time I looked, there was nothing in the law against people getting together and passing the time," Duran said.

"We were just visiting, Sam."

The detective leveled his gaze at Lisa. "I thought you would be the sane one of the group."

"I am. There's nothing sinister going on here. We were just talking to Kevin and straightening out a few minor misunderstandings. I think we've got everything under control now, right, everyone?"

Like puppets on a string, we all nodded our heads at the same time.

Villari sighed and turned to Kevin. "Where do you work?"

"At a restaurant."

"The name."

"Jamie's Café," he answered reluctantly. I knew the last thing he wanted was a cop snooping out his relationship with Jamie before he was ready.

"I'm being taken for a runaround here," Villari said, bluntly assessing the situation. "I know Maggie well enough to know that this is not a tailgating party. Something crappy is going on, but I don't have time to hang around while you four play verbal volleyball with me. So," he said, clamping my forearm, "I'm going to take the kingpin here and drive her home. Where's your car, Maggie?"

"It's in the garage," Lisa chirped happily. Even in the worst situations, she was a romantic through and through. Nothing made her heartstrings thrum more than Villari doing his best he-man imitation and hauling me off to his cave.

"But . . ." I protested, stumbling as he led me toward his car.

He stopped and faced Kevin. "Unless you want to press charges for something I don't know about?" he asked, letting his question dangle in the air.

"No, sir, nothing happened."

"Fine," he said, spinning around and heading toward his car. "Let's go."

"But . . ." I stammered helplessly again.

"Do yourself a favor, Maggie," he said quietly as he pushed me none too gently into the passenger side of the car, "and shut up."

Fifteen long miles stretched out ahead. I clasped my hands together while my stomach sank to the soles of my feet. With just a little luck and a few extra minutes, Lisa and I could have been driving away from the parking lot instead of getting caught by a man who looked angry enough to order my execution.

"Where are we going?" I asked, suddenly realizing that we were heading south on I-25.

"Downtown," he said tersely. "To meet Michaels."

"Dylan Michaels?"

"Yeah."

"Where?"

"Impounded vehicles."

"What?"

"Permission was finally granted to remove materials from Riley's car."

I shook my head as though to clear it. "Mind speaking in English?"

Villari shot me a glance that told me in no uncertain terms that I was currently not on his hit parade. "First of all, the only reason I'm taking you along is that I don't have time to drive you all the way home and back. Second, I'm fully aware that whatever you were doing in that parking lot was on the back side of legal, and my guess is that you're damn lucky I was the one who answered that call, and third, Michaels has been very helpful in the Riley murder case."

I decided to ignore his second comment. "How's that?" I asked as casually as possible.

He raised his left eyebrow as he shot me a cool glance. "And why would you need to know?"

"No reason," I said, shrugging my shoulders. "You're the one who brought it up."

"You're good at that, you know," he said, the corners of his mouth lifting a fraction. "I have to admire the way you can twist anything around so that it's the other guy's fault."

"Fine, don't tell me anything," I said, slouching in my seat.

"And when it doesn't work, you pout," he said, the corners lifting even further.

"I do not pout," I insisted.

"Sure you do. And it works pretty well."

"Not always," I muttered.

This time it was a full-out grin. "Often enough," he said.

Now it was my turn to smile. "What about this time?"

"Pushy little thing, aren't you?"

"Is it working?"

"Well enough," he said, reaching over to skim his knuckles down my cheek. "But this doesn't mean we're not going to talk about the real reason you and your two chums were huddled together back there. You're involved in something and I want to know what it is before we end up talking to each other through opposite sides of steel bars."

"Any chance you might be overreacting a little?"

"My guess is I'm underreacting, but right now, I don't have time to shake you down."

"Sounds fun," I replied, arching my eyebrows in what I

thought was a passable Mae West impersonation.

He rolled his eyes. "Give it up, Maggie. You're very pretty with a smart mouth on you, but you've got a ways to go before you perfect sultry."

"Can't blame a girl for trying," I said, raking my hands through my hair. "So tell me what Michaels has done."

Villari sighed. "When you sink your teeth into something, you just don't let go, do you?" he asked rhetorically. "We knew that Riley was a special agent—worked for the IRS ferreting out fraud cases. What we didn't know was that while he was tracking down people who were illegally withholding taxes for one reason or another, Riley himself was up to his ass in criminal activities."

"You mean he wasn't paying taxes?"

"No, I mean he used the information to extort people." Villari took his eyes off the road long enough to note the confusion on my face and tried to explain. "This isn't my area, but the way I understand it, when the IRS goes after someone for fraud, they can't do it on the basis of one year. They audit the tax returns over a period of several years looking for a pattern of evasion or whatever."

"I'm with you so far."

"Apparently, in that set of folders Michaels took from Riley's office—which, by the way, Baxter was plenty pissed about—he found a file filled with tax returns for individual people covering different years."

"Okay, you lost me again. Try the *Crime for Dummies* explanation."

"I guess Michaels cross-referenced the names and so forth, and what he learned is that on some of the cases that Riley oversaw as a special agent, he pulled out certain returns, copied them, and gave away the originals."

"I'm still just as clueless."

"The IRS needs several consecutive tax returns indicating fraud in order to prove criminal intent. It looks like Riley extorted some of the people he was investigating by offering to sell them back one or two of their original returns, which would ruin the IRS's case against them. The IRS cannot use copies of tax returns—they have to have original signatures to prosecute. Riley makes a copy of the original return and puts the copy in the IRS file. He sells the original return back to the person being investigated, the key word here being *sell*. He charged a lot of money for the tax return and for removing the person's name from the list of people under investigation."

"So what does this mean?"

"It means that Jeff Riley had a lot of enemies. Being a Special Agent puts you at risk anyway—people aren't big fans of the IRS in the first place, but being a crooked SA elevates you to a whole other level. I'm sure they appreciated having their names wiped off the screen, but my guess is that Riley's services didn't come cheap."

"So why are we going to check out his car?"

"Because after hearing what Michaels found, Baxter agreed to let him search for files that Riley might have left in his car."

"Haven't the police already checked it out?"

Villari shook his head. "Not really. They just impounded the car, and it's been sitting in the lot since the murder."

"But what does Michaels expect to find?"

"More of the same—folders, files, missing tax returns, things like that."

"And you think the murderer might be someone that Riley was extorting?"

"I don't know, Maggie. I'm not at liberty to tell you anything more than I have. I just thought it might ease your mind to know *why* someone might have murdered Riley. But beyond that, it's off-limits."

Flashing his badge, Villari pulled through the chain-link fence topped off by some nasty-looking barbed wire. Parking the Bronco next to a small building, he gave me a no-nonsense warning about staying put which irritated me to no end, and walked inside. A few minutes passed, when a sharp rap at my window startled me out of the heated argument I was having with the detective inside my head. I jumped and swung around, ready to yell at Villari for scaring me and for treating me like a child. But to my surprise, it was Michaels knocking at the window and grinning at me. I opened the door and climbed out.

"Hey," I said. "I hear you're a regular Angela Lansbury, cracking a murder case right in front of the police."

Michaels shrugged. "I'm doing what I can," he said modestly.

"Villari tried to explain it to me on the way down, but it's a little over my head."

"It's still in the theory stage, that's why I want to get my hands on all the files I can."

I glanced sideways toward the building in which Villari had disappeared. "At least he accepts your help in these

258

matters. He blows a gasket every time I even try to ask a question or two."

Michaels's lips twitched in barely restrained amusement. "Somehow, I don't think a question or two would satisfy you, Maggie. You strike me as someone with unrestrained curiosity."

"*Unrestrained* might be a little exaggerated," I said.

"Maybe, but I don't think it's too far off the mark."

"Trust me, that's understating the situation," Villari said, coming up behind me.

"I reserve the right to disagree," I said stubbornly. "But apparently I'm not going to change anyone's mind here."

"Maybe later. Right now, we've got to check out Riley's car." The detective's gaze swept over me and he sighed. "I suppose it would be too much to ask that you sit in the car while we do what we came for." He shoved his hands through his hair, leaving it twice as disheveled as it usually is. "Of course, it might be easier for me to keep an eye on you if you came along with us."

"We'll have to talk later about that obnoxious tone of voice you keep using when you talk to me."

"Along with many other things," Villari said, his expression reminding me of where he found me less than fifteen minutes ago.

Villari made up his mind. I was tagging along with him, like it or not, which was okay with me. I would find out a lot more by staying with him and Michaels than sitting in the car. And right now, I really did want to know who killed Jeff Riley.

The men's long strides ate up the parking lot at breakneck speed, forcing me to jog in order to keep up. They stopped in back of a huge silver Mercedes, an expensive honey of a car that made my heart swoon with love. From his back pocket, Villari dug out a key with a small remote and punched a button, automatically unlocking the car. The trunk immediately popped open, causing me to swoon again because my Jeep didn't do anything immediately except die. Half expecting a dead body, I craned my neck to see what they were looking at, but the two men were hunched over and there was nothing to see but a couple of cute butts. Not that I was complaining.

I breezily wandered past the guys toward the front of the car. This was a real car. I coveted the bright, shiny exterior, trying to imagine what it would be like to trail my hand down the side of a car without getting paint slivers caught under my fingernails. I peered through the window on the driver's side. The leather seat, the new, smooth interior, the unlocked door—it beckoned, it called, it begged for me. I shot a glance toward Villari, who was still in deep conversation with Michaels. I could hear their voices but I couldn't see them, not with the trunk up. One minute, that's all I needed—what could one minute hurt?

I quietly lifted the door handle, pulled it open, and slid inside. I rested my hand on the gearshift, my foot on the pedal, and leaned back and inhaled the most beautiful fragrance in the world—fresh leather. The car hadn't been locked up long enough to smell musty. I closed my eyes and dreamed of driving, threading my way up tight mountain roads, accelerating and hugging the curves, the mountains on my left, the ocean on my right. The wind blew through my hair, and since it was my daydream, it was long and straight.

Then suddenly, abruptly, the door was yanked open. I had stayed in one minute too long, and now I would have to pay for that mistake. Villari was not a happy camper. He pulled me out of the car and locked the door. After banging the trunk down, he consulted with Michaels for a few moments, directed him toward the building where he would have to sign out, and then turned to me and said tersely, "Let's go."

I did as I was told and followed meekly behind—one wrong move and I was dead meat. Getting in the car, Villari jerked it into reverse and pulled out of the parking lot. I looked back through the window and waved weakly at Michaels, who was grinning. I felt transported back to grade school, listening to the class chant, "Ooooooh, Maggie's in trouble," when the principal's office called my name over the intercom . . . a rather frequent occurrence.

The drive home was even longer than the earlier drive. Nothing was going to humor Villari out of his bad mood this time, and it probably didn't help that Michaels left empty-handed. Apparently he didn't find anything important in the trunk. After telling a few lame jokes that fell on deaf ears, I settled back, folded my arms over my chest, and gave up.

Twenty-five minutes later, we arrived at my house. I hopped out of the car and began trotting to the front door, stopping when I realized that Villari was not following me.

"Aren't you coming?" I asked, spinning around.

He rolled down his side window. "Don't worry, I'll be back. Keep dinner open."

"Maybe I have plans for dinner."

"You do. With me."

Being ordered around by General Patton was not my idea of a good time. "Look, Villari, I realize that maybe I overstepped a few lines today, but I don't think I deserve to be treated like a junior cadet in boot camp."

"Count yourself lucky I was on call today, Maggie. Any other cop would have made life a lot more difficult for you. You have a way of putting yourself in sticky situations. We need to talk about that."

I'd rather not. "Andy's taking me to check out some new cars this afternoon," I replied. "I don't know what time I'll be home."

"I know how to use the phone. I'll call," he said as he was leaving. "Make sure you pick up."

The guy was obviously more irritated than I gave him credit for.

Chapter Ten

I picked up on the second ring.

"Can you make it to Roy's tomorrow, Mag? Maybe in the afternoon?" Andy asked, explaining that he couldn't get off work until late that night. After a few moments of whining and complaining, I agreed. After a few more minutes of typical sibling bickering, we laughed and hung up at the same time. The way Andy and I fought and then moved on like nothing happened vaguely reminded me of my relationship with Villari—the two of us didn't seem able to move from Point A to Point B without crushing each other's toes. Lisa said these little tiffs were just our way of getting in the mood, but I was beginning to feel like foreplay was way overrated.

After the phone call, I walked back to my studio. No matter how disorganized or cluttered my life got at different times, working with clay always pulled me back to my center. Some people exercised, some people meditated. I stuck my fingers on the clay and my breathing automatically started to relax. My hands seemed to absorb a sense of peace, actually soaked it up like a sponge without doing anything more than resting my palms on an unfinished clump of red earth.

My mind traveled back over the day and I wondered at Kevin's reticence to tell Jamie about being her son. I understood the feeling, or rather, the fear of being rejected, but having lost my mother at such an early age, I didn't know if I could have kept our relationship a secret. But it wasn't my place to say anything, although that didn't usually stop me from voicing an opinion.

On another note, though, I had to admit that Villari may have been right. The fact that he answered the call this afternoon was a real stroke of luck. Any other cop would have pressured the four of us for the whole story, and I was pretty sure one of us would have caved in, even though there wasn't any proof that we'd done anything illegal.

In the end, however, after all was said and done, the three of us hadn't accomplished a thing except break a couple of laws and put ourselves in possible danger. I mentally ticked off the steps we had taken: First, I borrowed a phone number . . . well, in truth, I stole a sheet of paper with a couple of numbers written on it, one I recognized. Two, Lisa and I tracked down the owner of the unknown number—a private investigator. Three, after snooping around in Sutherland's office, we found Kevin's picture inside a folder labeled

Jamie's Café. Four, Duran finessed an address from an innocent, unsuspecting young man. Five, after letting myself into
Kevin's apartment uninvited, I played a message that re-
vealed a mother-son connection, a connection that Kevin
himself later confirmed. I heaved a sigh. So what? All in all,
the Three Musketeers ended up with a big fat nothing.

Nothing but one faint, nagging little detail.

In a daze, I slipped off my stool, rewrapped my clay with
the heavy tarp, and walked down the hallway to the phone.
I made a quick call and then gingerly lowered myself down
onto the couch, moving so slowly that anyone watching
would swear I was pregnant. I don't know how long I was
sitting before I heard the horn outside. Grabbing my purse,
I stepped through the front door and headed to the car.

We were quiet as we drove. I retold the whole story,
explained what I was thinking, and then fell silent. Lost in
our own thoughts, nothing more was said until we pulled
into the familiar driveway. Fortunately, she answered the
door.

"Hello, Mrs. Riley."

"You'll have to excuse me, but I don't know—"

"I'm Maggie Kean and this is Henry Duran," I said, indicating the man standing next to me wearing a pair of
Santa-red trousers and a blue-and-green plaid shirt.

"Please call me Hank," he said, bowing his head an inch.
Always the gentleman.

"I'm afraid—"

"You probably don't remember me, but I met you the
other day at your husband's memorial service. Well, actu-

ally, it was after his service—at the wake. I came with Dylan Michaels, the man who is temporarily taking over your husband's work at The Outlook."

"Oh, yes, I know Mr. Michaels."

Of course she did. The guy was brilliant with the grieving widow, while all I could do was stammer faster than a coked-up woodpecker.

"What exactly can I do for you?" she asked in that very quiet, very refined voice.

"I was wondering if I—if we could come in and talk with you a few minutes. I promise we won't be long."

"I suppose so, if you think it is important."

"It is," I said firmly, stepping forward. I didn't want to knock the lady down, but I didn't want to give her time to rethink her invitation, either.

She backed away from the entrance and let us in, leading us into the living room where she had graciously received a long line of sympathetic well-wishers just a few days before.

"Please," she said, gesturing toward the white-on-white couch as she took a seat on an upright chair beautifully covered in ivory-colored silk. The entire house had that light, Greek island feel, so fresh and clean, I was disappointed a cool breeze didn't drift through gauze-curtained windows and lift the hair off my neck.

"Why did you leave The Outlook so quickly the night your husband was murdered?"

The room was so silent, I could hear the blades on the ceiling fan slicing through the air. Muted voices from down the hallway floated into the room—the television or the servants or both. Duran shot me a look I interpreted as

"Bingo!" but I couldn't be sure. With him, you never knew. It could have been heartburn.

"I don't know what you mean," she said, her spine stiffening.

"Your husband attended a show at The Outlook the night he was killed. His body was found in the studio in the back," I said slowly. "You were there."

"I'm afraid you're mistaken, Ms. Kean," she said, her voice growing softer and more lethal. "I was not feeling well that night and did not attend the show." She paused for a moment as a light of recognition flickered in her eyes. "It was your art, was it not?"

I nodded. "Yes."

"Now I understand why your name sounded so familiar. Jeff spoke to me about your work. He thought you were quite talented."

"Thank you, but that's not why I am here."

"Perhaps you could explain exactly why you are here."

Quite a genteel way of asking why the hell I was bothering her. "Because you were at the opening, Mrs. Riley. No one saw you, but you were there."

"Ms. Kean, I don't have time for this nonsense. I believe I've been very patient with the statements you've made today, all of which are completely untrue and sound vaguely threatening. I'm sorry, but I don't have any more time to give you." She stood up. "I have previous plans and would like to get ready. Please see yourselves out."

I stood and gave her my best stare down. But this lady was not easily cowed. "Please sit, Mrs. Riley. I'll make this as quick and easy as I can, but if you want to make this difficult, I am willing to go to the authorities with my information. I'm sure they would be interested in knowing why you denied being at The Outlook on the night your husband was murdered."

She pinned me with a stare hot enough to burn a hole through a two-by-four, but I stood my ground. I had to. There was no way to gracefully retreat without embarrassing myself and looking like a total idiot, but my threat to go to the authorities was nothing but bunk. The last thing in the world I needed was another opportunity for Villari to witness me sniffing around where I didn't belong.

"If you insist," she said stiffly. Like a noble descendent, she lowered herself onto the straight-backed chair, her spine erect and rigid, crossing one foot over the other. She had a quiet strength that I admired—the antithesis of my loud, sloppy style. But as my eyes drifted over her stately composure, I was thankful that for such a composed, majestic-looking lady, she had very thick ankles. It sort of evened the field.

"I won't go into all the details, Mrs. Riley, but I happen to know that the car sitting in your garage today is your husband's. It's the car he drove to my opening and which you drove home that same night. The police impounded your Mercedes the night he was murdered. They assumed, logically, that it was his car, since it was parked in the lot."

"I see." The woman didn't even blink. She simply stared at me, folded her hands, and continued. "And exactly how do you know it wasn't? What would you know about my husband's car?"

She made it sound like Jeff Riley and I had a torrid affair in the backseat of the Mercedes.

"I sat in it."

"Pardon me?"

"The other day, when I was here, I was getting a case of wine from the garage. A black Mercedes was parked there and I opened the door and sat in the driver's seat."

Mrs. Riley lifted one perfect eyebrow a fraction of an inch. "Do you normally sit in other people's cars?"

"No," I said hurriedly, "but I'd been having so much trouble with my own—" I stopped when Duran put his hand over mine.

"Perhaps I could continue the story," he said, leaning forward conspiratorially. "You see, Miss Maggie here has a trash heap for a car, held together with nothing more than a spit and a shine. When she walked into that garage and saw your big shiny Mercedes, well she just couldn't help herself. She walked right over, pulled open that door, and threw herself in. I daresay she'd still be there today if she didn't have to eat and powder her nose once in a while."

Okay, this was way past folksy. He pulled this hillbilly stuff with Kevin, and admittedly, it worked, but this was above and beyond the call of . . . of reasonableness. Surely, he didn't think Mrs. Riley would fall for this load of— whatever you call his backwater, let me pluck old Grand-pappy's fiddle, routine. I wasn't sure if my stomach was strong enough to handle it twice in one day.

But Duran was completely oblivious to the queasiness roiling in my stomach.

"I see," she said calmly.

"Of course, she didn't do anything but some harmless pretending."

"Mr. Duran, I'm more than willing to ignore the fact that Ms. Kean got into my car without my permission. And although I'm not accustomed to strangers putting their hands on something that clearly does not belong to them, I suppose I can understand what transpired here."

"Now, that's mighty neighborly of you, Mrs. Riley, and if Miss Maggie didn't have the curiosity of a cat, I suppose we would all be headin' home about now. But the truth is, my friend here didn't stop with your car—"

"I went to the impound lot today and—"

"Ms. Kean, my husband just died a few days ago," she interrupted. "No, let me amend that. My husband was murdered, quite violently, I might add, on the night of your opening. I've only started to grieve, and I am quite appalled by your lack of manners. I don't know you, or your partner," she said, glancing in Duran's direction, "and I don't care to discuss this any further."

Her words settled over the room. I didn't respond. Neither did Duran.

"Now, unless you've come to tell me something important, I must leave."

"It fit. I fit."

"Pardon me?" she said again, exasperation creeping into her voice.

"Today. When I sat in the car—I fit."

"Ms. Kean you are truly trying my patience."

"I'm told your husband was tall, over six feet." I said, continuing as if I hadn't heard her. "The car I sat in today—the car that Detective Villari was examining today was supposedly your husband's car. But when I got in—"

"Why in the hell did you get in?" she asked angrily. "Didn't your mother teach you to keep your hands off of other people's property? What kind of trash are you?" she hissed like a threatened cat.

"Excuse me, ma'am," Duran said, smooth as silk. "But I think ever'body ought to take a deep breath and simmer down. Miss Maggie came to ask a few questions, that's all."

"Oh, shut the hell up. I don't believe your line of bullshit any more than I believe she just couldn't help herself. I don't know what the two of you want, but I'm through listening. I want you both out of my house now."

"Forget it, Mrs. Riley," I snapped back. "If I wasn't convinced before, I am now. You know damn well what I'm talking about. When I got into your husband's car this afternoon, I didn't notice anything at first because I was too busy daydreaming about owning a Mercedes myself. But a few hours later, it hit me right out of the blue. His car fit me. When I got in, I didn't have to adjust the seat for my legs. I could reach the pedals just fine, which should have tipped me off right away. Your husband, as tall as he was, would have had the seat adjusted for his height, making it very difficult for me to reach the pedals. But that wasn't the case."

"This is—"

"Give it up, Mrs. Riley, I'm not leaving. Not until we

finish this." I took a deep breath and went on. "The discrepancy struck me later. The car in your garage . . . it was perfect, too. Which makes sense. You've been driving it around; you've adjusted it to your height. But the impounded car. It was fit for your height, also. Why? Then suddenly, it made sense to me. You drove to The Outlook that night in the silver Mercedes. That's your car, isn't it? That night, you parked it and went in the back so no one would see you except your husband."

I had to hand it to her, the woman was made of steel. She never moved a muscle; nothing gave her away except for a certain blankness in her eyes. She looked no more excited or bothered than if I'd been her interior decorator suggesting different colors for the living room.

"Did you plan to kill him? Or did it happen by accident?" I asked, keeping my voice low and menacing. "When you left, you took the closest car, the black Mercedes, the one that is now parked in your garage. It was easy, wasn't it?" The music playing in my mind was swelling to a crescendo. "The keys to both cars are on your chain, you jump in, and without thinking, you push the memory button. The car seat adjusts automatically to the secondary seat placement. You drive home, and no one ever knows you've been to the gallery. No one suspects that the car left in the parking lot that night is really yours. And no one notices that the seat isn't adjusted for your husband, which it wouldn't be, because it's *your* car." On that last word, I wanted to throw my arms out and tap-dance a big rousing "Ta-da!"

Fortunately, I didn't. For the first time in my life, I actually clamped my mouth shut.

"Did you want to say something, Mrs. Riley?" Duran said gently, toning down the country act.

Then I noticed it. The look she had on her face moments before, the blankness that flattened her eyes—it wasn't fear or regret or anger. It wasn't any of those things.

"I didn't go to the museum to kill my husband, Ms. Kean."

"Then why—"

"You got some of the story right. I did leave my car that night. I panicked."

"Please explain," I said, trying to understand.

"My husband was having an affair." She spoke with the quiet dignity of someone who had been hurt over and over again and still somehow managed to survive.

"Jeff was a weak man," she began, staring over my shoulder and speaking in a soft, earnest tone as she narrated the story of her life. "I knew it from the beginning, but he was so charming, so boisterous and full of life that I was willing to ignore what was right in front of me," she said, clasping her hands in her lap. "My parents hated him on sight. They despised his loudness, his crudeness, his roving eye, but I told them they were wrong. I convinced them to let me date him. And finally, against their better judgment, they give in. They were never able to deny their only child anything."

I waited.

"So we dated," she said with a small smile. "They were wonderful, lovely days, full of magic and fun, the way a first love should be. At least, it was for me. For Jeff, it was a little more work."

I frowned a little. "Work?"

"Well, of course. He was desperate for my money," she explained emotionlessly. "Jeff came from a very troubled home and I was his ticket out. I can't blame him, really. My parents were very wealthy, I was young, unmarried, and not without a certain amount of beauty. To him, I was a walking gold mine. And he was able to manipulate me quite easily, right from the beginning. I fell in love with him, at least with the person he presented to me, but I was not completely innocent in all of this. I loved the idea of taking someone less fortunate than myself and supporting and helping him become somebody 'important.' "

"But there's nothing wrong with helping someone realize their dreams," I blurted without thinking.

"They weren't his dreams, they were mine," she said sadly. "Years after we were married, he used to call himself my little pet monkey. He said I took him in and taught him 'tricks of the rich,' as he liked to call them—where to live, how to dress, how to entertain."

"Sounds to me like the boy indulged in a large share of 'poor me' whining," Duran said.

"My parents said much the same thing."

"But you didn't want to listen, right?"

She shook her head. "Not right away. But it wasn't long after we were married that I knew we—or I—had made a terrible mistake."

"What happened?" I asked, blundering in naively.

"He had his first affair. I caught him in bed with the maid." She shrugged. "It's an old story."

"Not to me," I said.

"Not to anybody with an ounce of integrity," Duran said

274

firmly. "Any man who can't keep his hammer in the toolbox, doesn't have any business being married."

She smiled then. "Do you really talk like this?"

I nodded. "Believe it or not, he does. He tends to embellish the countryisms when it suits him, but, at the bare minimum, he's always outrageous." Then I just shook my head in disbelief. Here I was chatting merrily with a woman I just accused of murder.

"You still think I killed him, don't you?" she asked, catching my look.

"I don't know what to think. I mean, it's lousy, what he did—if it's the truth. But you don't kill someone because they . . . uh, took the hammer out—you divorce them. It's quick, clean and doesn't carry a prison sentence."

"That's exactly why I went to The Outlook that night. To ask him for a divorce," she said, tightly lacing her fingers and resting them in her lap. "We had a terrible fight earlier. I refused to put up with his affairs any longer. I suppose I was used to the idea that he didn't love me, that he never had, but I was tired of his reckless philandering. I confronted him and he stormed out of the house as he always does when things are unpleasant—to be comforted by someone who could soothe and reaffirm his wounded masculinity." She stopped and glanced over at Duran. "I realize that I am talking in very stereotypic terms, but Jeff was a cliche . . . the misunderstood husband, the spoiled wife who didn't appreciate how very hard he worked." She paused. "Of course, I wasn't any better. I had the education and the resources to move on, to go someplace better, but I stayed."

"But why?" I asked.

She shook her head. "I'm sure a therapist could explain it better—God knows mine has tried countless times, but in the end it was nothing more than an ego problem. He couldn't give up the idea of all that money, of moving up in the social stratosphere. It was what he had always dreamed of as a little boy—to have enough money to do anything and everything he wanted. And even though he berated them when we were alone, he loved hobnobbing with the rich. Don't get me wrong," she said quickly, "we're not the Kennedys or members of the Hollywood jet set, but we do okay."

"But you—"

"Yes, you're right. I could have left him, but I didn't. My parents have never understood. I suppose I don't, either, not really. But in the end, it was nobody's fault but my own. I loved him. As time went on, I didn't like him very much, but I still loved him, which makes his death very difficult. In the back of my mind, I held on to the idea of transforming Jeff, much like Eliza Dolittle in *My Fair Lady,* with a gender twist, into some bright, articulate man who moved smoothly into my world. And no matter how he fought it, I was determined to change him into someone that fit, that belonged. Of course, he knew what I was doing, and as much as he hated it, he wanted the same thing. So we stayed together. Our marriage was a tug-of-war; we pulled against each other, then ran around and pulled on the same side. It was a senseless struggle on both sides."

"What happened on the night of his murder?" I prompted.

She sighed and crossed her ankles. "I had discovered, or

more accurately, uncovered, Jeff's latest infidelity. I should have been used to it. I'd turned the other way before, certainly I could do it again—"

"But?"

"Not this time," she said firmly, shaking her head. "I brought it up before dinner. I accused him of seeing other women, but before I had a chance to show him the evidence, he walked out. Normally, when we fight, I throw myself on the bed and cry in frustration, but this time, a strange calming sensation washed over me. This time I was really angry. I was mad. Not only did I want a divorce, I wanted to catch him red-handed. I was tired of all the excuses and rationalizations. I wanted to see him snuggled in some corner with his latest bimbo and try to explain his way out of it with me standing there in person." She looked up and smiled sadly. "I suppose it sounds sadistic, really, but it's the truth. I wanted to see the expression on his face when he looked up and saw me. I wanted to savor that one precious moment when he realized that his money ticket had just walked out the door."

"I'm not going to pretend that I know what you went through, but from over here, it seems that you were awfully patient with a guy who didn't deserve it," I said sympathetically. "I'm not sure I could have stopped myself from punting his wandering private parts right up to his throat."

"You do have a nasty little temper, don't you," Duran said, wincing.

I ignored him. "But how did you know he'd be meeting someone at the gallery?"

"I found a note in his coat pocket."

"A note?"

She nodded and walked over to a small birch table tucked into one corner of the room. A stone lamp the color of eggshells stood on top. Mrs. Riley pulled open the drawer and withdrew a long folded envelope. Walking back, she handed it to me silently before returning to sit on what had to be the most uncomfortable chair in the house.

The envelope was slit across the top. Inside was a single sheet. I looked up with a questioning look, and when she nodded, I pulled it out and read the lines scrawled across the page.

> *Our involvement must end now. Now. Believe me, I thought long and hard before writing this note, but I simply don't have the strength to fight any longer. I'm tired of the lies and the secrets. I'm through with it, all of it. I can't continue this way any longer, and unless the current situation changes, I am willing to face the consequences.*
>
> *In fact, in a strange way, I look forward to it. It would be a relief.*
> *Jamie*

For a few moments, I didn't say anything, just passed the letter and its envelope to Duran. He read quietly and refolded the letter, slipping it back inside the envelope. Without a word, he handed it to Mrs. Riley, who dropped it on the end table.

"Jamie?" The single word hung in the air.

"I knew who she was—a friend had used her before,

and I knew she was catering your opening. You can see that the letter was written on the café's stationery."

"And you expected to walk in on the two of them playing kissy-face," I finished for her.

"Not the term I would use, but yes. As I said, by this time, I wanted a divorce, but I wanted a little revenge, too."

"It was the perfect setup." I said.

"Yes. At least I thought so at the time."

"What happened that night?" Duran asked.

"I drove to The Outlook and parked in the back. Jeff had been on the board for years, and we had attended several shows there, so I knew my way around quite well. I slipped into the studio," she said, turning to me, "you know, where some of the artists work, and . . ."

And where I found your husband's body, I thought.

She drew in a deep breath and clasped her hands. "I was heading toward the bar where the caterers usually set up, when the door swung open and Jeff walked through . . . alone. I don't know who was more surprised, him or me. For a few moments we just stood and stared at each other."

"What did he say?"

"He regained his composure and sneered at me— wanted to know why I was there in the first place. Having fought earlier, I was the last person he expected to see." She straightened the hem of her skirt and continued. "Obviously, the evening wasn't going to play itself out the way I had hoped, so I told him then that I wanted a divorce. He shrugged it off. I'm sure he thought he could talk me out of it—he'd always been able to maneuver his way out of any sticky situation. But this time, I held my ground. I told him about the note I'd found and I told him it was the last note I would ever find, because I wanted him out of the house that night."

Mrs. Riley crossed and recrossed her ankles and re-straightened her perfect hem, signs I recognized as a polite form of fidgeting. I wanted to say something soothing and sympathetic, because at this point, she was definitely beginning to suck me in with her version of the story. Right now, Riley sounded like the sludge found at the bottom of a week-old coffee cup. But I couldn't be sure. What murderer ever admits they've killed someone? *"Yep, that was me. I whacked the guy."*

"I take it by the look on your face that Mr. Riley didn't much cotton to the idea of leaving," Duran prodded.

"No, he didn't 'cotton' to it at all," she repeated, a bemused expression flickering across her face.

"What'd he do?" he asked casually. "Throw a few clay pots around the room?"

"He got angry," she admitted, knowing what he was suggesting, "very angry."

"Wasn't the first time, was it?" Duran said astutely.

"No, it wasn't," she admitted sadly. "Don't get me wrong, he wasn't a drunk, and he didn't use his fists very often, but every once in a while, he would become so enraged that he would have to punch something."

"Every so often, that something was your face, wasn't it?"

She leveled a direct gaze at Duran and nodded ever so

slightly. "My parents never knew, and truthfully, it didn't happen often enough to be a real problem."

"At this point, I'm going to have to side with Miss Maggie here. That man needed to have his two eggs scrambled—if you get my drift."

A ghost of a smile settled on her lips. "Well, you're probably right. At any rate, I'm sure my father would have agreed with you."

"Did he hurt you that night at The Outlook?" I asked.

"No, but he was heading in that direction. The signs were all there—the clenched fists, the tight jaw, the flushed face, the rapid breathing. It didn't take a genius to figure out what was happening. So I left."

"And he ran after you?"

"He tried. As I turned to go—run, rather—I saw him lunge for me out of the corner of my eye. I didn't stop, just kept going, but I heard a crash—more of a thud, really. Without thinking, I spun around in time to see his head hitting the corner of the table. He fell to the ground, facedown, not moving." She stared unseeingly into space. "The world just stopped. I stood there, looking down at him, not knowing whether to laugh or cry or scream. Finally, I leaned over and touched his neck, looking for a pulse. And then, without waiting another second, I ran out of the room. By the time I reached the parking lot, I had my key ring in my hand and I raced to the first car I could find. You were right, it was Jeff's Mercedes I drove home that night. He was parked closest to the door, and I carry both sets of keys. I jumped in the car, punched the seat adjustment setting, and took off." She blinked then, as though she was wiping away the visions of that night. Mrs. Riley looked at Duran and me and said somberly, "When I left that night, my husband was very much alive."

NOT long afterward, Duran and I left. As he drove me home, I stared out the window. Forest-green mountains stood tall and proud, their jagged silhouettes scraping the darkening sky. Peace pulsed from the sheer strength of the land, a strength that weathered the continual changes that shook and balanced our existence. I loved the strong palette of colors: the jade pines, coffee bark, and flaxen plains propped up against a soot-gray sky. I wanted to reach out and wrap them around me like a scarf, to protect me from the thoughts swirling through my mind.

A man was dead. In the center of everything stood that one irrefutable fact. Jeff Riley was dead. No one seemed to know why. And despite everything I had seen and done over the past few days, I was no closer to solving the riddle. Of course, Villari would say it was not mine to solve. But I couldn't shake the feeling that there was some single thread that connected all the different fragments I had uncovered, some legally, some not so legally.

"I still don't know why she ran," I said to Duran.

"People do awful strange things when they're scared."

"Do you think she was telling the truth?"

He lifted his shoulders. "My gut instinct says yes, and my gut's got a pretty strong track record."

"But why didn't she go get help? Her husband was knocked out and she just leaves him on the ground?"

"She panicked, just like she said. My guess is that she'd been beaten down for so long—and I don't just mean being slapped around, there's more than one way to grind down the spirit—she probably didn't stop to think about what she was doing. She did what all spooked animals do—got the hell out of there."

"But why not tell the police afterward?" I protested.

Duran glanced at me with one eyebrow arched to the roof. "Sounds mighty funny coming from the girl who slides under the radar whenever possible. When was the last time you came clean with that boyfriend of yours?"

"It won't be long," I muttered. "He's coming over tonight to launch his lecture series."

He chuckled. "You could consider gussying up a tad—might muddy his mind a little."

"This isn't the 1950s, you know. Women aren't running around fixing dinner and meeting their men at the door with a pipe and slippers. If he wants to yell, let him yell. I'm a big girl and I can handle it. I can yell just as loud as he can."

"Shit, howdy, Miss Maggie, how do you expect to land a man with that kind of attitude?"

"The same way Mary landed you, Duran."

"What the hell are you talking about?"

"You're not fooling anyone with all that blustering you do around her. She's got you folded up and tucked neatly into her pocket to pull out whenever she's good and ready. And don't give me that stuff about the one love of your life. I'm sure it was wonderful, but you're lucky enough to run into it twice. Admit it, you got your britches caught on your own pitchfork," I said in my best Texas twang.

"I don't know what the hell you're talking about," he said, clutching the steering wheel.

We were pretty quiet the rest of the way home. Duran muttered to himself periodically, but I couldn't make out what he was saying. Besides, I had my own worries. The closer we got to my house, the more nervous I got. Despite my brave facade, I was in no hurry to face Villari. Unfortunately, though, it was like having an abscessed tooth removed—it had to be done, although I wasn't convinced I'd feel better afterward.

Duran dropped me off, still mumbling under his breath. I waved to him once from the porch, which I don't think he saw, and then unlocked the front door to let myself in. Villari called a few minutes later to say he was on his way. I was in the kitchen making a pot of coffee for the two of us when I heard his knock.

"You made good time," I said, opening the door.

"Much to your dismay, I'm sure," Villari replied, rather curtly. He walked in, shrugged out of his jacket, and dropped it on the back of my sofa. He unfastened his shoulder holster and placed it next to his coat. I was thankful for small favors. At least I wouldn't get shot tonight.

Silently, he followed me into the kitchen, where I handed him a cup of coffee. I poured one for myself and sat down on one of the kitchen barstools. He paced around the room while I sat there swinging my legs and blowing the steam across the rim of my mug. I didn't say anything—neither did he. My plan was to wait him out. I wasn't going to help him stick my finger in the light socket.

But as the minutes ticked by, I shifted in my seat, cracked my knuckles, counted to ten a zillion times, and drummed my fingers on the counter until I couldn't stand it. "Okay, just spit it out, would you? I've been geared up for your lecture all day, you can't disappoint me now." All right, perhaps it wasn't the most subtle approach.

Turning to face me, he stopped and said quietly, "I'm not going to say a word, Maggie. At least, not right away, not until you tell me what's been going on and what you're involved in." Villari moved forward, grasped my upper arms, dragged me off the barstool, and sat me down in one of the wooden dining chairs. He pulled out a chair for himself and placed his cup on the table between us.

"Here are the ground rules. You and I've known each other for a while now, and sadly, we've been in a similar situation before. I know how you react and you know how I react. So we're going to bypass a lot of crap and save a lot of time."

"I don't think—"

"Be quiet, Maggie, and listen. I want you to start from the beginning, and judging from the look on your face, this story did not start at Kevin's apartment." He leaned back in the chair, folded his arms across his chest, and stared at me, his face set and his jaw rigid.

He was serious this time, really serious. Villari wasn't moving until I told him the whole truth, all of it.

So I began. I told him everything, right from the get go. Way back to the beginning when Mark told me about the problems he and Jamie were having. I described the trip up the mountain, the numbers I found in what I thought was Jeff Riley's car, and so on. I skipped the part about breaking into Sutherland's office. I made it sound like Lisa and I searched the place while the private eye was going to the bathroom. After all, the guy was a cop, and snooping around an office was a whole lot easier to swallow than breaking into a locked office. Then there was the small break-in at Kevin's apartment. I tweaked that part of the story a little, too. I told him I went up to his apartment and knocked on the door. When no one answered, I turned to go, but thought I heard music inside, so I checked the doorknob, and what do you know? It was open. By the time I got to the part about walking in and accidentally leaning on the message machine, Villari had his elbows propped on his knees, his forehead in his hands.

"This is not what I wanted to hear," he said, groaning.

"It wasn't my idea to say anything."

He looked up. "There's more, isn't there?" he asked, but it was more of a statement.

"Just a little," I hedged.

"I can imagine," he said, plowing his fingers through his hair.

So I went on with the story. I told him about the seat

placement and how I realized that it was Jeff Riley's car, not his wife's, in his garage. I saw his eyes widen when I got to that part, but it was nothing compared to the expression that fell over his face when I told him about my meeting with Mrs. Riley that afternoon.

"Tell me I didn't hear you right," he said, practically flying out of his chair and standing over me like the Leaning Tower of Pisa. "Tell me that you didn't really go to see a woman you thought might have killed Jeff Riley. The man was thrown into a kiln!" he said, his voice rising to a healthy yell. "Did you think you were going to sit and drink tea while you accused her of murdering her husband?"

Villari shoved his hands into his pocket and walked away. At that point, I think he was seriously considering the pros and cons of strangling me. I was afraid the pros were winning.

"I wasn't exactly alone. Duran went with me."

"That's such a relief," he said dryly, his words still outlined in anger.

"I didn't think I should go by myself," I started, "but—"

"But you didn't think about me, did you? Why is it that I never come to mind when you decide to go chasing after some murder suspect?" He stabbed his fingers through his unkempt hair again. Things were going from bad to worse. "Aside from everything obvious—snooping, breaking laws, stealing phone numbers—the thing that bothers me most is how little you trust me."

I didn't say anything. What could I say?

"We went through this with Elizabeth Boyer's murder, and as angry as I was, I could understand. We hardly knew each other. Why would you believe me, or trust me?" He stopped moving and turned to face me with the saddest, most vulnerable expression I'd ever seen on a man. "But now, we've been together for a long while and I've fallen in love with you." Villari paused for a moment. "And you've fallen in love with me, at least I thought you had."

Something was wrong. This discussion was taking a sharp wrong turn and it was scaring me.

He sat down and reached across the table for my hand. He turned it over and lightly traced the lines on my palm with his fingertips. The room was still, the air heavy with unspoken feelings and thoughts. "I thought I was okay with you keeping me at arm's length. I knew about your mother's death, about the impact it had on your father and on you . . . how important Andy is in your life," he said quietly. "My plan was to keep loving you, surround you with so much love—well, what else could you do," he asked quietly, glancing up at me, a half-smile playing on his lips, "but fall madly in love with me, too?

"But you can't force things to happen. I tried not to, but maybe I came on too strong, too fast," he said, his smile fading as he lifted his shoulders. "I'm pushy and bossy and I want things done my way, my timeline. Just ask my mother."

My throat was tight trying to hold back the sobs welling up in the back of my throat. He was letting me go. I could feel it with every fiber of my being and I didn't know how to stop him. I laced my fingers through his and held on, trying to say anything that would stop him from taking this conversation to its inevitable end.

"Maggie—"

"Villari—"

"Shhh," he said, gently disengaging my hand and putting his finger to my lips. "Someday you're going to meet a guy—the right guy—and you're going to want to tell him everything, everything that goes on in that mixed-up, crazy maze of a brain of yours. He'll turn your insides out and you'll come back for more because you can't stop yourself. You'll run after him and hang on for dear life." He gazed deep into my eyes and smiled sadly. "I want that for you, Maggie, because that's what you did for me. And I've had the time of my life." He leaned over and softly kissed my forehead.

I broke down then. Tears streamed down my face as I looked up at him. He brought his thumb to my face and smoothed away the tears, but they kept coming.

"Maggie-girl, it's going to be okay."

I shook my head and tried to speak.

"I've got to go," he said, his voice thick with emotion.

"Don't go," I said, between broken sobs.

"I have to, Maggie. It hurts too much to stay."

And then he was gone.

Chapter Eleven

Daybreak slapped me in the face with its cheery brightness and early-morning birdsong. Lying in bed, I stared out the window through puffy lids, idly wondering where I could borrow a shotgun to blow away the noisy little creatures. I could see the forest that edged the back half of my property and the tip of the Front Range Mountains peeking over the top. They were dark today, almost a midnight blue, with fresh, unmelted snow drizzled across the peaks.

But today, I didn't care. I didn't care about the colors or the shafts of sunlight or anything. The only thing that I cared about had walked out my front door yesterday and my emotions swung between sorrow and intense anger. Villari always said that anger was my emotion of choice, and maybe that was true. The saddest part, though, was that it had been less than twenty-four hours since he left, and already our relationship was past tense. How could that be?

I cried for hours yesterday. I couldn't remember crying that much for anything or anyone, not since my mother's death. The sobs welled up from somewhere deep inside me and came rushing forward so hard and so fast that nothing could stop them. After the tears subsided and the weeping stopped, it only got worse. Grief slipped in and settled into the emptiness that was the only thing I had left.

The phone never rang and I never called. Melancholy seeped through me so deeply, I didn't have the strength to pick up the receiver, much less hold a conversation. At this point, I wasn't sure what I could say to him. He was right in so many ways. I hadn't given him any reason to believe that my feelings for him were anything more long-lasting than a strong dose of lust. Of course, I knew, had always known, that my feelings ran much deeper than what I expressed, but even now, I was at a lost to explain why I had been so reluctant to let him in on the secret.

The heat of the covers was suffocating and I threw them aside. The way I saw it, I had two choices: Lie in bed all day or get up and work. The former sounded much more appealing, but if I stayed in bed any longer, I would either drown in my tears or swallow a handful of pills to escape my misery.

I pulled on a worn flannel shirt, a pair of old sweatpants, and thick wool socks, and I padded into the kitchen. It took forever for the coffee to brew, and all I could do was stare blankly out the window. Nature seemed to be mocking me with all its vivid colors while the chickadees went about their daily business, chatting on the phone lines and pecking at the feeders for breakfast. I thought seriously about returning to bed and pulling the covers back over my head.

The phone rang then, piercing the oppressive silence.

I turned from the window and stared at it without moving.

It continued to ring. And ring.

Blinking my eyes to clear the thick fog shrouding my brain, I reached for the receiver and picked it up.

"Maggie? Is that you?"

"Andy?" I choked out, those damned tears jamming my throat again.

"What is it?" he asked, his voice immediately filled with concern. "What's wrong?"

I shook my head. "Nothing," I managed to choke out.

"What happened?" he persisted. "Are you hurt?"

Hurt didn't come close to describing it. "No."

"Then what's going on? Come on, Maggie, talk to me. You're crying and you know I can't stand that."

Which was true. Andy never could handle a crying woman. Drove him crazy.

I took a deep breath to steady myself. "It's okay, Andy. Villari came over last night—"

"You two have a fight?"

"More than a fight. I think it's over."

"Over? But why, Mag?" he asked, genuinely confused. "It's obvious the guy loves you—you love him. I don't . . ." Then he went silent. "He doesn't know that, does he?" Andy said softly. "You never told him."

"But I don't even know—"

"Don't give me that line of crap, Maggie. You've known it all along. You're just too busy hanging on to that pride of yours to admit it. You've got some weird idea that being independent is going to keep you from getting hurt," he said, his voice rising with frustration. "It doesn't work does it? You kept everything locked in that skinny little chest of yours and you still got hammered, didn't you?"

"Look, Andy, I don't need—"

"The hell you don't. Mom died, Maggie. It was horrible, it was unfair, and it screwed up a big part of our childhood. But the fact remains, she's gone," he said. "But here's the other unfair part—life goes on. It moves right along like nothing ever happened. Babies keep getting born, kids grow up, and guess what."

"Andy—"

"People are going to keep right on dying."

"I know that."

"Then why the hell don't you grab on to what you have and wring it for all it's worth?"

"It's too late, Andy. He walked out."

"Did you go after him?"

"No, but—"

"I didn't think so. Look, we've got an appointment down at Roy's this morning," he said, abruptly changing the subject. "Are you still up for it?"

Andy always shut down when he was really irritated. I think he was always afraid he'd pop me one if his anger got the best of him. There were plenty of times when we were growing up that I saw him clench his jaw as tightly as his fist . . . but suddenly, with his face closed up, he'd back off and walk away . . . just like he was doing now.

"Well?"

"I don't think I can deal with Roy right now," I admitted. "But I could use a ride to The Outlook if you're going into the office."

"I thought the police had cordoned it off."

"Not anymore. Mark called me yesterday. They're through in there."

"I'll pick you up in an hour," he said, and hung up.

If I thought the last twelve hours were bad, sitting in the car with my brother was no picnic. We didn't exchange more than ten words between us. By the time we pulled into the parking lot, I popped my door open before he came to a complete stop. Things would ease up between us, they always had, but when Andy wanted to make a point, he could really drag out the silent treatment.

It was too early for the gallery to be open, but I was hoping to get in through the back. Mark usually opened it when he arrived in the mornings, and today was no different.

The familiar smell of earth, of dirt, assailed my nose as I entered the doorway, calming the misgivings I had about coming into this room again. The yellow tape had been removed and the place looked as it always did. The floor was swept, the shelves straightened. Dropping my purse on a box in the corner, I went to the cabinet and lifted out a block of reddish-brown clay. I placed it on the shelf and unwrapped the plastic. Using a long piece of wire, I sliced off a thick piece and rewrapped what was left. On the wooden bench, I laid out a piece of canvas to absorb the moisture and began kneading the clay until I had a soft round ball.

I moved across the room, pulled up a stool, and plopped the clay onto the wheel. Flipping the switch, I put my foot on the right pedal and pushed gently. I could hear the high squeak and then the soft whir of the motor as I dipped my hands into the water bowl and placed them on the ball, one on top of the other, tugging on the wet mud until it was spinning dead center of the wheel. I kept wetting my hands, slowly pressing my two thumbs into the top, carving out the center, rotating the wheel faster and faster until my mind emptied.

Finally, an hour or so later, I lifted my foot and turned off the machine. In front of me was a tall pitcher—not my best work, but not my worst, either. It needed to dry for an hour or two before being moved, so I left it sitting on the wheel. I rinsed my hands off in the sink and glanced up at the closed door leading into the firing room. I knew I had one last fear to lay to rest. Crossing the studio, I hesitated outside the small room. Taking a deep breath, I turned the knob and pushed open the door. I don't know what I expected, but I was a little surprised to see everything looking exactly as it had before I found Riley's body.

I went to the shelves, leaned over, and checked the vase I had placed there the afternoon of the murder. As I started to turn away, I noticed an odd impression on the clay. Squatting down, I saw the distinctive marks on my vase, a print I had not put there myself. I ran my fingers lightly over the design and realized that I did not need my glasses to know what I was touching and who put it there.

I got up and walked out the door.

. . .

"LIKE I told your friend, I haven't found a thing. Her husband lives like a damned monk. Goes to the grocery store, picks up the dry cleaning, drives his daughter to the park. Once in a while, he has a beer after work with his buddies," he said, leaning back in his chair. "No women, though. Hell, the guy doesn't even flirt with the waitresses."

"Hmmmm . . ." Yeah, that sounded like Joel.

"I said I was just wasting my time and her money."

"That's not exactly why I'm here—why we're here, rather," I said, indicating Duran, who was sitting next to me.

Sutherland stuck a toothpick in his mouth and waited.

"Have you ever been to The Outlook?"

Something flickered in his eyes, but his face never changed. "The gallery downtown?" He shook his head. "Nope, can't say that I have. Driven by, of course, but art's not really my thing."

"But you were there on the night of Jeff Riley's murder."

Sutherland didn't move a muscle except to keep digging between his teeth with his toothpick.

"Do you want to explain what's going on here?"

"It's simple, actually. Riley was killed in the studio and you were the last person to see him—a person big enough to pick up an unconscious man and stuff him into a kiln."

He stopped stabbing at his teeth, clasped his hands together, and placed them on the desk. "From over here, it sounds like you're accusing me of something," he said dangerously, "and I don't like being accused."

"I *am* accusing you, Mr. Sutherland. You saw Joanne Riley leave the studio and you went in behind her. Her husband was on the floor knocked out. She made your job a lot easier. All you had to do was dispose of the body."

"Like I said, I don't like being accused. I suggest you leave my office now and we'll pretend this little incident never took place." He glanced at Duran. "And take this fat ball of wax with you."

Duran, who hadn't said a word since we arrived, didn't budge an inch. He reached over and patted my hand. "Been called a lot worse in my day."

"Save the stories for someone who cares, old man," Sutherland said, rising. "Now both of you get the hell out of here while I'm still in a good mood."

"I have evidence, you know."

He stared at me, but I never flinched. Slowly, he sat back down, his eyes never leaving my face. "What evidence?"

"Your back pocket."

"Look, lady, I don't have time for games."

"You carry a thick wallet, Mr. Sutherland, with the Star of Texas hooked—"

"My father's money clip?" he interrupted. "It was the last thing he gave me before he died. I almost lost it once, so I quit carrying money in it, just slip it on my back pocket. Kind of a good luck charm." He leered at me. "Now, it's awfully flattering to think you were noticing my ass, but I don't see how it constitutes evidence."

"That little star's going to land your butt in jail," Duran said smugly. "Personally, nothing gives me more satisfaction than to see the Texas justice system at work."

Sutherland narrowed his eyes and turned to me. "Do you want to explain?"

"Like I said, you walked in, found Riley on the ground, but he was still alive."

"And the cops are going to believe this crap?"

"Sure," Duran interjected proudly, "because your big fat ass left a perfect imprint on Maggie's work."

"You dragged Riley across the floor into the firing room and backed into the shelf of sculptures waiting to be fired. You bent over, the clay was soft, and the star of Texas is now branded on my vase."

A sheen of sweat glistened on his forehead, and though he tried not to show it, Sutherland was obviously nervous. His face looked red and feverish, as though he was sick, and he picked up the toothpick again and started gouging his gums for the umpteenth time. He looked upset, and as the clock ticked away, I couldn't stop from fidgeting myself.

"Why didn't the cops pick this up?"

I shrugged. "My guess is they thought it was meant to be there—a decorative design. Lots of artists left their work to be fired. After the murder, the cops closed off the area and the pieces simply air-dried. If I hadn't created the vase myself, I might not have looked twice."

Sutherland put down the toothpick and stared out the window for a few moments. Then he pulled his gaze back to me and started drumming his fingers against the desk. Slowly, so casually it seemed unintentional, he dropped his right arm and tugged the right-hand drawer open a few inches.

"Hold it right there, son," Duran said, "nice and easy."

Sutherland's hand froze over the drawer. I whipped my head around to see Duran pointing some kind of pistol right at the PI's chest. "Now, we don't want any unnecessary trouble, and I sure don't want to have to hurt anyone, so listen carefully, because I get real irritated when I have to repeat myself. Do like you're told, and I won't have to fire this damn thing. For such a small gun, it packs a mighty powerful punch and makes quite a mess of things. So hold both of your hands real high like you're praying to Jesus," he said, nodding when Sutherland did exactly that. "Now, take your left hand and shut that drawer.

"Close your mouth, Maggie," he said, his gaze never wavering from his prisoner, "before a swarm of flies set up housekeeping in there. Now, Mr. Sutherland," he said mildly, "what was so all-fired important that you had to go and kill Mr. Riley?"

All the fight was gone now—his face the color of wet flour. He slouched in his chair and shrugged. "I didn't have much choice, you know. Riley and I had a good thing going there for a while. He'd pull out cases he was working, cases where the owner had a thriving business, but were being audited for some reason or another. Some were innocent people, some not so innocent with something to hide. Then I'd track these people down and suggest that they might want a little extra protection to keep the government from digging too deeply."

"It's called extortion."

"Whatever," he said, rolling his shoulders. "Most of them didn't like the price, but they were happy to pay the bill, considering what might have happened if the IRS went after them. We gave them their original tax return. They gave us money. All in all, a sweet deal for everyone."

"But Riley didn't need the money."

He shook his head. "Wrong. His *wife* didn't need the money. Jeff didn't plan on staying with her too much longer, but he'd gotten a taste of the good life. He couldn't make that kind of money as a Special Agent, not without a little lucrative business on the side."

"You were after Jamie McGuire, weren't you?"

"Yeah, but she didn't want to pay—she fought back. She started threatening Riley."

The note, I thought. *The note Joanne Riley found in his coat pocket was about blackmail, not an affair.*

"She wanted to go to his boss, to expose him. She was going to blow the whole thing wide open. He told me to take care of the bitch."

"It was you. You were the one who took her up the mountain pass."

"How did you know about that?" Sutherland asked. Suddenly, he leaned forward as understanding sparked in his eyes. "So *you* were the one behind us."

I kept quiet.

He studied me for a moment before continuing. "I didn't know who it was but I knew someone had been tailing me for several miles. Next time you want to follow someone, pick a car that doesn't stick out like a sore thumb."

There was no use pretending. "The black pickup—" I started.

He lifted his shoulder. "Friend of mine. I called him on

the cell phone, told him to give you a little scare, whoever you were."

"Did he show up at Riley's service?" I asked, thinking of the parked truck.

"Not that I know of. Why?"

"It doesn't matter," I said. "Go on. What were you doing with Jamie?"

"I just tried to scare her, told her how I could dredge up her past, bring it all out in the open. I knew things she'd tried to keep hidden, like that boy of hers who was working in the restaurant—but I could tell she wasn't buying it. Besides, it didn't much matter anyway."

"Why not?"

"Because Riley was getting ready to skip town. He'd been avoiding me the past month, wouldn't answer my calls, didn't pay me my cut of the deal. I started snooping around and found out his boss was getting suspicious, even without Ms. McGuire's help, and was starting to breathe down Jeff's neck. So Riley started hiding some money offshore on one of those islands where banking laws are a little more flexible and they don't ask questions about large deposits. He was sneaking off while the IRS snooped around, leaving me to face some stiff jail time alone." He sighed. "Seems like his wife and I had the same idea that night. When I got to the gallery, I saw her running out the door and taking off in Jeff's car. I didn't know what had gone down, but when I saw him lying there, I thought she had killed him. She did the next best thing—left him conked out on the floor. Didn't take me long to haul him into that big oven, flip the heat on, and take off."

"Is that enough for you, Sam?"

"More than enough, Hank," Villari said from behind. He moved quickly into the room, arms outstretched, a revolver held in two hands. Two men, both with guns drawn, followed closely behind. Villari stopped in front of the desk, next to Hank. His men split and moved around opposite sides of the desk, one retrieving the gun hidden in the drawer, while the other handcuffed Sutherland and pulled him up out of the chair.

I stood and planted my hands on my hips. "It took you long enough."

Villari lowered his arms slowly, until his pistol was at his side. He cocked his head toward the door. "Take him outside and read him his rights," he said to the cops as he shoved his gun into his holster. "I'll meet you downtown."

Sutherland didn't put up any resistance as they led him outside.

Then slowly, ever so slowly, Villari turned to face me. "I got your message."

"And?"

"We still have work to do on the concept of you staying put."

"And?"

"It was a helluva message," he said.

"And?"

But I didn't wait for an answer. I tripped over Duran's feet and ran to Villari, vaulting into his arms and wrapping my legs around his waist. "You're the right man, Sam."

"So you said."

Then he smiled that goofy, lopsided smile that melted my heart.

Chapter Twelve

H is mouth covered mine hungrily, his kiss hard and urgent. My lips were on fire and I wanted to devour him, to be devoured. My breathing was fast, my skin was hot, and just when I started to chuck my sweatshirt—

Duran cleared his throat. "Uh, I think I'll go outside and get some air."

Sam extracted a hand and held it out. "Thanks for calling, Hank."

"You called him, too?" I said accusingly.

"Damned straight, I did," clasping Sam's hand. "I had a feeling about this Sutherland guy. I wasn't going to come over here without some backup."

"I told you I'd already called Sam and told him what I'd found."

"No offense, Miss Maggie, but you've been known to tell

a story or two to suit your purpose. How'd I know you weren't stretching the truth just to get me to drive you over here? If I'm going to put my ass on the line, I'm going to make damned sure that line's extra sturdy."

I laughed and went back to burying my face against Sam's neck.

"I still expect that sculpture of yours," he said.

"Don't worry, you'll get it," I said, my voice heavily muffled.

Duran ambled out of the room.

"Maggie?"

"Hmmmm?"

"Honey, I've got to let you down."

"Too heavy?"

"Skinny as you are, you're no featherweight," he said, grinning. "But that's not it. There are cops waiting outside. I've got to run down to the station and take care of Sutherland, not to mention the paperwork. As much as I'd like to, I can't stay in here alone with you while everyone mills around in front." He released me. "They might get suspicious," he said with a slight moan as I slid down his body.

"Are you coming over later?"

"Nope," he said, shaking his head. "You're picking me up for dinner at your parents' house tonight."

"How am I—"

"Andy's going to take you to Roy's to get a new car."

"How did you—"

"He called me this morning. We had a nice long talk."

"Andy called you? What the hell? How about the Pope? Did he call?"

"No," he said, shaking his head, "but my mother's working on it."

Epilogue

The way the critics kept poking their noses under my sculptures, it was obvious they were looking for another dead body. I could see it in their faces—the immense disappointment that everyone in the room still had a pulse. Whatever they wrote about my work in tomorrow's heading would be tinged with the frustration that Maggie Kean hadn't stumbled over another corpse.

My second showing was not nearly as dramatic as the first, but I wasn't complaining. There was no yellow *Caution!* tape and no cops, except for the good-looking detective who escorted me in my slightly used, cherry-red Volkswagen. Sam and I had drawn a truce . . . well, much more than that, actually. I was crazy about the guy, and he knew it—an awfully big step for a girl with a smart mouth and a lot of old wounds. The wounds were starting to heal now, though, something Sam took a lot of credit for—credit I gave him and some he simply took for himself. His ego had done nothing but expand exponentially since we decided to admit our feelings to each other and to the world. Of course, his family was thrilled. Mamacita was already freezing pans of lasagna for our wedding reception and knitting booties, several pairs in both pink and blue, for afterwards, and nothing we said about jumping the gun made a bit of difference. In fact, every time we protested, she whipped up another pot of linguini. We finally kept our mouths shut before she bought stock in pasta.

"I'm surprised to see you here," I said, realizing there were two cops in the gallery now.

He shrugged in his elegant blue pinstriped suit. "You're not the easiest witness to work with during a murder investigation," he said, leaning over to examine my work, "but that doesn't keep me from appreciating what you've done here."

I lifted an eyebrow. "You like art?"

Baxter straightened and turned to face me. "Pure lines—graceful movement—classic composition. Your pieces reflect a contrasting nature, each subject involved in seemingly innocent activities with an underlying intensity that belies the simplicity. Your work is a study in tamed emotions, of passion beneath a smooth surface. It brims with a complex mix of anger and strength, hidden behind a tranquil facade."

"My God, where did you come up with that?"

"Art major in college," he replied. "At one time I wanted to be a painter."

"What happened?"

He angled his head. "Do you really care about my history, Ms. Kean?"

I grinned. "I care about anyone who can come up with a line of crap like the one you just whittled off, Baxter—right off the top of your head, too."

A slow smile spread across his face. "You ought to hear me describe wine."

"Don't bother," I said, laughing. "Just do me a favor and go spout those pretty words to the art critics. I wouldn't mind seeing some of them in print."

"It would be my pleasure."

"Uh, Baxter," I began.

"Don't worry about it, Ms. Kean," he said. "No one's at their best around cops. Take care of Sam and I'll overlook your rather challenging personality. He's a good guy."

"Yes, he is."

"And—"

"Yes?"

"All kidding aside," he began, "your work is good. You should be proud."

I watched him walk away, wondering if he was a good guy or a bad guy. Things used to be so much simpler when anger was the only light I followed. Now that Sam was softening me up with all that love and kindness stuff, life was softer, grayer, and the line between black and white was a lot less defined. I still hadn't gotten used to it. The last thing I wanted was to slip up and turn into a "nice" girl. The first time someone described me as "sweet," I was going to deck them.

I was ruminating over my life, when Mark came up and gave me a quick kiss on my cheek. I smiled, looked past him, and saw Jamie and Kevin talking in the corner of the room.

I tilted my head toward the two of them. "Looks like they're getting along well."

"Things were a bit shaky for a while, but I think we're through the worst part."

"You're a nice man, Mark. It's not everyone who could understand Jamie's past and accept it."

He shook his head. "That's not nice, Maggie, that's realistic. We've all done things we weren't proud of. She's had a sad life and Jamie dealt with it the best she knew how. I can't fault her."

I agreed with him, but I still didn't think too many men could accept her short dalliance into the world of prostitution. When she became pregnant with Kevin, it took courage not only to have him, but also to give him up in the hopes of a better life. Jamie spent the next few years turning her life around—becoming a chef, saving money, moving to Colorado, starting her own business. And when she was faced with Riley's extortion, she eventually fought against it, even under the threat of exposing her past.

"I still can't believe she knew that Kevin was her son."

"One of those female intuition things, I guess. But once she got over the shock of seeing him in real life, she let him stay. They were both doing the same thing . . . getting to know each other under the guise of ignorance. When Sutherland went to jail, I think she was ready to talk to Kevin. In fact, I think she would have talked to him regardless of what happened. She didn't want to hide anymore, especially from her son. Jamie was ready to talk, and Kevin was old enough to listen."

"And the two of you?"

"When Riley came after her, she withdrew from me. She didn't want to drag me into anything sinister. By the time Sutherland threatened her, Jamie was barely acknowledging our relationship or me, but she was tired of running from her past." Mark gave me the sweetest smile. "When she stopped running, we talked. It helped."

"Go get your own girl," Sam said, coming up from behind me and slipping an arm around my waist.

"I think I'll do just that," Mark agreed. "Enjoy yourself," he told me before leaving to talk to Jamie.

I wasn't sure if he meant enjoy Sam or the show. "Where were you?" I asked.

"Trying to calm Hank."

"What's wrong with him?"

"He wants you to, uh, 'quit wasting time flapping your gums talking to folks who ain't gonna do you a damn bit of good.' Translation: I think he'd like to see you mingle a little more—be more aggressive about selling your work."

"What did Mary say?"

"She told him to shut up and let you enjoy the evening."

I laughed. "Sounds like her. You know, he's never going to leave me alone until I finish that piece for him."

Sam smiled. "Honey, I have a funny feeling you're *never* going to get rid of Duran."

I wrapped my arms around his neck, stood on my toes,

and kissed him. Nuzzling my face in his neck, makeup be damned, I sighed. "I think you're right."

"How's that?"

I looked up and grinned. "He may look old, but he's still got some snap left in his suspenders."

"Honey," my boyfriend said, gathering me closer, "I've got a lot more than snap."

"Is that an invitation?"

"Is that a yes?" he asked.

"Count on it."